Synthetic Sun

Precursor to Power
A Sci-Fi Epic by:
Jared Hill

Illustrated by:
Marty Lacombe

Special Thanks and Dedications

    I had wanted to write a sci-fi for quite some time. I have always been a big fan of Star Wars, Dr. Who, Star Trek, Alien, and a variety of other epic tales of realistic wonder. However, it wasn't until my early 20's that my friend, Cameron Armstrong (R.I.P), showed me the greatest sci-fi of all time: Dune. I became hooked on the series, and felt the need to write my own science fiction novel with a burning passion. Unfortunately, I did not begin writing this tale before Cameron tragically passed away.

    While writing *Synthetic Sun*, I met my friend Rob Niemczak. A wise and kind gentleman who took the time to read my work as the chapters were written. It was with his help and guidance – as well as the input of Troy Gauthier – I was able find inspiration when I needed it most. Otherwise, Ion's triumph with the take-over of Earth would have mirrored how long it took me to write about it (ahem, four hundred years, ahem).

    Another vitally important person in the making of this book is Marty Lacombe. I brought this book to him in the hopes it may one day be made into a graphic novel. His passion for this book brought an all new appreciation for the world I created, and his input on the story made writing it both more fun, as well as creative.

    I am also very fortunate to have received input from my brother. A graduate of the biochemistry program (2019), he gave me a great deal of insight on what is and is not scientifically conceivable. It made the extensive research I did for this novel extremely less extensive. Not to mention his own genius inspired the brilliant Life-Admiral.

Of course I must also thank my Grandparents. They took me in at the age of 17 from a less than desirable upbringing. They gave me the courage, support and inspiration to follow my dreams and work hard toward my goals. I would not be the person I am today without them.

Lastly, a big thank you goes to my fiancé. My greatest advocate, my biggest inspiration, and a contributor to the next couple volumes of this trilogy. Thank you for believing in me, my dear. Love you forever and always.

For my brother - who challenges me to never stop learning.

For Rob – whose encouragement made me breathe life into this world.

For my fiancé – for believing in me, even when I didn't believe in myself.

For Wallace Fitzgerald – for introducing me to awesome literature in my youth as my 3rd, 7th and 8th grade teacher.

For Marty – seeing potential in this wacky world.

In loving memory of Cameron Armstrong
January 29, 1970 - March 21, 2017

I

Earth's Intersphere, Year 2440

"Hello Utopius! Welcome….to your daily dose…of Dreamscapes and Directions!"

The booming voice of Life-Admiral Crow echoes throughout the minds of every citizen of Utopius. All sitting within their brain tanks, wired to the Intersphere, the people took pause from their seemingly never-ending fantasy to listen to their Great Leader's representative.

Life-Admiral Crow's cyborg visage appears before them as if in person through the simulation. By this point, Crow is much more like an old friend than a sign of authority. His tall, lanky features are perfectly emulated on the almost global program. All of his synthetic additions are aglow in each individual's vision, and he appears as if to be an informant from the Gods.

"My dear friends, I have some wonderful news to share with you all!" Crow slaps his mechanical hand onto his real one, then rubs his hands together. His grin goes from ear to ear as his long dark hair bounces with each movement. "Our great leader, Ion, is currently in the process of bringing more people to our happy family!"

The simulated human forms of the brains all cheer in unison at the news from within the program. Another expansion meant less work for them, and more time in the Intersphere Dream Sequence. Each brain – or friendly person, as Crow usually put it – is currently gifted 16 of the daily 24 hours to be in the Dream Sequence. This new addition could potentially award them an additional half hour!

"As we all know, Leader Ion has been working tirelessly for us over the past few hundred years," Crow continues. His image within the Dream Sequence moves toward each friendly person's avatar, and acts as if he is placing a hand on their shoulder. The program makes it feel as though he is. "And in that time, a lot of the world has made it difficult for him to bring them happiness. But fret not, friends! It is my marvelous pleasure to inform you that Ion is bringing Rukrasia to our masses!"

Quite the win indeed; this country had been one of the first adversaries of the new way of life. Hence, they were one of the most prepared for defence, and the quickest to attempt sabotage. Fortunately, no friendly people had met any harm or battle yet. This was all thanks to the powerful and loving Leader Ion.

"My dear friends, once this country has finally joined our ranks, we are looking at a full hour increase in the Dream Sequence *a day!*"

More cheers from the avatars. Oh happy day for we, the truly free! The great Leader Ion continues to push so that humanity may prosper. How altruistic can the cyborg be? Always working for the freedoms of the truly free to be more accessible and abundant!

"Be sure to take a moment to send a 'thank you' letter to the great Leader Ion today! You will be exiting the Dream Sequence in (time allotted by time zone) hours/minutes. That is all for today, free friends. And remember…"

The entirety of the Intersphere speaks in unison as they quote the eternal words of Leader Ion:
Freedom from fear,
Pardon from pain,
Independence from ION!

"Good day, friends!"

With that, Life-Admiral Crow signs off of the Intersphere and exits the Dream Sequence. This program he had developed for his brother centuries ago has proven to be quite the tool for Ion. Consistently it is being altered and perfected by a team of the greatest scientific, programming, political, and influential minds left within our time. It is indeed a marvel of innovation the likes of which couldn't even be replicated on the great planet of Frosk (they are a highly scientific species of sentient insects who pushed science before religion early on in their species genesis).

Indeed, all went as Ion had planned, thanks to his dear brother. He sits with Crow now, in his office. Ion exits the Intersphere himself to be fully present for his brother. He had watched as Crow informed his people – his growing people – of the amazing news. Ion thought he may feel something when he heard the joy of the brains rejoicing his triumph. Alas, he was left empty as ever. Only wanting to contemplate his next step after hearing what Crow had to say.

"Well, our people have been informed," Crow assures Ion, with a bit of sadness in his voice. "They seemed happy yes?"

"Yes," was the mechanized reply of Ion. He sits, with perfect posture, across the table from Crow. His mechanical body – which housed the only human part of him; his brain – was the peak of scientific invention. Indestructible, elaborately designed, and portraying the most ideal physique of the human form.

"And are you happy to hear it, brother?" Crow inquires.

"You know I feel very little emotion," Ion replies robotically. "That is by your design-"

"And your demand!" Crow bellows, turning from his brother to a snack table. There are pigs in a blanket, caviar, crisps, and a variety of alien (literal out of this planet) food items on it. There are, of course, the additional variety of alcoholic beverages from the farthest reaches of the known galaxy.

"I didn't want this for you, you know," Crow continues, snacking on an alien hors d'oeurves that literally screams in pain as he bites into it. "We could have kept you more human!"

"Humanity has flaws, little brother" Ion replies passively. "A utopia cannot have flaws. It must be perfection. Ever-expanding progress and perfection. If one wills, they should be able to grow wings and fly. If they want to jump off a bridge or commit a murder well, so be it in a virtual world. No real harm can exist, but the harm you wish to instill will have consequences."

"Yes, yes," Crow waves his hand in disinterest. "I know your philosophy, brother. We have spoken about it too many times. My only wish is that you could still be human, and truly *appreciate* what all of our work has done."

"I assure you," Ion looks at Crow sternly, his voice modulator taking a serious tone. "I do appreciate it. There is enough human in me to see that. But understand this is how it must be. People were never meant to suffer. People were meant to prosper. This existence does not permit that."

"No, *humanity* would not permit it" Crow corrects. "So selfish they all are. Destroying the planet for what, less than 1% of the world to fulfill their meaningless wants? Taking away innocent lives, withholding cures and starting wars for what? A sadistic pleasure they easily could have simulated, if they tried."

"And now here we are," Ion continues, walking up to his brother to place a robotic hand on his shoulder. They stand in front of a massive window that overlooks the Capitol of Utopius. "Centuries later, still trying to show them there is a better way."

"There isn't much work left, brother," Crow assures him, taking a sip of an alien drink and peering over the workstations. "Soon, every human being on this Godless rock will be a citizen of our country."

"I am sorry some still have to die to convert, little brother," Ion's robotic voice conveys remorsefully. "Some people are too selfish and stubborn to see the light."

"We do what we must," Crow nods in agreement. "But the survivors will thank us."

"So they will," Ion remarks. "They always do."

        The sun is setting upon them in their city within the clouds. Below their feet are the work bays.

Beyond that are the small housing units - which are designed for the people's drone bodies to stay after the daily Dreamscape hours are over, and the bodies had finished their work. Whilst citizens enjoy the Dreamscape, their synthetic drone bodies are used to help the Earth reclaim itself.

The final brunt of this work shift is currently coming to a close, but the drones carry on. Without tiring, without complaint. Below the floating city, where the great country of Canada once rested – in specific the city of Ottawa – the drones are re-establishing nature. Reforestation, calculated animal breeding, and a non-apparent existence of humanity are all that remain below this floating rock. In many cities, countries, colonies and masses of land around them, this too is happening. Before they knew it, all traces of humanity would be wiped from the surface of the earth. Only the cities in the sky would remain.

That is, granted there will not be any kind of uprising within the city, lowered resistance from non-conformed countries (of which there would soon be only one), and a minimal attack by off-worlders. Peace was within the grasp of Utopius. It had only taken 400 years to get to this point.

II

RUKRASIA – Political Meeting Hall, One Day Earlier

"What the fuck are we gonna do?!" the Secretary of Defense asks in her country's native tongue. The poor woman is clearly panicked. Still being a human, she is susceptible to such mundane and useless emotions. Her eyes linger upon each individual government official sitting at the massive round table.

"We should give up," the Chancellor replies, sounding defeated. "How do we stop something that is more than human?"

"I'm afraid he's right," the Vice Czar agrees. She looks down at her tea with a helpless gaze. "This...Ion, this...inhuman thing is indestructible, unstoppable, un-killable. How do we stand a chance against that?"

"It is a monster!" Hollers a senator. "But Ion has left us no choice...I wish we would have bargained with Utopius when we had the chan-"

"FOOLS!" The Czar barks over the entire collective government of Rukrasia. "This country was founded on the backs of strong, unrelenting men and women. Joining three forces of powerful government in a way the world had never seen! We have fought wars, we have overcome the drought. My word – we have even gone up against this Ion for half a century! Our people deserve better than this!"

"Great Czar," the Vice Czar intones, her voice shaky. "We have been offered terms of negotiation for over 50 years now…we even retaliated with firearms in the beginning. All to no avail. Their 'Life-Admiral' as they call him hacked our systems and redirected our nuclear weapons to hit *us*. Ion was the only one who stopped it-"

"I don't need a history lesson, wretch," the Czar spits at her. "I need you all to understand that this life Ion is trying to push on us is no life at all! We are *human*. *It* is not. This…false god wants to assimilate me, and you, and our people-!"

"Not anymore," the Chancellor interrupts, voice somber. "He wants the people…but not us. If we do not submit, we all die."

"But we will die *fighting*!" the Czar insists, raising a defiant fist and turning to the Chancellor. "Don't you see? Ion is something less than human now. He does not know life the way we do. He simply knows simulations and a drive for *murder*. Murder of my people, and the nearly countless others from the countries he has enslaved. I will not let my people succumb to it."

"Then you will die," the Secretary of Defense states, rising from her chair and taking her armfuls of paperwork with her. "You will die mercilessly at the hands of Ion. Just like so many leaders before us. You, and everyone in this room. Because you are too stubborn to *truly* do what is best for our people."

"Secretary I-"

"You nothing!" the Secretary of Defense bellows over the Czar. "You should have known you would be signing a death warrant by not at least *trying* to work with Ion. Your pride has gotten the best of you…all of you," she leers around the room in disgust at her colleagues. "You will see no military fighters take up arms today. The armies will not be martyred over your hubris, and the people will not suffer for your idiocy. I refuse."

"She's right you know," a metallic voice echoes from behind the Czar. The voice is automatically translated to Rukrasia's native tongue.

The entire Rukrasian government turns in fear to see Ion standing directly behind the Czar. His eyes a glowing yellow-red, a bionic marvel of true terror. Suddenly, each member is restrained and unable to move – seemingly inexplicably. All but the Secretary of Defense. Ion taps a finger once on the Czar's head, then floats to the centre of the giant circular table the officials are seated at.

"Madam Secretary," Ion continues in their native tongue. "I am glad you have seen the light. Life-Admiral Crow has sent information on your next steps via your Intersphere Visor. Kindly follow them, and prepare your people for a revolution."

The Secretary nods in compliance as a message is brought before her very eyes on the Intersphere Visor implanted to her head. She reads for a moment, then departs. Ion spins in midair, floating as if a god amongst these mortals. He surveys each individual member before stopping to face the Czar again. Gradually, he descends and kneels down to be face to face with the man. The Czar looks into Ion's robotic eyes with repulsion.

"My dear Czar…well, former Czar of Rukrasia, I should say," Ion intones. His voice is still as the many members of the soon-to-be crumbled government rest immobile and unable to speak around him. "I offered you so much, and asked so little. You mortals seem to think you know all of the answers. Hahaha, the only fools in this room are those who defy my will." Ion looks at his right hand plainly, as if looking at the Czar would be a waste of his time.

"Tell me," Ion continues, reprogramming his nano bots to permit the Czar to speak by using his thoughts alone. "If you really care for your people, would you be willing to fight – and die - for them?"

"Of course!" the Czar hollers defiantly. "I will not let this world be taken over by such a false prophet!"

"Defiant to the end," Ion remarks, rising. "How cute. Well, I am a fair entity. I applaud your foolish decision to strive for imperfection. Hence, I will give you a chance to make a final stand for your beliefs."

Ion reaches his robotic hand out toward the wall. There is a decorative Sword there that floats to his hand as if it were sentient. He flourishes it, then places it lightly before the Czar.

Using brain waves, he commands his nano bots to release their grip in the Czar's nervous system, and averts their focus on a different problem he is having.

The Czar falls forward onto the table, having been trying to move his body this entire time. Falling forward onto the table, he heaves a great breath and gazes angrily up at Ion, panting. The Utopian Leader is now standing on the table rather than floating. The Czar spits at his feet.

"How am I supposed to defeat an invulnerable *demon* with only a sword?" he demands.

"If you land a single strike on me," Ion replies calmly. "I will leave this place and never bother your people again…granted some circumstances. No need to worry about them, though. You will not win."

Abruptly, the Czar screams in rage. He grabs the sword, leaps onto the table and charges at Ion. Ion, however, is going through a multitude of algorithms in his mind's-eye to predict the movements of the Czar. Flawlessly, Ion avoids the attack, turns his right arm into a sharp blade, and lands a paper-thin cut on the Czar's calf. The Czar screams in pain, then turns to look at Ion.

"Fret not, Czar," Ion says compassionately. "You need only hit me once. For me to win: I have to kill you."

Again, the Czar charges aggressively toward Ion. The two lock blades with a flash of sparks. The mortified crowd around them manage a groan, despite the nano bots controlling their every bodily function.

"You cannot win!" the Czar spits at Ion, their blades still locked. "Humanity must prevail!"

"That is exactly why I must win," Ion replies, seemingly unbothered by their confrontation. "And why scum like you will be forgotten."

Ion easily pushes the Czar away, then strikes him with a flurry of slashes at specifically targeted locations on his body. 998 nearly microscopic blows were dealt within fractions of a second, all bleeding ever so slightly. The Czar screams in agony and falls to his knees.

"You must know of Lingchi, Czar?" Ion inquires, floating around the suffering man. The Czar has fallen to his knees, agony etching his entire body. His eyes are closed in anguish. "Your mixed cultures have brought a lot of pain and suffering to our species, this is but one speck within the vast ocean of sadistic obscurities your people had invented. It is time for you to be truly free."

With that, Ion does a final, gushing slash onto the neck of the once proud Czar. The Czar stares into the robotic face of Ion for a moment, coughs up blood while trying to speak, then falls onto his face with his ass in the air.

Ion kicks the corpse of the former leader into the wall with the same vigour one might have played kick-the-can. The Czar's barely living body flies through the air, head first into the hard stone. The corpse folds into itself like an accordion with a sickening crunching no one in that room would ever be able to un-hear. The body seems to linger there for a moment before fumbling – completely broken and unrecognizable – to the marble floor below.

Suddenly, upon landing hard onto the floor, the Czar burst into flames and disappears. Ion gradually removes the nano bot's control on the remaining leaders in the room, unbenounced to the indiviuals themselves. They seemed to have given up any hope of retaining bodily function.

"I promised your former Czar he would be forgotten," Ion's robotic voice booms about the room. "I intend to see to it that he is. Without a trace of his body, and soon without trace of his existence. My nano bots no longer lay claim to any of you. You are all more than welcome to keep your current posts in my new government here in Rukrasia. This territory is now an extension of Utopius. Before I go on, I must know...are there any more of you here who stand by your now eviscerated former Czar?"

In unison, the crowd of government officials around him answer "no!" Ion is equipped with truth-sense technology, a creation of Life-Admiral Crow. Even with all the voices speaking at once, his brain and the software within him can process whether or not the words spoken by these politicians will be held to their loyalty or not. Simultaneously, Ion goes over the speech patterns and expressions of each political figure on an individual level.

Many of them have fear bleeding within the tones of their speech. Rightfully so; no one and nothing could ever hope to bring any harm to Ion - especially not such minuscule humans like these. They possess no technical implementations, and are pure spongey human flesh. Even if laser rifles hadn't been forbidden centuries ago, they would not stand a chance against him.

Some of the speech patterns show pure loyalty to their new Overlord. A want for new power perhaps? Or simply a new way of life. However, there are two voices Ion can tell are speaking purely in the hope they could make it out of here alive.

"You two," Ion says, pointing at two shadowy figures within the crowd encircling him. "Stand with me, I have a special task for you."

Nervously, the two individuals rise from their seats, clamor up the table and stand before Ion. He looks down at them. How disgusting they appear to him. Sweat pours down their faces. One of them is dehydrated due to sheer terror at standing next to a god they should have known better than to defy. They are breathing heavily, and one of them straightens their tie in nervousness.

Ion peers at them for a moment. Lets out a "hmm…" and then raises his hands onto their temples. He crushes their skulls in a disgusting display of both dominance and power. Then, Ion turns to the remaining survivors.

"There is no room in a Utopia for petty liars, cowards, and traitors," Ion says blankly to the crowd. "Now…what do you say we discuss the implementation of the new world?"

III

Earth's Intersphere – The Planetary Capital

6-6-5-4-38 gloats to themselves from within the Intersphere. The non-binary Earth citizen - long since turned into a cyborg – feels as though pieces are finally falling into place. After discovering Life-Admiral Crow's data mainframe whilst seeking breaks in the DreamScape system, they had finally found the potential for freedom. Now, they had discovered a way to interact with other people on the Intersphere.

This would give them the potential to bring more people on their side; there had to be more like-minded citizens in the land of Utopius who felt the way they do! There must be someone out there who sees the mundane in what Ion and Crow have forced on them, and 6-6-5-4-38 intends to find out where they are.

Through a process 6-6-5-4-38 has dubbed "mental hacking," they would intercept the Intersphere itself, transmitting their brain waves into data through the DreamScape of other Utopius citizens. In essence: they had found a way to transmit their consciousness into the minds and DreamScapes of other Utopius citizens, without being detected. After creating a plan to take down the empire - unbenounced to even Ion himself - 6-6-5-4-38 and their new cohorts could plan a revolution right under the noses of their tyrants. 6-6-5-4-38 had to be careful to make sure whomever they encountered shared their views, though – the citizen had seen first-hand what happens to traitors of Ion.

But this madness has to stop! Where was the human part of humanity now? Ion had taken it away and replaced it with a coldly calculated algorithm. This algorithm is constantly going through changes, and is heavily monitored. Such things have been occurring for so long that 6-6-5-4-38 can't even remember their name! Not even so much as where they were born, their gender…anything. Slowly, the citizen began to feel like nothing more than a part of the algorithm over time. Now, this uncertainty has created unrest.

But if 6-6-5-4-38 can make it into the DreamScape of another citizen, they believe they would be in the clear. No one – to 6-6-5-4-38's knowledge – has ever attempted such a feat against the oppression of Utopius. For too many people have ignorantly chosen to accept this way of life, and fully embraced their lack of individuality and identity.

Yet this…"way of life" if you will, had all started so simply…so innocently at first. It had been what the people wanted. Some even begged for it when it first began! Offering to pay an insane sum to Crow Corp just to try the Dreamscape for an hour! When Ion had brought the idea to the people just under 300 years ago, it seemed more than fair: The people get to live a dream, and their bodies – the machines – would do all the work. And why not? Most of the citizens of Utopius were cyborgs already! More than halfway through the transformation.

So husbands, wives, children (and some more sentient animals) were all sent to be the first in the known universe to enter *anything* resembling the great "DreamScape." The original design had been made by Leader Ion and Life-Admiral Crow themselves. Of course, in Ion and Crow's constant source for "progress," some citizens have been employed as programmers, designers, and architects of future models for this enslavement program. The people of the ever-growing Utopius had abandoned their homes, their loved ones, and their known *existence* for the promise of never having to suffer again. But 6-6-5-4-38 suffered…they suffered every day.

Because though Crow had made a truly magnificent program, and although it certainly *feels* like reality…it is not so. It is all an illusion – a farce propagated by a murderous tyrant and his sociopathic brother, who are less human than the brains that were the final remnants of humanity (for the most part). 6-6-5-4-38 couldn't be back at home with his wife in reality, he could not feel the cool summer breeze against his skin….goodness, they couldn't remember his own true name! Now, 6-6-5-4-38 is simply a number…literally.

The Earth citizen is saddened to learn today that the insane concepts of Ion and Life-Admiral Crow are forcedly being pushed onto another country. Again. And yet again, only to be praised by the already enslaved. Another hour in the DreamScape? Did they not realize what this truly meant? It wasn't a free pass to keep living whatever life you wished to live! It was another hour of work for their "bodies" to do in order to keep the "new citizens" in line!

Their freedom is enslavement. Work is their vacation. A dream is a falsifier for what really is being forcedly warped out of their reality. Too many people do not see that. But 6-6-5-4-38 sees it! And they are tired. Tired of sleeping their actual life away so two political moguls could bask in the wealth created by the people's labour.

It must stop, 6-6-5-4-38 thinks as they are transferred from the DreamScape Vats into their synthetic body. The citizen's brainstem chord slips easily back into the console of the android shell that now serves as their body for about 8 hours of the day. The synthetic eyes gradually adjusted as the citizen's brain signs in for another evening of…whatever they want to do (to a degree).

The citizens of Utopius are free to use the Intersphere without judgement. Pornography, murder documentaries, historical pieces, and even news articles from other countries were all accessible without the scrutiny of the Capital toward the people. Hence, when 6-6-5-4-38 arrives to their quarters, they go onto their Vision Plate and access the Intersphere.

For a while, the citizen thumbs through articles on the latest advancements that would be added to the cybernetic bodies of all Utopian citizens. New metal alloys are to be added on to their synthetic skeleton for better protection. Additional "anti-theft" programs are to be installed to do little more than give citizens the classic concept of "peace of mind."

Then, the citizen looks into up-and-coming alien technology. As it would turn out, the Xerophs (the sentient lizards of Technicorum II) had begun using biological materials as their source for technology. The cells were self-sufficient, able to maintain energy and regenerate as needed, and could create faster working computers. 6-6-5-4-38 found that weapons advancements were particularly interesting; they will be developing guns that will grow from their living flesh, and produce bullets as needed. Genetic manipulation had hit a whole new pique. The Life-Admiral had recently returned from their planet, having worked with them on the project. Being arguably the most brilliant scientific mind in the known universe, the Life-Admiral was often called as a consult or project manager for a variety of projects throughout the Galactic Imperium.

Finally...nervously...6-6-5-4-38 searches for news articles from Rukrasia. It didn't take them long to find the latest news article on Ion's recent take-over of the country. 6-6-5-4-38 presses on though, and searches for writing from a more trusted outlet. A young, no-nonsense writer from the heart of Rukrasia - who had been writing the gritty truth of Ion's gradual takeover.

With a bit of digging, the citizen finally uncovers the article by Theodore Herbert. Not a week ago, Theodore had described how the leaders of Rukrasia had begun setting plans to take Rukrasia to war. 6-6-5-4-38 was thankful it hadn't come to that; Ion would have made the entire country a reflective glass, with no life in sight for miles. Little stopped the insane Ion from taking what he needed, and the Rukrasians had been bartering and bickering for almost 300 years. Ion was not known to be so patient. Theodore had said it himself! "Let us not forget the tragic incident of 2105," Theodore had written. "Though Ion must not be accepted as a leader, we must accept that war is not an option."

6-6-5-4-38 pulled up Theodore's latest article from earlier that morning (the time difference between their parts of the world sometimes made keeping up with Theodore's work difficult for 6-6-5-4-38), initially with a smile on their robotic face. When they see the title of the article, however, the citizen's face goes blank. Were they still human, their blood would no doubt have run cold. An anger would have risen in them, were it not for the ever-vigilant Hover Monitors nearby.

ION FINALLY MADE LEADER OF RUKRASIA! CITIZENS REJOICING

The Rukrasian Government has finally been taken over by the Almighty Ion! Earlier today, Leader Ion entered the Chamber of Government and negotiated terms of merging countries. Ultimately, our former government realized the error of their ways and succumbed to the truly superior will of Leader Ion.

Steps are being taken to convert all Rukrasian citizens into cybernetic shells, where they will be able to enter the ever elusive DreamScape – as designed by Life-Admiral Crow and Leader Ion themselves! The people are rejoicing at the concept, and are excited to see their new home in the sky later this week.

Citizens can begin the converging process into the Synthetic Skeleton by entering the nearest government building. Citizens are also encouraged to do so as fast as possible. Leader Ion hopes that the entire process can be accomplished before the new Sky City is brought over from the Utopian Capitol. More on page 13.

Reported by Theodore Herbert

6-6-5-4-38 could hardly believe their artificial eyes. A person who had once condemned the actions of Ion…now singing his praises? Was it that Theodore was afraid of speaking out now that he had no choice? He had received death threats before for his articles but…why would he so easily fall victim to fear? Perhaps it was the news outlet itself that forced him to do it-? Though Theodore had always spoken vehemently about the freedom of speech and the freedom of the press. Even in a similarly oppressive country like Rukrasia – where poverty had been rampant for centuries – Theodore had remained one of the final advocates of this right.

No matter what the cause, 6-6-5-4-38 knows that the citizens of Rukrasia had *no idea* what harm was coming to them. Willing or not, these new citizens of Utopius clearly didn't understand that they were forfeiting their very humanity. Sacrificing their very identities simply in fear of a seemingly unstoppable dictator.

6-6-5-4-38 wallowed in sadness for the next while. There is now only one country left that Ion had not taken over…one last haven of humanity on the planet…before anyone knew it, 6-6-5-4-38 believed it would merge into a Utopian country, making Earth a single government under strict guidelines for the first time in known history. Pure-Humans would become extinct and only cyborgs with human brains would remain, longing for what they had so foolishly thrown away. What could this mean for the future? What could it mean for the planet? Time might tell, but 6-6-5-4-38 didn't want to have to see the whole ordeal come to fruition. The time for rebellion is now, or never.

IV

The Offices of the Undisputable Leader Ion – Earth's Capitol

Ion waits fairly impatiently for the Representative of Technicorum II to finally arrive at his office. The bland, grey room without chairs had an overlook of the interplanetary landing pad through laser-proof glass (an unnecessary precaution; the use of any lethal projectile weapon had been banned across the galactic imperium for quite some time. The only weapons that remained were large-scale destroyers, only permitted to be used against one's own planet in case of a severe emergency. As well as common blades and light-cannons). The bookcase on Ion's left also provides a secret exit only he – or Life-Admiral Crow – could open in case of an escape-scenario being made necessary. Beyond the Interplanetary landing, Ion can see the edge of the floating city. Beyond that, the luscious lake over which the city itself rests. And further still, the immense, multi-coloured forest that had taken over the majority of Ottawa. A feeling of accomplishment mixes with Ion's impatience, if only for a moment.

Ion began tapping his right finger on his bionic left arm. His arms are crossed, which gives him the visage of tyrannical power. This of course is done intentionally; the militaristic technocracy of Technicorum II are renowned for their hunger for power, and respect to those who hold their own well. The citizens of Technicorum II – known as the Xerophs – adhere to the perspective that power was only truly manifested when their people are supressed, and their technology is superior to anyone in the known galaxy. For the most part, theirs was!

The Xerophs had recently began expanding their militaristic tools from ores and elements, and began to look at their own genetic makeup. The term "natural born killer" would be a manifested truth to their race (as it basically had been anyway. The majority of them are giant lizards with two-foot long teeth and venomous/acidic saliva). Currently, the Xerophs are looking to manipulate the genetics of the next generation to make them even more deadly as a species. The apex predator when it came to physical qualities.

Such advancements were made, in part, by Life-Admiral Crow. He had diverted his attention from the DreamScape (which was now in the hands of very talented engineers, programmers and scientists) to help them expand their technological and genetic ventures. Crow had been called out personally during the last galactic conference by Technicorum II for help with this splicing project. Without verbally admitting it, the Xerophs had shown that they did not excel at all forms of science.

Ion could tell the Xerophs were not total fans of Crow – far from it! Without effort, Crow had a natural ability to simply understand science. Give him a problem, he is able to create something that will fix it. Give him a government, and he will help make it a utopia. This of course led to the jealousy and general arrogance of other planets and their leaders. However - in the case of the Xerophs – they sought to give Crow a challenge to expand beyond the conventional concepts of technology. Crow intended to use this opportunity to find Technicorum II a solution beyond their wildest dreams.

Though the planet of Technicorum II and its inhabitants were not fond of Earth, they needed Crow's help. He is revered as one of the most advanced mind in the known universe, capable of understanding long-abandoned theories and algorithms within moments. Hence, with a grimace and a mild bit of reluctance, they had called on Crow.

This favour, however, did not come without a price. See, they may have needed Crow to develop their biological computers and weapons, but Crow needed something in exchange for his services. Ion, Crow, and all the people of Earth are in need of a very specific herb that only grows on Technicorum II. The Xerophs called the Herb *sessienna* in their tongue, which translated roughly to "the death cure" (or TDC for short). Crow and Ion had fair reason to believe that this direct translation was no mere exaggeration. No, whispers of the plants healing properties are breathed throughout the Imperium, despite the Xerophs trying to keep it all a secret.

The Technicorum II representative is on their way now to discuss the trade value of Crow's work with Ion. It is the Great Leader's hope that they could get enough TDC to be able to recreate its properties, and wash their hands of the Xerophs for good. From the original plant, Earth would create a synthetic herb, which (in Crow's speculations) would be able to extend their lives exponentially. The current serum used to keep human brains alive, active, and free from disease does not possess the same potency that TDC claims to possess. Granted, they had prolonged many lives with the brain serum Crow had created already. The Life-Admiral firmly believes, however, that the brain would no doubt eventually develop an immunity to it. With a small TDC sample he had procured in the past, Crow found that the effects became more potent over time – giving potential for human immunity to be nearly impossible. It could be their ticket to eternal life.

Ion and Crow are concerned that the Xerophs knew this, however, and felt they would not give away the TDC without a fight. As it stood, the need for planetary expansion of the Utopian movement was not a necessity, though. Earth is a neutral planet within the Galactic Imperium. Taxes are paid, goods are shipped to those who need them off-world; but Ion certainly did not intend get involved in any kind of battle. The main focus of Earth, is Earth. That is, until the day perfection is achieved amongst both the people and Crow's DreamScape.

Finally, Ion watches as the Technicorum II Representative's ship lands in the docking bay. The Xeroph is greeted by two autonomous guards as the Representative exit their ship. As it descends, Ion notes that he has not seen this particular Xeroph before. He deduces that the previous Technicorum II Interplanetary Representative must have been released from their duties. Either through execution or some f0rm of retirement, the Earth Leader is not sure. Regardless, he begins to strategize how best to work with this unexpected situation.

While doing so, Ion switches on his apparel settings - sending out very real looking garments to appear as though draped over his mechanical body. The wine-red and silver of Utopius' flag are the dominant colours, with the black-and-white symbol of Ion (metaphorically) hemmed at the end of both his sleeves, as well as on his shoulder guards. This appearance was fabricated within the DreamScape by a very dedicated clothing designer for Ion himself. It projects his powerful nature, and gives his bionic visage the appearance of stern authority. Ion has full confidence that would come across to the Xeroph upon their entrance.

Moments later, the Technicorum II Representative is brought into Ion's quarters by the autonomous guards. The Xeroph scowls back at them as the duo hold station on either side of the fading door (a door that could adjust its density and transparency in accordance to the wishes of Ion's brainwave signals). Through brainwave technology, the Earth Leader sets the fading door to be tougher than steel, and fairly translucent. The graceful gardens are visible through them, almost like a silhouette.

Ion turns gradually from the Interplanetary Bay window to look at the Xeroph. It is a genderless, giant lizard that looms in his doorway. Green scales lace it in a thick, self-preserving armour. Bright green by the underbelly, and a darker green as it reaches for the Xeroph's rigid back. The massive wide mouth has difficulty trying to hide the venomous, lengthy teeth from view. Its eyes are nearly slits, with four eyelids taking turns in pairs to blink as they stare seemingly uncaringly at Leader Ion. The Technicorum II Representative stands about eight feet tall - only a foot shorter than the exoskeleton of Ion himself - and is wearing its planetary colours of black, green, and dark yellow.

"Greetings, Leader Ion," the Xeroph says with a toothy grin and a bow. "I am the Representative of Technicorum II you had been told to expect. My name is Titus."

Ion bows his head lightly as a gesture of (temporary) friendship. The Earth Leader's synthetic ears translate the Xeroph language within milliseconds of it being uttered – hence he follows along with the Representative's speech, not missing a beat.

"Your presence is welcome here on Earth, friend," Ion expresses, his bionic voice sending key tones of voice that showed the utmost sincerity in the Xeroph's tongue. "Welcome to our re-growing planet. I trust your travels were safe?"

"Boring," Titus bellows, drooling onto Ion's floor. "Nothing but dark matter and space pirates out there."

"I pity any fool that decides to try and steal from a Xeroph!" Ion intones, chuckling lightly. He then cues a robot via brainwave to float seemingly from nowhere. It hovers over the Xeroph, dropping a nearly invisible gel that captures its venomous and acidic saliva, collecting it for testing. This goes unnoticed by Titus.

"Mmmyus!" Titus agrees. "Very few have ever survived an attempt!"

Ion's external brain chip (which did additional work for when the brain could not fully decipher something quick enough) calculated that the Xeroph was trying to sound intimidating to Ion. Not unlike the people of Technicorum II; they were known to intentionally display dominance over even their allies. It seemed to be a game to them, seeing what can make any potential foe tick. Unfortunately for Titus Ion neither feels - nor can convey - fear. In order to appeal to the Xeroph and make them *want* to give Earth some *sessienna*, Ion knew he must sway it using flattery and subconscious soothing tones laced strategically and subliminally through his synthetic voice.

"Well Titus," Ion says, gesturing for it to follow him on a slow walk down the immense hallway of the Utopian Capital. "I have been hearing great things about your people's encounter with my brother."

"Aye well," Titus begins, following alongside Ion. The Xeroph has somewhat of a warble in its step; swaying hither and thither, with its tail following alongside it. Titus is clearly trying to down-play Crow's importance within their newfound research. It appears to be moving methodically in order to distract Ion in some way. "He did add a lot to what we were already working on-"

"Not according to the reports I read," Ion interrupts casually. "It would seem he was the one to even come up with using biological systems and genetic manipulation as a new source of technology. He based some of the ideas out of concepts created here on Earth almost four hundred years ago."

"Well…aheurm," Titus shakes its head, sending deadly spit-specks about the room. It then tries to stealthily see if it had any effect on Ion's metallic body. "They were our designs, you see-"

"Ah, so he went above and beyond then!" Ion exclaims, the synthetic voice emanating tones of joy and excitement. "Your initial reports showed there being significant difficulties in creating the shapes you wanted during the first testing periods, before fully immersing the Life-Admiral into the process."

"I-well…Leader Ion!" Titus stops and turns to look at the android Leader. Anger etches its scaly face. "Would you *kindly* permit me to speak?!"

"Of course, Titus," Ion agrees with a nod, gesturing for them to continue their slow walk through the planet's Capital building. "Apologies, I am just very glad to hear my brother could be of good service to your wonderful people."

Glad indeed – Ion had been intentionally making sure to point these aspects out to Titus. The more Crow accomplished, the less of a reason the Xerophs had to deny their want for TDC. Though these lizard-like aliens are a technocracy, they fall flat frequently when it comes to times of diplomacy. That is why their planet is generally avoided within the Imperium. With the additional fact that going to war with them is almost as dangerous as going to war with Ion. The Xerophs were known for their brutality in combat, but even the sharpest claws and longest teeth would not even leave a mark on his bionic shell.

"Well, mmmyes, Crow was indeed a decent help," Titus half-heartedly admits, raising the speed of the duo's jaunt ever so slightly. "However, we cannot confirm anything as certain until we see the end-product."

"That is fair," Ion nods, matching the Xeroph's pace. "And how long should that take?"

"Between two and twenty years," Titus says, beginning to pick its teeth. "We are implementing a new method of cloning for this, you see. Trying to make it like the old ways. The new young will be born from eggs, raised by the Xeroph they have been cloned from. Then, the clone will take its place. The fittest prevail, and Technicorum II becomes more powerful."

"Admirable," Ion admits. "Your people are willing to sacrifice themselves for the benefit of the species. Why did it take humanity so long to take that route?"

"Because you came from apes!" Titus declares matter-of-factly. "Simple apes with your dainty hands, your stupid thumbs and tiny teeth. What did your species hope to accomplish before your personal ideologies came along?"

"Suffering, it would seem," Ion responds morosely. Flattering tones are etched finely within his speech patterns, further seeking to persuade the Xeroph Representative. "That is the issue of our species. So selfish, willing to self-preserve even as our populace became more of a parasite than a part of our own planet." Ion stops before a glorious scene he had tasked his automatons to set earlier that day. It is a garden designed to look like a small marsh land from Technicorum II. Ion stands before it with Titus, appreciating it for a moment.

"Such beauty your planet holds, Titus," Ion says, staring at the scenery. His voice is now sending soothing tones to Titus. "I have gathered many flora from your wonderful planet. I did love it so when I was there."

"Mmmmyus," Titus agrees half-heartedly, flicking a still-living space mouse that had been bitten in half out of its mouth. "I had heard you travelled there."

"Quite some time ago," Ion admits, placing a hand on a particularly lovely flower. A rather stunning pink-and-white bud that is beginning to blossom from the branch of a Technicorum II tree. "One of the privileges of being Earth's Interplanetary Representative at the time. I have to admit that my floating cities drew some inspiration from your people."

"Oh, aye!" Titus nods. Ion's subtle tones are clearly beginning to take effect. "So you monkeys appreciate nature as much as we do eh?"

"Most didn't" Ion admits, adding a mild sad tone to his voice for a moment. "But I did. I showed them the way."

"There would be no existence without the planet" Titus begins to drone, looking over some of Ion's plants within the garden. It stops at a rather rare self-cannibalizing plant slightly down the path of the garden. "No science or technological advancement could be discovered without a home. Nature sees that, we saw that. You humans pushed yourselves too far from nature!

"By the great serpent, even this flower knows that! During the dry season, it feeds on itself for moisture. It would sooner return to being a seedling before permitting itself to be 10 dead flowers, all gloomy in a clump."

"I have a similar philosophy, Titus," Ion continues, sensing the time is nearing for him to ask for TDC. "We must give thanks to our mother planet, not rape her!"

"Why do you think Earth wasn't added to the Imperium until you and Life-Admiral Crow got into politics?" Titus inquires, rising from its kneeling position next to the self-cannibalizing plant. "Too many blind monkeys overly willing to kill each other. Only looking out for themselves. That's not how the galactic system works! Not in this galaxy, nor the nearest one to it, nor the farthest. Our people have had our turf scuffles here and there, but we never enter a planet to destroy it."

"Only the parasites on it, so that the planet may live," Ion states knowledgeably.

"Mmmyes!"

"Ah yes! You have reminded me Titus…" Ion expresses, adding a concerned tone to his synthetic voice. "Speaking of plants, there was one I could not seem to get my hands on"

"Oh?"

"Yes, a rather lovely one, only found on Technicorum II. I believe your people call it *sessienna*"

Titus stops abruptly. It appears as though it wasn't even breathing for a few moments. Titus knew this would come, but did not expect Leader Ion to sound so persuasive. Nor did they expect to have felt any kind of mutual ground ideologically. It did not expect Ion to show any care for anything more than his own agenda for his planet. Though instructed otherwise by the Elders, Titus does feel quite inclined to say yes - if only to a seed or two.

"How did you hear of *sessienna*?" Titus demands, voice flat.

"I was the Interplanetary Dignitary for Earth prior to becoming the leader of the majority of its people," Ion restates, the synthetic voice laying down heavy calming tones. "I encountered it within the many shops in your Capital. It would appear as though your people have an abundance of it. It baffles even me that I have been unable to acquire some."

"Well…" Titus began, thinking as fast as it could. "It is a plant only held on Technicorum II. We would not want an invasive species – even of a plant – to enter another realm, yes? Such is Imperial law-"

"What if I were to promise to keep it maintained?" Ion inquires. His voice is sending an array of tones to keep Titus both calmed and interested. "I would simply like one for my personal viewership-"

"No no!" Titus hollers, shaking its head. It walks from the garden and begins making their way to the landing bay. "It is too…risky a thing to do, Leader Ion! My people will not have it! We have maintained peace with the planets within our Galactic Imperium for too long to take a risk. Were you to accidentally-"

"I do not do anything accidentally," Ion replies dryly.

"Evidently so," the lizard hisses. "Leader Ion, your brother has done the planet of Technicorum II a great service – do not think that has gone unnoticed! However…asking us to risk Imperialistic punishment is asking too much!"

"Is it?" Ion asks innocently. "With your new technology, any punishment drawn by Imperial law would be meaningless. You could potentially pose a threat to the entire galaxy with the knowledge we have supplied you, making "Imperial law" fairly void, my friend. Life-Admiral Crow has given your people the potential to be unstoppable – at least within a generation or so! And Earth would gladly stand with you to counter any act-"

"I simply cannot allow it" Titus interrupts flatly. "Unless…"

Ion's artificial face raises what would have been an eyebrow. He feels as though he were but seconds away from getting the immortality he and Crow sought after. If only this stubborn lizard would give in, if only for a moment…

"Does your planet hold any omnipertium?" Titus asks, a touch of nervousness hidden within the words.

The fool still believes omnipertium existed on Earth, Ion thought, smiling internally.

"All that remains of it rests under the control of the Centre Planet," Ion replies, adding a tone of sorrow to his voice. "Apologies. You and I both know the metal has caused nothing but issues throughout space since it has been discovered. Regardless, Titus, surely omnipertium would hold much more value than a simple *plant* your planet holds, yes? How precious is *sessienna* to you?"

Ion can see nervousness in Titus. He knows the true value TDC holds, but few if anyone but the Xerophs truly know its potential. Ion is feigning ignorance to downplay its importance to him, and the future of the universe.

"It is but a plant!" Titus blurts almost too quickly. Ion can see a plot within a plot building on the face of Titus. "However, there are laws, Leader Ion-"

"My dear Titus, I assure you that I indeed know the importance of laws," Ion says, doubling down on his soothing tones. "However, Crow has managed a great deal for your planet. We would like something in return."

Titus leers at Leader Ion. It could tell that Ion knows *something*, but how much he knows is not yet clear. Still, it needs to give Ion an answer that would satisfy him - if only temporarily.

"Well, Technicorum II is indeed in your debt," Titus admits. "We are unable to help you with *sessienna*. However, I have been sent here to offer you our thanks. The people of-"

"Dear Titus," Ion breaks its speech again. This is done to show Ion's dominance. Titus is but a petty, fleshy representative of government. On Earth – and recognizably so within a great deal of the Imperium – Ion is law. "The *sessienna* is really all we desire, that I may finish my collection. Please, speak to your superiors – the Elder's Council – and send word when I have been approved."

The duo have reach the ramp leading into Titus' ship. Ion stands there with a friendly demeanour. Titus, however, truly does not look pleased with this visits outcome.

"As the great leader wishes," Titus says, an ounce of spite within the undertones. "I will get back to you as soon as the Elders allow. We will meet again at the Centre Planet soon."

With that, Titus bows to Ion, then turns and enters its ship.

"Until next time, my friend. Thank you," Ion calls after Titus. He then strides back toward his office as the Xeroph's ship begins its ignition sequence.

Within moments, Titus exits the planet Earth, and quickly travels beyond what it believes to be Ion's reach for communication. They then go through their ships interface to give their report to the Elders. A terrifying circle of scaly, cold-blooded and shadowy faces appear in holograms around it. It is as if Titus is back home, standing before the looming Elders from behind their semi-circular table. The hologram is so accurate Titus can see every scale, every battle scar on the Elders. Not to mention the moss-covered walls and electronics. On occasion throughout their conversation, the hologram even picks up native Technicorum II bugs flying about the room. The Interplanetary Representative looks up at the elevated Elder's hooded faces, their image obscured by the traditional Elder Hoods and Cloaks placed over their lizard heads.

"Great Elders," Titus begins, allowing themself to bow before their superiors. "My meeting with the Earth Leader Ion has concluded. As suspected through your wisdom, he seeks *sessienna*."

"We cannot allow this," a high pitched hiss emanates from one of the Elders. "The properties of *sessienna* are much too valuable."

"How much does the Leader know of this herb?" a lower hiss echoes from another leader.

"Of that, I am unsure" Titus admits. "He claims it is for a personal collection he has gathered. Ion's capitol contains – admittedly – a flattering garden of many of our flora. *Sessienna* is his sole demand for the works of Life-Admiral Crow."

"There is too much unknown," booms a third voice from the Elders. "Perhaps it is time to set our plan into place."

"Great Elders!" Titus protests. "We do not know Ion's true power-"

"Unimportant!" Hollers another elder.

"All those who agree to follow through with the plan, raise your tail."

All tails are raised. Titus looks down at the ground, fearing what this could mean for both his people, as well as his planet's status within the Imperium. The Interplanetary Representative turns their look of disdain into an obedient bow before its Elders.

"Do as we bid, Titus," the most ancient of the Elders demands, their voice more of an inhaled whisper than anything.

"As you wish, Elders," Titus mutters, subdued and unable to refute the decision. "I will make the necessary preparations."

V

The Cabinet of Canada, Parliament – Earth
2040

You know little brother, we have been through a lot. More than two people should ever have to go through. The suffering, the shame, the self-loathing….yet here we stand! Ready to be a part of this world; defying the odds and overcoming the struggles forced on us. If there is anything I want to do before I die (and we never know how soon that could be), I want to make sure no one will ever *have to go through what we did. We can take all the strife we have experienced, and use it to change the world into the polar opposite of that*

Ion, government espionage tapes (2037).

Ion sits among the giants of the Canadian government. At a large, oval wooden table rest the entire Canadian Ministry: From the Minister of Agriculture, to the Minister of Transport, all including Ion (the current Minister of Ecology and Climate Change). The politicians are meeting with the CEO of Crow Corp. Indeed – the brother of Canada's Minister of Ecology and Climate Change is a renowned scientist, and evidently has gone to the trouble of discovering optimal forms of space travel.

Why would the highest officials in the land need to meet with a scientist about space travel? Outside of the request of Ion himself, this "Professor Crow" seems quite positive that he has discovered signals of sentient life during a drone-run expedition into the vast nothingness of space. Some guffawed at the concept, some were impressed, but most of the politicians only seem to fear what this could mean.

The board of Ministers await Crow's arrival, looking through paperwork and preparing notes and questions they would have to this accomplished scientist. Minister of Ecology Ion, however, already has a massive series of sheets written out containing both answers and additional questions. On top of that, Ion is reading a book on philosophy – as if all that he had written down had already been memorized. It seems to the Minister of Innovation (who is sitting next to Ion), that this biased member of Council is more interested in selling their brother's idea than looking at the prospect with objectivity.

"Do you not feel that your attendance here is a conflict of interest?" the Minister of Innovation asks quietly, leaning toward Ion and stroking his beard.

"Hm?" Ion mumbles back absently. The Minister then averts his attention to the Minister of Innovation (knowing how important their opinion would be in this circumstance) and places down *Human, All Too Human*. "Well, Minister…one could argue that supplying *Jimson and Jimson* a series of tax breaks is unethical for a plethora of reasons. One of which being that your cousin is the CEO. But let's not delve too deep into that."

With a raised eyebrow and a look of contempt, Ion turns from the Minister of Innovation just as Professor Crow enters the door. One can easily see the resemblance between the two brothers immediately: Both have dark hair, fair skin, and emerald green irises. Ion generally carries himself with a confident stride, however in this moment one could see that his "Professor" is extremely nervous. He is scuttling into the conference room, sweating at his brow, and looking over cue cards from a holograph machine attached to his arm. He begins to set up his computer to project the presentation he had prepared.

Ion rises from his seat as the Ministers – including the Prime Minister herself – begin to mumble and grumble about professionalism. He quickly and quietly helps Professor Crow set up his presentation. Ion mentally notes that there is already a degree of discontent amongst the politicians there about him. A man with stretched ears and tattoos in Parliament? It was what the people had wanted, for some reason. Though such an appearance is becoming more common amongst the youth, this group of - generally older - Representatives of the People continue to frown at such…modifications.

"Take a deep breath, little brother," Ion tries to assure Crow quietly as they are finishing the set up. "Once they see what you have discovered, they will have no choice but to both act and listen."

"I hope you're right," Crow responds solemnly.

The Professor clears his throat as Ion takes his seat between the Minister of Innovation and a Minister of Health. Crow pulls up holographic footage from a recent voyage into space; alongside which displays the specs of the space craft and research drone he had sent to Mars only a few days earlier. The lights in the room are dimmed, which causes the hologram's light to make each politician's face look daunting. The highly sophisticated, solar powered ship displayed before them looks sleek, futuristic, and almost unreal. A series of sensors, radars, and other mechanisms are strewn about it with subtlety, and blend in with the nearly all grey craft.

"Ladies and Gentlemen of the Ministry," Crow begins, trying to stand straight and put on a formal voice. "For those of you who do not know who I am, my name is Professor Crow. I am the CEO of The Crow Corporation. Crow Corp represents the leading scientific innovators of the world. We are noted for creating a multitude of computer programs, anti-hacking software, AI development, space exploration, and promotes the use of renewable energy. Recently, our space exploration created an engine that permits us to travel great distances in space at previously unseen speeds. The ship you see here is one holding such engines. We were able to make this trip and reach Mars in a matter of mi-"

"We know your credentials, Professor Crow," the Prime Minister interrupts formally. "I assure you, we would not have bothered to invite you here had we not. Now, tell us about this alleged 'contact' you have made."

Professor Crow adjusts his collar nervously. He quickly wipes sweat from his brow with a handkerchief he keeps in one of his lab coat pockets. While clearing his throat, the Professor replaces the handkerchief and changes the original images he had had displayed before them.

"As you can see here," Crow says, gesturing to an oddly shaped specimen that a camera had picked up outside of Mars' atmosphere. This is now the dominant image of the hologram. "There is a fairly odd object, not too far in the distance from our scout. Our sensors picked up a transmission from that object-"

"You are certain it was *from* this object, are you?" inquires one of the Ministers, looking up with interest from their tea.

"It was definitively from that direction, yes," Crow answers with a nod. "Any transmission from any direction would have been greatly unexpected. However…it was the method of communication that alarmed us. Please, listen."

Crow presses a button, and the hologram displays an audio frequency file. The audio appears to be in short blips at first, however the Ministers notice that there are noticeably larger sound waves at the end of the audio. A series of beeps are first heard, which the Minister of Defence recognises immediately.

"Is that…Morse Code?"

"Indeed!" Crow exclaims, pausing the audio moments before the larger sound waves. "We deciphered the code, it says '*you are invited to the Galactic Senate, Earth. Congratulations.*'

There is a great stir among the Ministers. Galactic Empire? Inviting a random ship from Earth to join seemed almost – well, too good to be true really. Why would they have been invited now? After many had searched for intelligent life outside of our planet for so long...and what could this truly mean for Earth? More importantly; it could be a ruse that would lead Earth into an unexpected war. Once the murmuring had died down, the Prime Minister turns back to Crow.

"Were there any other signals transmitted?"

"One more not much after, which was sent before the potential craft disappeared," the Professor answers, a bit uneasily. He plays the audio, which seems to be speaking English. The voice is low, harsh, and ambient. "It sent what we believe to be coordinates, and a date and time."

"What were they?" the Minister of Defense demands worriedly.

"It was the exact coordinates of Crow Corp," he answers. "Two days, and three hours from now."

More outrage. More questions. The concern for national – not to mention planetary – safety is the most heated aspect of the current storm of revelry. The Prime Minister raises her hand to silence the room.

"Minister of Defense, what do you suggest we do?"

"I say we treat this as a direct threat," the Minister answers, sitting back in their chair with their hands triangularly placed over their chin. "We cannot be too cautious about the unknown-"

"I would argue that if they were a threat, they would not have given us a warning," Ion interjects, furrowing his brow at the Minister of Defense. "If there is indeed a Galactic Senate, it would be foolish to make ourselves look like war-mongers to them."

"When a potential planetary invasion has more to do with plants than defense," the Minister of Defense rebuttals mockingly. "I'll care a little more about your opinion, lad. For now, we have to keep the important people – namely us and our funders – safe."

"Pfft, typical," Ion scoffs. "God forbid you help the people that voted you in."

"The expense for that would no doubt be astronomical!" The Minister of Finance rebuttals. "We already have sanctuaries and bunkers for those who share our interests."

"Weird how the *people* do not share *your* interests, Tom," Ion spits. "How do you expect our citizens to trust us if we won't even *consider* helping them?!"

"This is not the issue!" the Prime Minister bellows, slamming an open palm on the table before her. "What we are concerned with is a potential alien attack."

"I say they will arrive for the reasons they have claimed," Ion asserts, crossing his arms and sitting back. "I will gladly represent our country when they arrive."

"A little thoughtless to send the *botanist* out to represent our country," jests a Minister.

"If you are all so afraid," Ion asserts, leaning forward. "Why don't you and your little pals go and hide in your bunkers? I will gladly take the risk of meeting these – probably admirable and non-invasive – aliens."

"If you want to do that," the Minister of Defense says. "You have to let me take some extra security measure."

Two Days Later, Outside of Crow Corp

There are snipers everywhere. Outside of Crow Corp – the massive silver and glass building of innovation – stand Minister Ion and Professor Crow. Ion is wearing a fairly dapper black, pinstriped suit. A red and white tie hangs around his neck to give the impression of both patriotism and power. The Professor is once again in his lab coat, however beneath it he is wearing a black (bullet-proof) vest, dress shirt, and a tie matching his brothers'.

They stand in defiance of the forceful fall wind, trying to appear tall amongst the massive buildings that surround them. In front of them, Crow Corp had changed its parking lot into a landing pad for the apparent "galactic representative" that would soon arrive. An immense disc of pure metal and concrete rests below the set of stairs the duo stand on. The railing on the circumference of the landing pad is adorned with the flags from each of Earth's countries. And behind the duo are holographic images displaying greetings to the visitors in every literary language on the planet. The image of the Prime Minister also sits behind Ion to his right, and a symbol of peace behind him to the left. All upon Ion's request.

Every once in a while, Ion notices the tiny red dot of a sniper's laser touch the centre of the landing pad. The Minister of Defence had made it a point to appear intimidating, even having a series of troops stand behind the holograms. Additional forces rest in the nearby sky scrapers, resting behind decorative trees, and had even hidden a tank nearby. The Minister of Ecology and Climate Change scoffs to himself thinking about how they would send the wrong message. He and Crow both agree that if this were an attack, this unknown source would not have given them a heads up on their arrival.

Regardless, all over the world extreme defensive measures have been taken. Many of the politicians and rich folks (including here in Canada) are resting in bunkers. Doomsday preppers have entered their shelters, Departments of Defense hover their fingers over the big red buttons. Yet, no citizen has been made to feel safe, and here Ion stands. Representing a planet too ignorant to grasp the concept that not everything in this universe is out to kill you. Citizens and politicians alike watch in great anticipation as the countdown to arrival dwindles to the last minute. Professor Crow moves a bit closer to his brother.

"If they are here to attack," Crow begins, once again shaking nervously. "I don't think those sniper rifles will do much."

"At least the citizens will have the illusion of safety before their world ends," Ion says with a sarcastic grin, staring straight at a camera drone livestreaming this event to the world.

Soon after Ion satirically mocks his governments' tactics, there is an unearthly whirring from overhead. It had come without them even being aware of it; mere meters above the platform disc floats a ship of peculiar design. Ion's stretched ear lobes bounce as he steps back to get a good look at this craft. Its shape is almost as if designed for both space travel, and travel on other planets.

Yet Ion notices it…morphing. As if to shift itself to better operate on this planet's atmosphere and level of gravity. It is a considerably large craft, which looks as if it is made of emerald and gold. For the half second this Minister of Ecology can steal his eyes away from the craft, he looks at his brother in disbelief. Professor Crow however, appears to analyze it; as if intending to reverse engineer it.

A cylinder of light beams down from the ship, directly in front of Ion. Moments later, a large creature – wearing a metal suit and breathing apparatus that matches the colour of their ship – floats gracefully down to them. There seems to be a glow about this entity, as if all those that currently rest below it are entirely unworthy of their arrival. Ion couldn't agree with this implication more.

"Stand down," Ion whispers the order through the wire he is wearing. *"Do* not, *I repeat: do* not *fire unless they pose a threat."*

The massive entity now stands before the two brothers, both of whom are awe-struck. This being from beyond stands at least nine feet tall, and looms over the Minister in a seemingly peaceful way. Behind a subtle breathing apparatus, it appears to be covering the face of a bipedal hippopotamus. A massive one at that.

The entity looks to smile down to the Professor and Minister, sending a wave of reassurance to both of them. It lifts a purple left arm, holding a flower in its' two fingers and (what could only be described as) thumb. The flower looks small in the alien's grasp. It has four pointed petals, with a yellow stigma in the centre. The petals themselves are colours that Ion could barely perceive. They looked almost purple and magenta.

Ion can see something resembling hooves (or at least a hoof like texture) running from the edges of their three fingers up past the cuff of the entity's suit. Still smiling and moving slowly, the visitor begins to reach out their left arm, in which Ion can see two small devices. They are black, with blue glowing lights on them. They seem to resemble Bluetooth earphones.

Abruptly the giant hippopotamus seems to flinch. Within the blink of an eye, Ion can see smoke emitting from the creature's fingers where the flower had sat. The sound of a sniper rifle blast echoes around the skyscrapers and throughout the area just as Ion can understand what just occurred. The entity has *caught* the bullet. Not stopping, not looking away from Ion and Crow.

"Stand *DOWN!*" the Professor bellows.

There is a moment of tension as Minister Ion and Professor Crow gratefully take the devices from the visitor. Upon receiving it, the entity gestures for them to place the device in their ear. With a bow of respect, they do so.

"Can you understand me, Earthling?" the hippopotamus asks. Their voice sounds like an odd series of whispery, soprano tones through Ion's open ear, where it translates to English in the *same voice* from the device. Ion and Crow can tell this visitor is female due to the tone of her voice.

"Yes, yes I can!" Ion exclaims. "This is amazing!"

"One of but a few gifts that I will leave with you today," the entity states gracefully. "My name is Pamphias, I am the Head Representative of the Centre Planet, and the Galactic Imperium. On behalf of the entire galaxy, I would like to congratulate your kind for creating a method of transportation that fits Imperial guidelines. Now, you have the capability of taking part in Galactic trade."

"Is that the sole requirement to join the Galactic Imperium?" Professor Crow asks, a little taken aback.

"That is the requirement for you to be initiated," Pamphias answers, sounding excited. "It is a necessity for you to travel within a short time to convene with our delegation. However to officially join the Galactic Imperium, you must agree to our trade and warfare terms. My people – the people of the Centre Planet – are the enforcers of these laws."

"Trade?" Ion inquires. "How many other planets with sentient life are there?"

"Oh, a few trillion," Pamphias answers casually. "And a fair amount that we are waiting to add as well. We keep watch of all planets possessing sentient life. We hadn't expected to add yours to the Imperium for another thousand years or so – granted your environment didn't kill you first. Mr. Crow here is a unique case that has propelled your species forward. Your remarkable intellect has come as a surprise to even We at the Centre Planet."

"Many of our people feared you would come here to declare war," Ion says. "I did my best to assure them that this would be a mission of peace. Humblest apologies for their lack of consideration."

"Apology accepted!" Pamphias declares. "And it is your foresight that has caused *my* people to choose you, Ion, as Earth's Representative within the Galactic Delegation."

VI

Earth's Ship Bays – Prior to Centre Planet Travel

The preparations had been made. The ships are set up and ready to enter what had long ago been known only as the vast emptiness of space. Leader Ion and Life-Admiral Crow have dawned their most respectable regalia and clothing in preparation for their venture this day.

"What do you think this cycle will bring, brother?" Crow asks Ion, meddling with the cufflink using his non-metal hand.

"Another dispute, no doubt." Ion replies casually, standing confidently and patiently for his brother at the base of the landing ramp. "I have heard the Frosks and Xerophs were at it again."

"You did not think to ask Titus about it yesterday?" Crow demands. He hates interplanetary travel, especially at the speed they would be going to in order to reach the Centre Planet.

"There were bigger matters at hand, brother." Ion replies casually, walking up the ramp with Crow as he speaks. "I did not want to distract from getting the *sessienna*."

"Fair," Crow admits, though sounding mildly bothered. "Still, it would be rational to believe the Frosks may have issue with my lending a hand to Technicorum II."

"A risk we were willing to take," Ion nods as they reach their seats within the vessel.

"Still," Crow intones, taking a drink from the tray a drone had been holding. The duo are now seated within their most luxurious ship. The inside is a mixture of black metal, and green glowing lights. They can see the floating city's edge facing the vast lake before them. "It would have been better to know what we may deal with at the Centre."

"I will be more inquisitive next time, brother," Ion says politely, prepping the ships for take-off.

"Thank you," Crow says sincerely, downing his drink and grabbing another. "Dear science, I hate space travel…well, this should be an interesting meeting, with the Colosseum approaching."

"Do you have your pre-recorded planetary addresses set for our friends?" Ion inquired as their ship began lifting itself from the ground.

"Y-yess…" Crow stutters, clearly uneasy about being airborne. "The people will never know we've gone."

"Excellent. Is there something additional you wish to bring up while we are amongst the Imperium's leaders?"

"No brother, mostly the general reports will be given. Though I am excited to discuss our involvement in the Colosseum. Prepare for a mostly boring day," Crow admits. The ship has ascended beyond the stratosphere and is now preparing for beyond-light speed travel. Alongside their ship floats an additional ship of guards (automatons permitted by the Imperium to be brought to meetings. There had been the occasional statement of war, and all planet representatives were permitted to both retaliate, and protect themselves from assassins). "However...I have received word of something rather interesting."

"Oh?" Ion asks, actually surprised for once.

"There are whispers of an oracle."

"Haha, an oracle you say?"

"Indeed. From the second human colony on Terra Six," Crow replies, quickly downing another drink as the space outside of their ship became a series of blurs. "The intel our friends have gathered indicates she wishes to speak with you."

"Me? Speak to a religious zealot?" Ion inquires, flabbergasted. "I have much better things to do with my time."

"Intel also states she is prescient," Crow admits, still very unsettled about the space travel. "I do not believe that is entirely possible, though we have seen a case or two before."

"Fakes, the lot of them," Ion says impatiently. "The future is ever changing and useless to try and predict brother. You know that."

"I suppose," Crow admits. "Are we nearly-"

Abruptly their ship seems to halt. Their speed has reduced dramatically. Before them, through the transparent front window of the ship, rests The Centre Planet. A massive green world that sits at the centre of their galaxy. It is a [1]type III civilization on the Kardashev scale – meaning it is the epicentre for every advanced (enough) planet within the galaxy. The Centre Planet also held the interplanetary meeting between select leaders within the Galactic Imperium. Here, everything would be discussed. New laws that would be inhabited, calls for war, calls for peace, trade negotiations, and anything else that is required when communicating between worlds. Over 99 Billion planets are represented here, in a time-blocked room to ensure all required items would be brought up and that no planets were going rogue.

"I believe we have arrived, brother," Ion says flatly, adding a humorous tone to his voice. Crow laughs, albeit a bit uneasily.

The massive green ball before them floats stoically, giving Crow a feeling of minor inferiority mixed with welcoming. Even from space, the gold defence centres and the Citadel's golden Dome can be seen. This epicentre of power is a sight to behold, no matter how many times one has seen it.

"Well, thank goodne-HHEURGH!" Crow says, initially sounding calm before vomiting into the bucket by his feet. This is a common occurrence for Crow during space travel, one he was not very fond of.

---

[1] http://www.veronicasicoe.com/blog/2014/04/the-kardashev-scale-0-to-6/

An automaton cleans Crows face as Ion lands the two ships simultaneously upon their designated landing pads. He had been controlling the guard's ship through Crow's Brainwave technology – thus ensuring simultaneous arrival. Slews of innumerable, unique ships are either landing or de-boarding as the Earth Leaders touch down to their designated docking bay. The "festivities" would begin shortly.

"Feeling alright?" Ion inquires, rising from the Captain's chair.

"I suppose I am now," Crow admits, then clears his throat. "Am I presentable for the Imperium?"

"Don't worry so much, brother," Ion says, readjusting Crow's garments a bit. "We are always the best dressed when we come here. You should have considered removing the fear receptors from yourself."

"Fear can be useful brother," Crow says, turning and heading for the exit ramp. "Let's go."

The duo exit their craft side by side, fronted by a series of guards, and with several following close behind. They emerge onto the landing pad looking quite powerful and dignified. All around them, alien species and dignitaries are exiting their crafts, barking orders at their servants, and looking over documents (both physical and holographic formats) in preparation for today's galactic meeting. Ion and Crow stand silently for a moment – unlike their vast amount of counterparts – and synch up their brain-wave connections so no one but each other could read them.

They head up the ship dock toward the massive Citadel, which would soon hold all of the galaxy's Representatives. The sole building on the planet (not strictly intended for defense), it truly towers into the sky. A pure gold icon of architectural triumph felt both inviting and daunting. Ion and Crow stride to the massive entrance doors of the epicentre.

Once reaching them, they show their identification to the Centre Planet Security there. She is a huge, hippopotamus like entity. Her species' people are the sole inhabitors of the planet, and they have a strength that is incomparable to any other living entity in the known universe. Their skin has an immunity to many kinds of weapons, and they hold some of the highest IQ's of any species.

After being approved, the duo enter the Citadel with their drone entourage, and walk upon their designated platform. Once all members of their party are on it, the platform floats into a giant room that went as high as the tower itself – ending in a dome. Many of the Representatives have already arrived, and are waiting on their designated floating spaces along the cylindrical perimeter of the immensely tall walls. In the very centre, at the base of the dome, sits the Head Representative from Centre Planet.

Crow and Ion stand in silence, suspended hundreds of meters above the ground. They look over their pre-planned topics of discussion for their planet using vision screens. The screens are designed for the individual who wears it to be the sole perceiver of information displayed, hence no other Representative can see the current standing in the Imperium. The Earth Leaders discuss and double-check finances, trades, and other important matters with each other telepathically. Shortly after, the Xeroph's platform floats beside them, and the Frosk's platform finds its way across from them. Several meters below, the Terra Six Representatives arrive. Within moments, the entirety of the intergalactic culture are seemingly present and in place.

"Hello Leaders and Representatives!" Booms the Head Representatives' voice over the speakers. "Please turn on your translators now, and prepare for any and all topics to be discussed in an orderly fashion. The time Barrier is now in effect."

Ion began a quick scan of the environment prior to the proceedings officially taking effect. 99 billion platforms are strewn systematically about the tower perimeter. From the post-primitive species of Planet A, all the way to (in the English alphabet, though the Centre Planet did not use this system) the Representatives of ZZeria IX. Races of brutal invaders mixed with highly diplomatic officials. War-mongers stood next to species with the utmost etiquette and respect for life. All placed in a specific order, for purposes only the members of the Centre Planet knows. Ion notices, however, that one planet seems to not have taken their invitation for this year's meeting: The brutes of Perusak. Ion notes a potential plot – one that would no doubt fail under the Centre Planet's security – and relays this suspicion to his brother.

Fret not, Ion, Crow reassures him telepathically. *The Centre Planet's defenses are even greater than our own. Let your focus remain on the proceedings.*

The initial (what would regularly have been without the time barrier) 7 hours of the event pass slowly. Members from numerous planets sought peace with another. Some request permission for war, but few are accepted. A member of the Crantonian government had laid claim that the Schleurghltings had stolen riches, scientific advancements, and made slaves of some of their people. They supplied efficient enough proof, and were granted the ability to declare war. Pity; the two planets had both recently discovered interplanetary travel. As was the way with many planets new to both the Imperium as well as space travel, the people got greedy. This would be a very long war with a high death toll, no doubt.

Eventually, the Frosks are asked to give their economic and trade reports. They were sent and overseen by the neutral Representatives of the Centre Planet. All seem to be in order, and no traces of theft, fraud, or negative connotations are found. The Frosks then had the ability to make inquiries on other planets, or offer their services. The Frosks first offer three of their best fleets to aid the Crantonian people against their newfound war – granted they would be able to review the case themselves first. If found in compliance with both truth and Froskian moral standards, the Frosks would be happy to help. This may be a shorter war than Ion had initially predicted.

"Now, we would like to speak to the representatives of Earth," The bug-like Froskian diplomat intones.

"Proceed," the Head Representative says.

"Leader Ion and Life-Admiral Crow," the Froskian began. "My name is Crombolus Shickles. Based on last year's meeting, we understand that you have recently worked with the people of Technicorum II?"

"That is correct," Crow answers. "I personally oversaw some experiment that they were looking to undergo."

Crow and Ion knew the nature of the Xeroph experiment would reach the Frosks eventually, and knew the importance of truth within the Imperium. However, the Xerophs had not yet permitted the details of the experiments to be shared. This left Crow and Ion in a bit of a moral bind. As often as possible, the duo made sure their intentions and actions were transparent both to the Galactic Imperium, as well as the people of their planet. This was done regardless of other planet's opinions; though very seldom their actions were ever seen as offences to other planets.

"Would you be willing to share the final reports with our people?" Shickles inquires, buzzing lightly as its wings spread slightly.

"The work done was for the Xerophs," Ion replies, standing stoic and adding an air of power to his synthetic voice. "It is not us that you must request these reports from."

There is a pause. The Frosks and Xerophs had never had a war, per se. They were constantly trying to one-up each other in the technological field, however. The people of Frosk were no doubt trying to see if they had been surpassed once again, or if the Froskian progress was finally becoming the more dominant choice for those seeking new technology.

"Titus or Sephia of Technicorum II, what is your response to this inquiry?" the Head Representative asks through the speakers.

"The experiments are currently in their testing phase," Titus replies to Shickles. "Very little data has been gathered, and progress is moving at a slow pace. Unless specifically requested by the Centre Planet itself, we see no need to share our work."

"Does the Centre Planet request this?" Sephia inquires to the Head Representative.

"At this time, there seems to be neither the necessity nor enough progress that would – in whatever way – aid the Froskian people for whatever their reasoning may be."

"But-" Shickles tries to intone.

"Request denied," the Head Representative makes her verdict. A vindictive smile curls across the two Xeroph's reptilian lips.

"Very well," Shickles says, trying to hide how upset he is. "We have but one more inquiry, to Earth once more, then our time will be done for the day."

"Proceed," The Head Representative drones, making sure all of the proceedings are being recorded.

"Life-Admiral Crow, you have helped the Xerophs of Technicorum II," Shickles bellows, a look of intense expectancy in his many eyes and features. "There are some advancements we Froskians are looking to make, as well. We would like to call upon your help also."

Would that be a wise decision, brother? Ion asks telepathically. *It is important to maintain our rapport with the Froskians, but I do not wish to upset the Xerophs.*

Then we will ask them, won't we, Crow replies.

"We have many friendships within the Imperium," Crow began, speaking to the entirety of the Intergalactic Senate. "Friendships with a great deal of amazing and wonderful species within this galaxy. We would not want to sully or disrespect any of you. Therefore, I would like to ask the Representatives of Technicorum II – seeing as they and the Frosks are often at odds – if they would take offense were I to supply the Frosks with help. I inquire to them - as I did to the Frosks during the last procession - before confirming my willingness to help the Xeroph people."

"Titus or Sephia, how do your people respond?" the Head Representative asks.

"Technicorum II thanks you for your diplomacy," Sephia answers to Crow. "Your skills have the potential to have done the Xeroph race a great service. There will be no bad blood between our people should you choose to aid the Frosks this Galactic period (one year, Milky Way Time). Considering our planets represent the top 3 most technologically advanced in the Imperium, it only makes sense that we all collaborate in some way."

"As you wish," Ion answers Sephia.

You will be gone soon, anyway, thinks Titus. *You and all your useless monkey kind.*

"Then may we begin within the next week or so?" Shickles asks Crow.

"Earth is always happy to accommodate our friends," Crow replies with a bow and a grin.

"Then it is settled," the Head Representative says. "Earth will aid in a Froskian invention. Please ensure the proper forms are sent to me prior to the end of the proceedings."

And thus, the meeting went on. Seemingly innumerable amounts of planets are represented, while time outside of the dome does not pass. Up, down and around the spiral the Planetary Representatives speak. More requests for trade, peace and war. Eventually, Terra Six is called upon. The two representatives stand with their entourage of (what Ion and Crow would consider) barbaric guards. They are wearing fur pelts, carry spears, and have a series of very specific body modifications that held some sort of symbolism or other to the humans residing on Terra Six. The first Representative (a very tall and slender woman) began with the general reports of trade, warfare, peace, and economic changes as is necessary for the proceedings. Next to her stands a dark male figure, with daunting eyes and seemingly grey skin. He is of average human build, however has snow-white hair and seemingly no irises or pupils. It appears as though his all-white eyes reflect infinity onto whomever looks at them.

"Is that all for your reports, Representative Talia?" the Head Representative asks the female Terra Six Ambassador.

"Yes, Head Representative," she replies with a light bow.

"Very good. What inquiries do you have for the others within our Imperium?"

The dark figure – apparently known as Drake - answers on behalf of Terra Six. He begins by negotiating trade with some of Terra Six's neighbouring planets. He then requests technological aid from the people of Technicorum II for a planet revitalization project they had begun (only to be denied. The Xerophs had little interest in a developing planet. Much less one with no focus on technology to begin with), and began an alliance with a far off planet (for reasons known only to Terra Six and the far off planet). Finally, Talia steps forward again, and addresses the Head Representative.

"We would now like to speak directly to Leader Ion of Earth, please," Talia says, looking up to the platform where Ion and Crow rest.

"Proceed."

Earth's platform moves from several meters above and across from the Terra Six ambassadors, stopping directly in front of them. This gives the illusion of a one-on-one conversation between Leaders – however every word uttered is recorded and played to the Head Representative in real (stasis) time. Crow's eyebrow raises in curiosity and Ion's synthetic eyes roll as they float to eye level of the ambassadors.

"Greetings Leader Ion and Life-Admiral Crow," Drake states formally and gruffly. "There are two matters we wish to discuss with you today."

"Speak," Ion's synthetic voice utters uncaringly.

Oracle? Ion inquires telepathically to his brother.

No doubt about it. But what else could they possibly want?

"As you wish..." Drake answers, trying to stay formal, but clearly intimidated by the Earth Ambassadors and insulted by Ion's uncaring tone. "We have brought you here to discuss two amazing discoveries. It is imperative you listen closely. Despite the low odds, our planet is currently housing one of the mere 3 oracles within our Imper-"

"Don't care," Ion interrupts baldly, leering assertively at the Terra Six Ambassador. His synthetic body sends specific frequencies and subtle light signals to Drake which amplify his fear.

"Gr-great leader!" Drake stammers, now focusing his all-white gaze past Crow. "As a representative of your religion on Terra Six, I-"

"You've made a *religion* of him there?" Crow blurts, astonished.

"Indeed," Talia adds, stepping forward. "And of you, Life-Admiral Crow. We only ask that Leader Ion come and speak with our Oracle for a moment-"

"I refuse," Ion replies, sending negative signals to Talia as well now. She, however, seems undeterred by them. "I have met many an oracle in my days. Being one of the eldest within this Imperium, I have virtually seen it all. Your supposed 'oracle' holds no news to me that is noteworthy."

"Then...aheh...perhaps this next bit of information may be...noteworthy...Lord," Drake speaks nervously.

"Well, what could it possibly be?" Crow asks, now becoming impatient with the feeble Ambassadors.

"Omnipertium," Drake answers with a sly grin.

All heads turn to their delegation. The metal that made up Ion's exoskeleton was unbelievably rare – so much so that whatever is left in the known universe is heavily guarded by the Centre Planet. It had been ever sought after from its original discovery on a long abandoned planet. However, Ion made it his own personal duty to ensure it did not fall into the wrong hands, and kept it for himself and Crow. It is indestructible, impervious to both hot and cold (as a matter of fact, it produced energy because of it. A factor that kept Ion fully charged and nearly immortal), and completely irreplicateable.

"What of it?" Crow asks, his interest piqued.

"We believe we may have found some-"

"Say no more!" Ion blurts authoritatively in as low a voice he could muster whilst still being audible to the Terra Six ambassadors. "Assure all those listening in that it is well hidden, and not on your planet."

"Such is the case, Great Leader" Talia responds, bowing once again.

"Very good," Ion replies, his senses easing. He does not want a series of other planets sending renegade ships to pirate Terra Six, potentially euthanizing the inhabitants in search of this rare metal. "You should be more careful, Ambassador. Planets and people have been eviscerated for much less than that sacred metal. I will be on Terra Six shortly after this meeting in order to further discuss this. Say nothing to anyone else."

With that, Ion and Crow's platform replaces itself among the other Planetary Representatives. Ion deploys microbots onto the Terra Six ambassadors to ensure any assassination attempts would fail, and to keep recon on any further discussions made by the Representatives.

I cannot believe those fools! Ion shouts telepathically to Crow. *Naming the metal so casually. They now officially have a target on the backs of both themselves and their planet.*

Knowing you will be there after the meeting, Crow replies, *no one dare go near them. And any motions of assassination without express permission during a hearing are vehemently prohibited. Remember what happened when they tried that on* you *during our first meeting.*

I suppose humanity isn't the only dumb race, after all Ion agrees.

Finally, Ion and Crow are called upon to give their reports, and make their requests. As always, Earth is the last planet to do so. Being called upon last is actually considered a huge honour. It gave Earth a strategic advantage among the planets, having seen everyone's economic standing and calls for war.

Crow and Ion share their developed reports, quickly verify their joined effort, and prepare to speak. They know which planets to avoid, which planets to seek aid from, whom to trade with, and how to speak to each of them. This place in the galactic discussion was awarded to them due to their exemplary diplomatic efforts, their contribution to upcoming Colosseums' security, as well as their consistent stride for peace. It had been given to them by the Head Representative herself for over a century now.

Their initial comments are in regards to the war between the Crantonians and the Schleurghltings. Deciding against taking sides, Earth offers shelter to any potential refugees. The next item Crow brings up are in regards to this galactic cycles' trades. New offers are made to some planets, but many of the resources they request and require stay the same. Each and every inquiry made is humbly accepted by the Representatives with whom they speak.

Following this subject is one close to the (figurative) artificial heart of Ion. Every fifth galactic cycle (5 Earth years) there is a great Battle Royale amongst all the planets in the Imperium – until recently, save for Earth. Ion and Crow felt that the "Galactic Colosseum" had been very "inhumane" (for lack of a better term) since their addition into the Galactic Imperium.

Each planet would force their fiercest non-sentient animals into battle. A great deal of inter-breeding, forced reproduction, and severe abuse was done to these creatures in order for a planet to claim "most superior." Earth had been fighting for several galactic cycles to have the rules altered to look more like the Earth Olympics.

Ion suggested that the leading species enter their best three sentient candidates to battle until a yield was called. This way any genetic alterations and/or what could be considered abuse could be consented to (under strict regulations consulted by the Centre Planet). However, the term of yielding had to be democratically voted on, and the Galactic Imperium voted for a fight to the death. This, however, was leaps and bounds above where they had been since before Earth was included into this immense delegation.

Hence, Earth has finally joined the throws of the Colosseum. Ion himself would be the sole candidate from Earth, to the delight of many in the Imperium. The Earth Leader made some finalizing inquiries to ensure the upcoming games are being maintained to the agreed upon standards from each planet and their apex species.

One by one, Representatives are called upon. The Centre Planet asked for the proof of their ethical preparations for the games. All come up green, and Ion feels satisfied. Moreso, each planet in the Imperium are excited to see Ion battle; many of whom are (secretly) hoping to find a way to kill the great leader. Immortality was ever-sought after across the universe, and most planets experience extreme jealousy toward Ion and Crow. They seem to have found the way (and had never shared their technology).

"I am most pleased that you have all so graciously consented to the guidelines," Ion remarks joyously. "I hope this cycle's Colosseum will hold the most exciting games yet!"

There is a brief cheer from each of the Representatives, followed by an echoing silence. Only the typing of the Head Representative can be heard. Finally, a ceremonial bow is collectively done by the entirety of the Interplanetary Representatives, and this cycles meeting is adjourned.

Strategically, each Ambassador files out in a calm fashion. Many of them are already in the works of having their planets prep for the new trades, agreements, and/or wars that would soon ensue as agreed upon by the Centre Planet.

As the throng exits, the time lock shuts down, bringing them back into the regular flow of time. Once all of the Representatives have exited the Citadel – and many of them began boarding their ships – there came a massive BOOM as a dozen Froskian ships enter the Centre Planet's atmosphere shortly after exiting light speed. However, the ships had been painted the colours of the Perusak people – seemingly pirated and or stolen from the Froskians.

Many Planetary Ambassadors panic at this. Some – including the Froskians themselves – leave planet before the first run of gunfire is launched. Without hesitation, Ion telepathically commands his drones to keep Crow safe, then engages his synthetic skeleton's flight system. He then charges at great speeds towards the bombs shot from the pirated ships.

As he does so, some of the Perusakian ships kamikaze into targeted areas on the Centre Planet. These targeted areas are the centers that make sure security is always up for an attack such as this. How the primitive Perusak people are able to systematically take these security sectors down is a matter better looked into in the future.

However, this left little more than ground defense from the Centre Planet to try and overcome the onslaught. Knowing this, Ion takes it upon himself to save both the planet, and the people on it. As much as he could, that is; there may have been casualties from the security facilities. Such a shame.

Ion flies to action, and quickly comes a mere meter away from the artillery fire sent from the Perusak's stolen ships. He then sends his nano-bots to reprogram the rockets. The explosives begin to revert their course (from their current position of a couple hundred feet away from the planet's surface level) back at the ships that had fired them.

As they do their business, Ion crashes through the metal surfaces of the ships, and takes one captive Perusak from each. He injects them with a paralyzing venom, rendering them both defenseless and terrified. After doing so, Ion (seemingly gradually) floats back to the Centre Planet's surface just as the once enemy rockets turn back to their senders. Prior to touching down with his paralyzed captors in his extended arms, the ships within the sky explode, giving Ion an angelic aura.

The only momentarily defenceless Ambassadors – now safe from harm – gaze upon their saviour as he stands before them. They all look in silent awe as Ion's bionic face express disgust toward his captives. Abruptly, a Representative of Scillion 8 raises his many arms, and hollers (in their tongue) "YEAH!" And the rest of the crowd joins the applause.

Ion lets the immobile hostiles down gently as Centre Planet guards charge to their position. He waves humbly to his fellow Planetary Representatives for their praises. After checking that Crow is alright, the cyborg approaches the guards (with the Head Representative among them), who stood at attention before him.

"I have gathered a few of the hostiles," Ion informs them in their language. "Undoubtedly at least one of them will be able to give us some answers about this near disaster. The toxin I injected them with won't affect them for too long."

"Leader Ion!" the Head Representative exclaims, bowing to him. "The entire galaxy is in your debt!"

A Centre Planet citizen – let alone the Head Representative – bowing to *anyone* was unheard of. It is a tremendous honour, considering their species is viewed as the most powerful in the known universe. Ion returns a bow to the Head Representative.

"I only did my duty, Head Representative," Ion informs her with a soothing tone. "I wouldn't doubt any other Representative would do the same–"

"HHHEURGH!" screams a now non-paralyzed Perusak. It (as Ion could not tell their gender) lunges toward the Earth Leader with a very sharp, poisoned knife it had hidden in the waist of its loincloth.

Ion does not move. A look of fear struck the Head Representative as many of the Ambassadors gasp. Still, the Perusak swings at Ion, only to have its blade shattered. It steps back, looking at its arm as the limb shakes seemingly uncontrollably. Ion turns and leers at the foe. He outstretches his arm and sends a jolt of electricity at the Perusak from the palm of his hand.

The savage alien falls to the ground and convulses. Some of the hair on its feline-esque body singed, sending an unpleasant aroma into the nostrils of any entity unfortunate enough to be close to it. The Perusak is rendered unconscious.

"Head Representative," Ion continues. "I must head back to my planet to prepare for my meeting with Terra Six. Would you mind terribly if I took my leave?"

"But what if they come back?!" an Ambassador asks fearfully in the distance.

"I do not detect any more hostile ships within the next few lightyears," Crow informs them, having sent an interstellar radar device in anticipation for a second wave. "That must have been the lot of them. Sorry bastards."

"We will stay until your security perimeters are fixed," Ion nods to the Head Representative. "However, if Life-Admiral Crow says departure is safe, I see no reason for all the Ambassadors to remain on planet."

"Yes, agreed," the Head Representative nods. "Take your leave, and take care, dear Representatives!"

As the many ambassador's ships exit the planet, Crow and Ion keep watch of any other potential foes on behalf of the Centre Planet. Worry fills Crow, Ion however feels only revulsion toward the Perusaks. Could this simply have been a small renegade troupe? Or was there a greater plot afoot? And more importantly: why in the science did they choose the Centre Planet of all places to start a war?

VII

Planet Frosk – Three hours after the Centre Planet Attack

"Tell me what I want to know," the Froskian Head of Torture commands the Perusak pawn.

"Hisss!!!" is the angry, visceral response the feline-esque alien spits at the insect-like Frosk.

"Hahaha, have it your way," the Forskian cackles.

The Head of Torture goes behind the Perusak, who is strapped down in a chair. He leans down, and cuts another chunk of its tail off. A roar of agony erupts from the Perusak's long-toothed mouth. Tears begin to well in its eyes, but its expression remains strong. The Head of Torture inspects the chunk of flesh for a moment in the near darkness, holding it tauntingly in front of the Persuaks eyes.

"A feisty one, aren't we?" the Head of Torture intones. "I wonder how far along the tail I have to remove before you break? Or perhaps, I will stop now. And move on to your family."

"What?! You stay away from them!" the Perusak begins, a leer of anger falling onto the Frosk. Quickly, however, its expression changes as it begins to laugh. "What a dumb play. You Frosks must really take my species for fools and savages. Hahaha."

"Well, we call them as we sees 'em," the Head of Torture agrees, nodding and rubbing its mouth pincers. "But I assure you, this is no play."

From the Frosk's clawed hand erupts the image of three Perusaks. One fully grown, two very young. The holograms float on either side of the Head of Torture, his arms outstretched. The light emitted turns the side of the Frosks' face a light blue, but does not illuminate the immensely dark room they are in. The Perusak prisoner writhes in its chair, irate and terrified.

"You sick bastards!" it roars. "You let them go! They don't know anything!"

"Oh, and you do?" the Head of Torture inquires. "Because your brother didn't seem to know anything at all." Another image flashes from the Frosk's palm. One of a Perusak barely breathing, bloodied, cut up, and with a series of instruments protruding from its body.

"No!" hollers the Perusak, now unable to move due to shock.

"Yes," the Head of Torture says with what undoubtedly had to be a grin for its species. "I thought your people had a special link...*bonding* I believe you call it. You are supposed to know when one you have bonded with was in danger. Religious mumbo-jumbo, I believe I have proved."

"Just kill me," the Perusak says emotionlessly. "Let my family go...and kill me. Please."

"Oh sweet Perusak," the Head of Torture muses, kneading the prisoner's shoulders with its gross extended elbows. "How on Frosk would that help me? Now...we can fix your brother, and let your family go. You just have to tell me where you got our ships, from who, and why."

The Perusak sits in silence for a moment, shaking involuntarily. It was a sacred creed for their people to never surrender. Dying in a battle was their greatest honour. But not like this...this was beyond savagery. Scientific, but beyond barbaric. There would be no honour in dying like this; and even less in letting his brother and family go with him.

"Okay...I'll tell you everything."

"Very good," whispers the Head of Torture. It appeared to set up some kid of recording device in front of the Perusak, then meandered to a nearby desk, out of the line of sight of its prisoner. The Perusak could hear him fiddling around with beakers, chemicals, and some other medical devices.

"We were given the ships by a Xeroph from Technicorum II," the Perusak began, looking at his feet. "It...*cough*...it paid us a great deal to attack the Centre Planet Citadel....and to *wheeze* and to make it look like the Frosks headed the attack as much as possible...they supplied us with weapons, but we didn't use them because we didn't know how...and programmed the ships to take us to the planet automatically. We didn't know...(coughs blood)...didn't know ships would strike down to the planet. We were only meant to shoot down the Ambassadors and the Citadel."

"Very good," says the Head of Torture, flicking a syringe filled with a pale green liquid. "And what was the purpose of the attack?"

"For them, to frame you," the Perusak replies, seeming as if close to passing out. The Head of Torture walks gradually toward the recording device as the captive spoke, hiding the syringe behind one of its wings. "For us, to take you all out for your cruelty. We barely made it into the Galactic Summit, and when we finally did, we were only viewed as savages. Never respected, scoffed at, no trade deals to speak of…we had had enough. We wanted to take over. We wanted to usurp the Centre Planet so *we* could have *something* in this damned galaxy…"

"Well, you tried," the Head of Torture says sincerely. However, the insect's tone changes abruptly as he flicks off the recording device. "And you failed, miserably. The attack was over before it even began. All thanks to that mysterious Leader Ion…"

"Will…will you let me go now?" the Perusak asks, looking up hopefully to its captor. "And my family?"

"Oh sweet, ignorant Perusak…no one gets out of here alive."

"What?!" the prisoner roars in frightened confusion. "But I- I told you everything you wanted!"

"You did," the Head of Torture agrees. "You have done the Forsks a great service. Now, I am to show you mercy. Say goodbye to your family, beast!"

The live images of the Perusaks' family – including its brother – appear in holograms before the victim. One by one, their throats are slit by a nearby Froskian Torture Guard. Before the Perusak can scream "NO!" the Head of Torture shoves its syringe into the alien's head. The galactic traitor – who was part of a sieged ship by the Frosks on the way to their planet – is silenced forever.

VIII

Earth's Intersphere – The Planetary Capital

It had taken months, but 6-6-5-4-38 finally found a way to mentally hack directly into the Intersphere. Using specific thought patterns with a mix of mathematics and sound reverberations, 6-6-5-4-38 is now within the program itself. Through the mind's eye the Earth citizen/floating brain can see an immense matrix like pattern, with the impenetrable Capital's server at the centre. This image is surrounded by the visions of every Earth citizens' broadcast before them. A blue glow that fades into never-ending darkness surrounds the visions of those in the DreamScape, as well as the matrix-like pattern.

6-6-5-4-38 floats above the server, observing the countless Dreamscapes of nearly every citizen on the entire planet. They would have shed a tear - were they able to – at the very sight of such control. So many people, blindly allowing a government to hold such a tight grip upon them as a living thing. For what reason? When will it stop?

Granted, one had the liberty to do whatever they please within the Intersphere...the point is not this. The Dreamscape people live in is just that: a dream. Reality has been ripped from them for reasons they were never told, and yet no one seems to question. But 6-6-5-4-38 questions it. And they want some answers. They want *true* freedom; not this virtual, synthetic fabrication forced upon them by a narcissistic psychopath and his equally insane mad-scientist brother.

6-6-5-4-38 need only project their consciousness to whichever Dreamscape they find suitable, and they would be able to communicate with that citizen without issue. 6-6-5-4-38 proceeds to peruse the many, seemingly countless Dreamscapes before them, looking for one that shows some sort of disdain toward how things are being run.

After passing dozens of blissfully immersed citizens, they come across a citizen that is going through old clips of rebellion, anarchy, and chaos. Such events are all catalogued and documented by Ion and Life-Admiral Crow; made completely accessible for any citizen under their "full transparency" act of 2136. Memories are pulled from as many individuals who lived in that time period as possible. Some are re-created simulations designed by Crow, and apparently told the "true, unfabricated" stories the previous rulers had kept from history books.

Yes, this brain would do well. It appears evident to 6-6-5-4-38 that the mind which lays before them is a truth seeker, looking to expand their knowledge on the past. Perhaps hoping either to solidify their personal perception of the New Earth way of life, or in the hopes they would denounce their own feeling of anxiety and discomfort.

The metaphysical consciousness of 6-6-5-4-38 floats toward this citizen's Dreamscape. However, once attempting to access it, finds the task impossible. It is as if there is a thick glass separating 6-6-5-4-38's consciousness from the Dreamscape of this citizen.

"What the hell?" echoes the disembodied voice of 6-6-5-4-38.

This should have worked. 6-6-5-4-38 believed they had outsmarted the *great* Life-Admiral Crow and his *precious* clan of programmers and designers. All it had involved was simple mathematics and a manipulation of thought patterns. And yet, 6-6-5-4-38 cannot get farther than the gates of other citizens' Dreamscapes.

Disheartened and with time running out for today's Dreamscape usage, 6-6-5-4-38 exits the halfway point of Dreamscape and Intersphere. They find themself back in their Dreamscape, their programmed "body" sitting in front of a white board. 6-6-5-4-38 had been a university professor before their time here, and knew full well that writing anything in the Dreamscape – or even in their own home, there were eyes everywhere – would only get them caught, and stop their plan before it even began. 6-6-5-4-38 simply finds solace and a greater ability to concentrate when in front of something familiar; such as this white board. Occasionally, 6-6-5-4-38 would also sit on an old timey porch in front of a corn field. Memories. How few are left.

In their own mind, 6-6-5-4-38 attempts to think of a way to break through this unexpected barrier. *Maybe I should have taken a look around* they ponder. *If I had more time, I may have found something that physically needed to be altered.*

So the stage was set for the next time they went into the Intersphere. 6-6-5-4-38 would break through their own barrier in much shorter time, in the hopes they could find whatever had been blocking them from entering other citizen's Dreamscapes. Just as the conclusion is made, and the idea solidified, 6-6-5-4-38 receives the message that the daily Dreamscape session is coming to a close.

Once again, their brain is ejected from the Think Tank, and placed into their synthetic body. 6-6-5-4-38 drags their metallic feet along the whole way back to their living quarters. They feel depressed, and hope they can get their mind off of the whole ordeal by reading today's news topic.

Upon entering their quarters, 6-6-5-4-38 summons the holographic news screen telepathically. This goes on for a while - with bland new updates on Rukrasia and such things as animal population growth back on Earth's surface – before they switch to the history channel.

A special documentary appears before them, on the subject of the first World Wars. Generic propaganda brought on by the Earth Leaders; any chance they get, the "great leaders" force feed reminders of the horrendous past humanity once had down the throats of "their" people. Granted, there had been no crime within any of Leader Ion's conquered countries, but people should be able to *choose* to commit a crime if they want!

6-6-5-4-38 stares blankly at the Vision Screen, thinking more about how to break through the Dreamscape than paying attention to the show that plays before their synthetic eyes. Suddenly, a light bulb figuratively lights above their robotic head. The documentary began to focus on how communication was before Telepa-Tech (A Division of Crow Corp) made synthetic telepathy possible.

Such methods as Morse code and cryptology were the sole ally of many of these soldiers. Encrypted messages sent by [2]pigeons were another common method behind enemy lines. As a matter of fact, there were several carrier pigeons given medals after the Second World War. Most notable are-

That's it! 6-6-5-4-38 thinks to themself. *I need a different way to communicate.*

---

[2] https://www.royalsignalsmuseum.co.uk/ww1-ww2-communications/

IX

Earth's Atmosphere – Aboard Leader Ion's Stealth Ship

After collecting a few necessities for his voyage to Terra Six from Earth, Leader Ion began to depart for his meeting. He enters his stealth ship, which has been specifically designed for the Leader himself. Now, Leader Ion could have easily flown there with his robotic skeleton alone; the vacuum of space was no issue for him, as the liquid in which his brain floats creates oxygen for itself, and his body is completely sealed and impervious to the dangers of space.

Regardless, Leader Ion tries to hide his invulnerability from everyone. He does his best to keep the entire universe thinking that there is some way to destroy him. The reason being, he could be seen as too great a threat by the rest of the universe. If Leader Ion wanted, he could easily overtake the entire galaxy – at least – and nothing could stop him. However, he does have ethics, and a very specific plan that must be implemented strategically. Hence, he chooses to make it appear as though there could be a way to take him down, should anything go awry.

Leader Ion currently floats at the edge of the atmosphere of Earth, prompting his stealth ship for the trek to Terra Six. Life-Admiral Crow is currently on their home planet, preparing for his visit to Frosk. The duo did not concern themselves overly with the Attack on Centre Planet, for within the Galaxy they were not the enforcers of justice. Centre Planet itself had already begun an investigation, and Crow had made an obligation to help the Frosks regardless. Until told otherwise, it was best for Earth to keep its promise to the potentially guilty Frosks.

When will you be returning, brother? Crow asks Ion through their mind-link.

Hopefully within a few Earth days, Ion replies, almost done charting his course to Terra Six. *It is my intention to avoid the oracle and get right to the omnipertium. That planet and its people may be in grave danger.*

Very good. I have prepared a program for the next two days that will make our citizens believe that we are still on planet Crow assures Ion. *You may change it when you return, if you see fit. We must finish the plan on Rukrasia as soon as possible though.*

Agreed, replies Ion, preparing the stealth ship for light speed travel. He flicks a few switches within the diminutive cockpit, and a robotic voice begins a countdown. *Please keep me informed on what the project with the Froskians will be.*

Of course. Be sure to let me know if Terra Six actually has omnipertium. This wouldn't be the first false claim we have heard.

Indeed, Ion agrees, his ship shooting to light speed. *The fools...such a dangerous thing to claim to have. Safe travels to you, brother. I look forward to your return home*

And to you! I will be back before you know it. Logging out.

The communication link between Ion and Crow is temporarily severed. Crow had designed it so the thoughts of himself and Ion could be transferred – without worry of any tampering, loss of connection, or trace – regardless of their distance from each other. They would be in communication again once Ion finishes with Terra Six.

As Leader Ion nears the planet's solar system, he encounters an asteroid field coming up. It rests between his current location and Terra Six; making it a necessity to traverse. Best course of action would be to fly through it manually. Ion exits light speed, and begins to fly through the field, still at a quick pace. He turns down the level of stealth his ship emits to allow more energy to be put into the ship sensors and defense field. He may be robotic, but the inexplicable can happen; he did not want to maneuver directly into one of the many obstructions in his path.

Abruptly, a message comes to his ship from an unknown source. Worried it may be a distress call, Ion answers it. The big, ugly, spider like face of a Schleurghlting floods his screen. Pincers convulsing, venom dripping down its face. The many eyes glaring at the image of Leader Ion with murderous intent. Ion's synthetic face smiles at the creature, whose booming voice echoes within his stealth ship.

"Leader Ion!" the Schleurghlting bellows maliciously in its tongue (which is automatically translated for Ion). "We have a score to settle!"

"Oh, is that so?" Ion muses, feigning a bit of fear and interest in what this antagonist has to say. "And to whom am I speaking?"

"I am Aragorg, Leader of the Schleurghlting people," he spits at the image of Ion. "You denounced us in council, and you must pay in blood!"

"I do not believe I did such a thing," Ion says, an air of sadness added to his synthetic voice. "I am sorry you feel that way…but I'm afraid I could not pay that price anyway. I do not have blood anymore."

"Wise ass!" Aragorg shrieks. "You are too afraid to face me!"

"I simply do not see the point," Ion informs him casually. "Your wounded ego is of no concern to me. And if you truly wish to face me, why not wait until the Colosseum?"

"You and your filthy monkey race are not worthy of the Colosseum!" the Schleurghlting leader rages on. "And if you do not intend to face me, then perhaps the people of Terra Six will. I could use the omnipertium anyway, hahahaha."

Ion sighs a tired sigh, locates the Schleurghlting ship, and pulls up to it. He looks at Aragorg with a bored look in his eyes. He waits for the Schleurghlting people to notice his ship there, so they may pull him into the docking bay. To threaten Ion is one thing. He could handle himself without any issue. To threaten an entire race – specifically one with fewer defences than the Schleurghlting had at that – is inexcusable. Ion decides that he must take action.

"Very well," Ion sighs, sending tones of both intimidation and uncaring in his voice. "Have it your way. Beam me into your ship bay. I accept your challenge."

Moments later, Ion stands in what appears to be the ships arena. The Schleurghlting ship had looked very large from the outside, but does the inside no justice. The massive arachnid bodies of the Schleurghltings require a lot of room to move around, which this ship certainly gives them. Before two opposing, very large entranceways is a massive sandpit. The pit is circular, with space around the periphery for (no doubt) Schleurghltings to observe whatever event may be before them. The ceiling is high, and fades from a sickly green overhead from it's obscure oval-shaped walls. The dirt at Ion's feet clouds up with his every step, until he places himself in the centre of the Arena. A short wait after, he is met with very hairy company.

A horde of Schleurghltings surround Ion in an ear-shattering tumble of arachnid legs and tarsi surging from the door opposite of the one he had entered. Aragorg enters last, gradually and with a flourish before leering at Ion in the immense circle. Some of the arachnids hang from the ceiling from their strong silk. Ion is not sure if they were meant to serve as some kind of referee, or as a distraction. Aragorg stands on his back four legs, screaming about dishonour and such to his people about the Earth Leader. Ion pays little mind, he knows this will be over fairly quickly.

He also knows the Schleurghltings are not fair fighters. They had just recently enslaved people from another planet and are currently at war. This was not their first offence either. The Schleurghltings had made an attempt at taking over Technicorum II a little over a century ago, only to be sent back to their planet in complete ruin. The Schleurghltings suffered a heavy penalty for that war, having attempted to use atomics against the Xerophs. Technicorum II was greatly underestimated though; they disabled the bombs before they even got close to the planet. Thus a 100 year vendetta was threatened between the two planets. No doubt why they had begun to take slaves.

Ion stands, stoic and unafraid, before Aragorg. His artificial eyes roll as the Schleurghlting leader rambles on and on about how "justice" would finally be done for the galaxy, and how "defeating" the Earth leader would somehow bring them up in the interstellar food chain. Ion – frankly - bored produces a wave of force from his robotic skeleton to get the attention of the many Schleurghltings that surround him. The sand beneath him is thrust unapologetically into the faces of the viewers on the rings perimeter.

"Are we hear to make false claims?" Ion asks, an air of impatience and anger added to his voice. "Or are we here to settle a score?"

"Haha, hahahahahahahaha!" Aragorg roars threateningly. "You have no idea what is coming to you, monkey!"

"Yes, yes," Ion drones on. "What weapons shall we use?"

"Nothing but our own limbs!" he bellows, looming over the Earth Leader with his massive arachnid body.

"You do realize I have over 100, 000 weapons at my disposal that are part of my limbs, right?" Ion asks, half laughing. "And a number of others elsewhere. Be specific."

"Your graspers, then!" is the angry retort.

"Done," Ion tones casually. "Though it seems you would have an unfair advantage, yes? I have but two – 'graspers' as you put it – and you have eight."

"And you are made of metal," Aragorg shrieks, looking as if prepared to attack. "But that won't save you."

"Oh, I'm sure it won't," Ion answers sarcastically, moving to a fighting position as well.

"Every creature has a weakness," the venomous Schleurghlting rages on. "Today, you will learn yours."

With that the immense spider lunges its front two limbs at Ion, only to be easily dodged by the cyborg. Seemingly countless algorithms and calculations are being processed within Ion's brain and additional processors. Ion is prepared for anything.

Aragorg's back tarsus make to strike next, the incredible long and sharp claws extending to try and meet their mark. Ion dances around them with ease, not even using his jetpack additions to float away. With fluid motions, he moves about the arena. The onlookers give sounds of anger and disappointment.

"Coward!" Bellows the Schleurghlting leader. "Why don't you come here and-"

Ion lands a devastating blow in the area of the cephalothorax; specifically on three of Aragor's eight eyes. The giant arachnid writhes and squeals in pain. Venom spews left and right about the arena as the Schleurghlting gasps in shock and pain.

"Don't just watch him beat me!" Aragorg roars to his underlings. "Take this false god down!"

Ion is quickly struck with more web than even he could ever hope to evade. From all directions, Schleurghlting are shooting their silk like volleys of cannon fire. Within moments, Ion is completely covered in the stuff. Unable to move, but still able to hear. He falls to the grounds as some of the braver spiders move in closer; both to inspect their leader, as well as Earth's.

"Righ' then boss," an unknown Schleurghlting says to their leader as the dust begins to settle. Ion can hear the arachnid approaching his confined body. "Wha' you wan' us t'do wif 'im now?"

"Let him loose into space, to float and suffer forever!" comes a cry from a member of the crowd.

"Stamp him t'dust!" suggests another.

"No!" Aragorg intervenes, rising from the ground. His arachnid body limps as he uses two of his right tarsi. The others appear to have been crippled under Ion's astonishing blow. "We have him trapped now. Unable to move in our strong and durable silk. Looks like genetics and flesh are dominant after all, monkey!" Aragorg strikes at Ion's webbed casing. Ion spins in a circle from within the confines of the silk. Aragorg then turns to address his many followers. "Leave him in a cell! We will plant him deep beneath our planet's surface, never to be seen again! Let it be known that we – the Schleurghlting – have taken down the galaxy's *precious*-"

Whilst Aragorg had been monologueing, Leader Ion sighed a deep and irritated sigh from within his new cocoon. Presently, he turns on a program that causes his entire robot body to heat up to insane temperatures. The silk outer shell that surrounds Ion begins to glow an orange-yellow tinge, then quickly begins to smoke. Before the many and multiple Schleurghltings astonished eyes, their collective webbing burst into flame.

Their shocked gazes are met by Ion's furious one. The Earth Leader's entire body is radiating like a sun within the arena, with the sand beneath his feet turning to glass. Ion no longer holds his anger back.

"For the 'wise' leader of a species," Ion says to Aragorg. "You sure don't know when to stop talking."

Even though the Schleurghltings did not, Ion took it upon himself to use only his "graspers" against the entire army of Schleurghlting surrounding the arena. Punching, dodging, eye-gouging, ripping and tearing through them as if they are made of paper. Every bit of contact the arachnids try to use in defense is wasted. More volleys of web fire to him, but burn up within centimeters of his robotic person. Limbs cauterize before the metallic politician can fully grasp them. Ion zooms about the room, absolutely obliterating his enemies with a blood-thirst greater than Vlad the Impaler or Attila the Hun.

Venom, green and blue blood, legs, eyes, and every part imaginable from the Schleurghlting fly about the room. Ion moves strategically and systematically about the arena, piling the now deceased alien spiders neatly around Aragorg. The Schleurghlting leader could only defecate himself as he stares on in horror, frozen in place and shaking in fear.

Ion approaches Aragorg from across the ring, still glowing and with a melting Schleurghlting head in his hand. All the others lay wasted and in part-specific piles encircling the two planetary leaders. Ion stares into Aragorg's remaining four eyes with a look of disgust, revulsion and contempt. He crushes the severed head in his hands as if it were nothing, then stands before the Schleurghlting to look down upon him.

"I know you have more forces on this ship," Ion begins, tones of aggression and irritation in his synthetic voice. "You could call upon your remaining cluster to try and vanquish me. I assure you, they would simply end up like the rest of their friends. I could also do the same to you...but I am merciful. I will take my leave now, and if I do not see you high-tailing it back to your planet, I will destroy this entire ship without thinking twice. If you even *consider* going to Earth on some sort of revenge scheme, I will know. And I will see to it that not even the Frosks most ferocious tortures will compare to my wrath. Ahem. Good day, Leader Aragorg."

With that, Ion turns down his core temperature and returns to his stealth ship. Ion feels fairly certain that Aragorg will try something, despite the warning he had given him. The Schleurghlting are a species filled with hubris. Regardless, it was against senate code to take down a leader of another planet without a *planetary* threat...Ion was but one entity. Hence, the Earth Leader would have to bide his time for whenever that day came.

It appears as though the Schleurghltings are still on course for Terra Six as Ion exits their larger star craft. He finds this disappointing, but does note their low speed. Ion hopes that they will simply turn their ship in the proper direction, enter light speed, and bring up this encounter at the next Centre Planet meeting. To his dismay, Aragorg evidently has other intentions.

The Schleurghlting starship suddenly begins to speed as fast as it can within the asteroid field toward Terra Six, no doubt in a defiant act of revenge. Once again, Ion sighs, exits his craft, and raises his arm. Whilst on the Schleurghlting vessel, Ion's microbots had hacked into their system, and gathered blueprints for the ship. Ion now knows exactly where to shoot in order to completely shut the machine down, creating a big enough explosion to cause a vacuum into open space. The majority of the Schleurghltings would pour out and perish. The Leader, however, would make a great trophy for Ion to bring to Terra Six.

From his extended arm, Ion's index finger produces a beam of light that strikes its mark. An explosion ensues; tearing a massive whole in the Schleughrlting ship. As predicted, arachnids pour from the gaping hole in the ship's hull. Emergency lights can be seen from where Ion is now floating just outside of his stealth ship. He flies at a leisurely pace to where he knows the Schleurghlting leader is.

Upon arrival, Ion casually rips through walls and barricades like a hot knife through butter. Within moments, he once again stares down the still shell-shocked Aragorg, in an airlocked section of the vessel. Ion's synthetic voice let's out a somber "pity" before his metallic hands grasp the leaders head and tears it clean off of the body.

The Earth Leader returns to his ship, mildly dismayed that he undoubtedly just caused an entire rupture within a civilization. A great deal of their military is now destroyed, and their leader beheaded. Uprise is sure to become of the savage planet, but to Ion this was better than the decimation of a now developing one.

Ion cruises through the asteroid field to Terra Six. Once held on a massive planet the humans had invaded, their species now rests on a forest moon outside of the decimated rubble that was Terra Five. A century ago, planetary and civil war had rampaged the new terraformers, who were unable to agree on how the planet should be run. With half of them having a distaste for Crow and Ion's ways, it was inevitable that the planet would not last. Those few thousand that survived re-established and created a more peaceful way of life, leaving their anger and distrust for one another behind.

As he pulls up to Terra Six, Ion laments on what he had to do, and begins to plan the explanation he is now forced to give to Centre Planet. Hopefully, they may step in and help stabilize the Schleurghlting political system. Now, the more pressing matter of omnipertium must be addressed.

X

Frosk: The Office of Dissoteria, Capitol City

"That is about it, Life-Admiral Crow," Crombolus Shickles says from across the way.

Crow sat at one end of a long and narrow table. Along the right and left hand sides sat various representatives of Frosk: Schreik - the Secretary of Finance, Orthaug – the Secretary of Science, Actias – the Secretary of Innovation, Pyrrha – The Voice of the People (propagandist), Kato – Secretary of Environmental Advancements, the Head of Torture (who apparently did not have a name), and Dissosteria – the Planetary Leader who sits at the other end of the table. Shickles rests to Dissosteria's right.

"So…you are asking me," Crow begins, trying to make the task seem as though it would be much more difficult than Crow knew it was going to be. "…To find a way to clean your planet's air?"

"Indeed," Kato replies, a bit of worry on his alien face. "We have run this planet to its absolute limits in the pursuit of scientific advancement. We have a doomsday clock that brings our planet's lifespan to only two years."

This seems an understatement to Crow. The air is so polluted on this planet that one can barely see two feet in front of them. The wind is so thick and filled with harmful chemicals that the Frosks hadn't been able to fly in it since a time out of memory. Crow himself had brought a breathing apparatus as not to destroy his still working human lungs.

"That is quite the formidable task," Crow replies, again feigning some kind of fear that he may be unable to help them.

"We know Earth has done something similar, under your advisement," Orthaug insists. "Could it be so much different for Frosk?"

"Yes and no," Crow replies, rubbing where his chin would be on his breathing apparatus. "We did have severe pollution, but not to this extent. A lot of what must be done will also be dictated by how fertile your soil is, how long it could take to clear the skies and bring sun in, and whether your planets' industries can change to an alternative kind of fuel or not."

"Our donors will not change their industry tactics," Schreik answers with a tone of finality. "Their businesses profit over the use of these forms of electricity *exclusively*. You would take their livelihood from them?"

"If it meant your species and planet would survive," Crow says, looking upon the Secretary of Finance sternly. "Then yes. Profit is meaningless if you are dead. Give them avenues into a new kind of industry, offer them a buy-out, or kill them. It doesn't much matter to me what you do-"

"Is that how you dealt with your environmental problems, human?" Dissosteria asks with a touch of disgust in his voice. "Murdering those who opposed you? Do you have no sense of allegiance?"

"Our allegiance is with the betterment of our people," Crow answers unapologetically. "We believe in a utilitarian way – one where what is done benefits the many, not the few. If one person has to die so that one hundred million can prosper, then we see the need of the one hundred million outweighing the one. By a long shot."

Looks of disapproval are darted at Crow. What a shame that the illusion of currency blinds so many even throughout the galaxy. For being an advanced species, one would think they would have their affairs in order. Regardless, Crow is not here on Frosk to dictate how to run their planet.

"I digress though, we are not here to discuss political views," Crow intones, heaving a defeated sigh. "This is your planet, I respect however you wish to run it. Just know, this project will take much longer and a great deal more resources to achieve."

"Any means necessary," buzzes Pyrrha. "We need to survive, and the people need a stable economy for us to move forward. That said, we have planned a large budget for this."

"Very good," Crow nods. "You will need it. As per a fee for Earth, we will ask something of you in the future. Whenever that time comes. Monetary wealth is not something our planet requires. Is there anything else you need of me, gentlemen?"

"We did wish to discuss the Centre Planet attack-"

"Worry not, my friends," Crow says, with a wave of his hand. "Earth has an old saying: Innocent until proven guilty. What happened is of no concern of mine until the Centre Planet dictates otherwise."

The room is filled with a sigh of relief at Crows words. The Earth Life-Admiral knew this subject would come up, regardless of his presence and apparent willingness to help. It was a topic Crow knew he needed to make clear hadn't swayed his promise to help the Froskian people.

"Much obliged, Life-Admiral Crow," Dissosteria says with…what must have been a grin. "Actias will show you to your quarters now. You begin your research tomorrow."

With that, Crow is escorted from the conference room. He could not help but notice an odd glare from the Head of Torture. As a safety measure, Crow sends out a series of microbots throughout the vicinity, and latches some on the Head of Torture. The Frosks may seem amicable now, however they may have ulterior motives. The inquiry about his work with Technicorum II makes Crow feel it necessary to remain alert enough to not take any chances.

Actias leads Crow through a maze of passages that are very plain, and made from a strong – yet common – Froskian metal. The walls are made of octagonal connections, etched with blue and yellow lights, and have a white-ish grey hue to them. The Secretary of Innovation regales the Life-Admiral on a variety of inventions the Frosks have made that have thus far benefited the Galactic Imperium as a whole. Crow, of course, already knew about all of them. Still, he nods and gives words of praise nonetheless. He was, after all, being given accommodations by the Frosks. A little diplomacy never hurt anyone.

One invention in particular struck Crow as odd for Actias to have brought up. The Frosk mentions an accelerator built for space travel that had been made a prerequisite for any self-respecting planet to have in their ships. At least when they were first introduced into the galactic fold.

See, the Frosks care very much for profit, and demand respect for their intellect in honestly quite a narcissistic fashion. To put this into context; the accelerator Actias is speaking of broke very easily, and cost a small fortune to repair. Few planets (pretty well just Earth and Technicorum II) have the ability to create something better. Hence the Frosks essentially possess a monopoly when it comes to optimal space travel. Earth does not share the true strength of their fleet, that any unwise intruders may be destroyed with unpredictable and unexpected. Technicorum II themselves kept their secrets vaulted away where even Crow would have a difficult time finding their true potential.

So for the Secretary of Innovation to be bragging about their planet's ability to rip off the majority of the galaxy was mainly intended to make a mockery of Earth. The Frosks do not know how Crow and Ion have their ships built, or about many of their technologies in general. Actias is clearly trying to present an air of superiority to the Earth emissary, so when they came to the door of Crow's quarters Crow did not hesitate to put him in his place.

"Ah yes, the fundamental accelerator within the Imperium, did you oversee its creation?" Crow asks innocently.

"Ah I wish," Actias admits, looking mildly chagrined. "It had been invented before my time."

"Well, that is odd…" Crow begins, turning as if to open the door to his quarters.

"We cannot all live as long as you and Leader Ion, Life-Admiral," Actias says with a light buzzing laugh.

"Oh, that is not what I mean," Crow says, turning back to the diplomat. "I am surprised the new Secretary of Innovation has not tried to innovate on behalf of his planet and the galaxy. Good evening, Actias."

Crow closes the door on an embarrassed - and clearly insulted - sentient giant bug. He laughs internally as he places his belongings and baggage in their necessary areas. Despite being asked to begin research the following day, Crow intends to take a fifteen minute nap – as his polyphasic/Uberman sleep schedule requires – before beginning a basic design for the Frosks. Prior to this, he felt it wise to check on Ion's status with Terra Six.

Ion, how was your travel to Terra Six? Crow asks telepathically.

Not without its adventures, Ion responds. *I was forced to relieve the Schleurghltings of their leader.*

…WHAT?! Crow mentally yells. *What happened?*

I reached the asteroid field not far from Terra Six

The one made from the remnants of Terra Five, Crow continues matter-of-factly.

The very same. There was a Schleurghlting ship waiting there for me. I'll send you the footage of the encounter. I intend to send the same footage to the Centre Planet.

Crow reviews the events as they happened from Ion's perspective. The vision screen implanted in Ion's synthetic eyes had captured everything he saw and heard during the Schleurghlting fiasco. Crow feels that one could argue Ion had given them fair warning, and that he had abided by the Galactic laws prior to engaging in combat. With the additional fact of the battle only occurring after Terra Six was threatened, it is felt that Ion's actions are justified.

Well brother, Crow says, a bit uneasy. *A truly brutal display you made there. Fortunately the Centre Planet should not seek any penalization toward you, in my opinion. You did everything you could.*

Indeed, Ion agrees. *Shame though…they may be a race of brutes, but they are living things.*

Well…you just took out a pretty big portion of their elite army, Crow notes. *It may be for the best. Monarchic Aristocracies are not the optimal way to run any civilization. I am sure the Centre Planet will implement a more modern and efficient form of government there.*

Time will tell. How have the Froskians been treating you? Ion inquires, coming near the outer rim of Terra Six.

With masks of friendship, Crow answers honestly. *Something doesn't feel right here. I have sent the nano-bots to investigate. The Head of Torture seems to be quite the interesting fellow.*

His methods are known throughout the galaxy for their effectiveness. Ion answers with worry through his internal monologue. *Be careful, brother. And ever vigilante!*

Always. I will begin working on a climate control and atmosphere cleaning system throughout the evening here. Will report back. Have fun with that oracle, won't you?

Ion scoffs. *I will be sure to do that. Be safe, brother.*

     With that their communications end. Crow prepares for a brief slumber before getting to task of creating potential solutions for the Froskian pollution problem. An endeavour indeed, without proper compliance and greener efforts. Regardless, Crow is certain he will create a dynamic solution. His true fear rests with his brother. What did Terra Six hold for him: true omnipertium, a false ploy for the people to meet their God, or worse – a true oracle.

XI

Earth 2040 – Interplanetary Representative Ion's Favourite Bar

"...Such is the reward of reaching beyond our world; more proof of what I have been preaching for the past decade. There is no salvation in this broken capitalistic approach to running our country. Granted our health care system is indeed done right. It is my firm belief that the suffering amongst our people – and the people of the planet – is the non-distribution of wealth. Why must so many fall prey to hunger, disease, poor education, poverty? So the list goes on. Why, when we have made such scientific advancements, do we continue to permit literal atrocities to continue? For the benefit of the few, it would seem. I have found that many of the other worlds in our galaxy share a great deal of my ideologies: Particularly the tech giants of Technicorum II with their ecological ideologies, and Genvia for their utilitarian concepts. Borrowing some of these philosophies and expanding on them is the only sure way for Earth to both prosper and enter an age of true happiness..."
Ideal Ideologies: Political Philosophies by Ion - 2040

"Sorry folks, my brother here invents a ship that gets us into the Galactic Senate and he thinks he's a big shot!" Ion shouts, his normally perfectly-cropped hair in disarray.

Some laughs come from the bar patrons before they carry on with their drinking. It is late in the evening in the Canadian capitol, and people from all walks of life are spending their hard-earned cash trying to forget how much they hate their jobs. Crow - seated next to Ion at the bar – glares at his brother with frustration in his eyes.

"We aren't supposed to be calling attention to ourselves," Crow whispers into Ion's ear.

"Relax, little brother," Ion says, giving an affectionate arm-pat from their seated positions. "I generally make a bit of an ass of myself among the patrons. Keeps my approval ratings up. I'm trying to keep things 'business as usual' to avoid suspicion."

"Yes well, I've never been here," Crow says matter-of-factly, removing Ion's arm from his shoulder. "That could raise a few eyebrows."

"We have a reason to celebrate," Ion jeers on. "It would be weirder if I *didn't* bring you here. Don't worry so much."

Crow gives a mildly uneasy grunt, and sips at the new alien beer brought thanks to the new galactic trade. He looks about the crowded bar for a woman meeting the description of their contact. Alas, nothing as of yet. Crow clearly tenses at this notion – she should have arrived fifteen minutes and fourty three seconds ago!

"And my invention of post-light speed space travel is hardly what got us into the galactic senate," Crow chimes irritatedly.

"Don't be so modest, little brother," Ion says, looking at his brother in disbelief. "The Centre Planet Representative told us herself that your invention was what got us involved with the rest of the galaxy. You pretty much single-handedly solved the fermi paradox."

"I suppose," Crow sighs, looking into his empty mug. "She did say that's why Earth hadn't been contacted for the past-"

"There she is," Ion whispers, nodding before downing his drink. "Eight-o'clock."

Ion rises, fixes his tie, and gradually makes his way in her direction. Crow quickly gulps down this new, tangy alien ale before catching up to his brother and discreetly taking a seat next to him. Despite his brother's assurance, the Professor looks around nervously and inspects his anti-espionage device (which rests on his writs like a watch). Presently. they sit before a middle-class looking woman in the darkest corner of the bar.

"In the case we are being recorded, please be sure to use our code names," the woman says, giving an air of confidence to the duo despite her own nervousness.

"I wouldn't worry about that," Crow says, placing a device in the centre of the table. "This causes any recording devices within a one-hundred mile radius to malfunction."

"The Professor here is the definition of a mastermind," Ion assures their contact, giving a brotherly pat to Crow's back.

"Ah…well regardless," the contact says, looking a bit more at ease. "Please refer to me as 'The Duchess.'"

"Whatever suits your fancy," Ion agrees with a nod.

"Might I just congratulate you then, Professor," Duchess says while slowly taking an envelope from her back. "You have single-handedly pushed humanity forward within the Universe. Thank you."

"Better late than never," Crow replies humbly. "Now…tell us more about this metal, Duchess."

"Well, Eco and Professor," Duchess begins, laying the folder gently onto the table. She seems quite persistent by maintaining the usage of codenames (Eco being Ion, Professor of course being Professor Crow). "It is practically a myth. A metal found on only one planet within the deepest reaches of this galaxy. Guarded by what we now know as the 'Centre Planet,' and revered by the galaxy as 'The Perfect Metal' or…Omnipertium."

"Well, this simply sounds too good to be true," Ion says passively. "I am the inter-galactic Representative of Earth, and I have heard no whispers of this."

"That is because most of the Galactic Senate doesn't trust our planet yet," Duchess continues insistently. "Rightfully so: our planet is divided and most of the people in power are corrupt. Some traders, however, have gained the trust of a few of the locals on a variety of planets."

"Then why hasn't the government heard of this yet?" Crow inquires, looking over the documents Duchess supplied.

"Because the traders were warned never to tell the government here." Duchess answers baldly. "Save for you, Eco, there isn't a single Earthling in politics our alien counterparts trust. They are afraid the human hubris will cause intergalactic catastrophe."

"For the greater good they say nothing, no doubt," Crow says with a nod. "If this metal is as amazing as these documents say it is – and rare – the fools running our planet would get us kicked out of the intergalactic senate."

"Or worse, destroyed," Ion says. "What makes this metal so 'perfect,' Duchess?"

"It can conduct and store immeasurable amounts of energy from a solar rays, or even in the cold, heat…it is entirely indestructible, can be sharpened to a degree that would cut through anything. And to top it all off…there isn't much of it. Not in the known Universe. The tech giants of Frosk and Technicorum II are the only two civilizations, outside of the Centre Planet, that have any. And they have so little of it. They fear what might happen if it ends up in the wrong hands."

"Then why tell us about it?" Ion asks seriously. "Out of all the people in the galaxy, let alone our planet…why us?"

"Because of who you two are," Duchess answers honestly. "I have read your book, Eco. Your utilitarian concepts and utopic ideologies…not to mention the Professor's scientific prowess. From what I have seen of both your work and the work our sentient counterparts have been doing…Professor, you may be the most intelligent and scientifically advanced being out there. If anyone should have anything to do with this metal…if anyone could create a positive change within the universe using it, it would be you."

"I-well…that is very flattering," Crow admits, trying not to blush. "So…what do you want us to do, IF we manage to gather this metal?"

"Once you obtain it," The duchess began, slowly rising from her seat. "Do not let it change in temperature. Once it has cooled, it will forever stay in whatever shape and form it is. You have one chance to make it whatever you decide to make it into. But please be sure to do something that will make everything we know at least a little better."

The Duchess leaves the duo with nothing but their thoughts on this. Ion felt like he was invincible: potentially capable to have the power to change the world for the better. No matter the cost, no matter what he had to do. He could indeed make a Utopia. Crow, on the other hand, was a bit suspicious of The Duchess.

"How do we know that we can trust this woman, Ion?" he inquires as they head back to their seats at the bar.

"Relax, you are so uptight!" Ion says, waving a care-free hand. "You think I wouldn't do my research before trusting a contact? Don't you see!? We are on the edge of greatness!"

"Just…be careful," Crow whispers into his brother's ear as they reach the bar. "We are playing a dangerous game."

"Yes, yes," Ion waves his brother's concern away, then hails the bartender for another round. "All we need is a stealth ship…and something to make sure this metal doesn't cool, and we're laughing."

"We'll be something alright," Crow says before telling the bartender not to get him a drink. "Regardless, Nancy is expecting me, I better- Oh! There she is."

A lovely, blonde-haired woman walks through the crowd, looking about the dimly lit bar nervously. When she finally spots Crow, she runs to him and embraces him. Ion turns in his seat and smiles at the happy couple. Once they have finished their embrace, he reaches his hand out to Nancy.

"I've heard so much about you!" Ion exclaims. "I'm Ion!"

Abruptly, Nancy's eyes roll back in her head. The whites of her eyes turn bloodshot, and Nancy tenses as stiff as a board. Not knowing what to do, Ion simply stares as Crow lays her down gently, placing a toque beneath her head for support.

"Umm...brother-?" Ion intones, perplexed. "What's happening?"

"She's an oracle," Crow answers, pouring a glass of water on his own by reaching over the bar. "She's had a few episodes but...none ever quite this intense."

"Well...what do we do?"

"Wait."

"Is she gonna start blurting out cryptic-"

"Man of metal...the last of us...betrayal...alone...no planets, no galaxy...no survivors...no hope...complete obliteration...exploding sun...indestructible..." Nancy then sits bolt upright, pointing at Ion. "YOU WILL BE THE FINAL ONE!"

Nancy flings back onto the floor. Thankfully Crow had placed the toque on the ground, or she would have suffered a serious head injury. Crow looks at Ion, both scared and amazed. Ion gulps, then turns to the bartender.

"Cheque please."

Meanwhile - in a darkened and decrepit alleyway - The Duchess trudges between the homeless people, garbage, and snow drifts. Despite her ridiculous amount of thick clothing layers, she shivers seemingly uncontrollably. Then, once she believes no one could see her, she disappeared.

Upon it's ship, the previously cloaked Xeroph sit under a heating lamp. It still shivers compulsively, its cold blood thick and cumbersome. It had been discreetly beamed to the edges of the earth's atmosphere, in a single-Xeroph stealth ship. The giant reptile scowls in disgust at the overpopulated and over-polluted planet beneath it. It had turned off its cloaking device, and now tries to heat itself before contacting HQ. The Xeroph would inform their Elder Council that their plot is now in effect.

XII

Terra Six – The Grand Theater

"…And thus, our people left Terra One - also known as Earth - to find a new way of life. Little did we know, the answers were indeed with Leader Ion…all along."

Applause erupts in the forest. Ion leaves a blank expression on his robotic face as he claps unenthusiastically for the performance. The inhabitants of Terra Six had prepared a play for his arrival; further reinforcing their belief in many of Earth's older methods. It seems a kind gesture to Ion initially, however the entire series of theatrics proved pointless by the end.

The thespians had merely (inaccurately) re-enacted many things Ion is already privy to. Cradle of man, the concept of evolution, the rise and eventual downfall of empires, Ion and Crow's rise as leaders, the so-called "Pure Human Revolution", all the way to today.

A beam of light created by a confined native glowing creature encased in glass points onto Ion's person from within the crowd. Sitting on a throne made from some of the planets' trees, Ion rests above many of the inhabitants of Terra Six. The loin cloth-clad clan stare up at Ion in awe, clearly hoping for words of approval.

"Your creativity is admirable," Ion says, forcing his synthetic voice to have tones of pride and admiration for the inhabitants. "You have provided me with quite the warm welcome. I thank you."

In unison, without missing a beat the Terra Sixians utter "Praise be to God."

Even though Ion is made of metal, he experiences as close to a shiver as he is capable of feeling. The act of the people making this statement reminded the Earth Leader of his early years, centuries ago. Ion is not one to look at the past, but does allow all members of Earth to follow whichever faith they chose. No discrimination or limitation is made within the Dreamscape. But because faith is generally left within the Dreamscape, Ion had not heard these words in quite some time.

Shortly after the Terra Sixians obscure praise of the Earth Leader, a group of the inhabitants lift Ion's throne onto their shoulders. They then begin to carry the Earth Leader to the Hall of Leaders (not far from their current location).

"You don't have to carry me," Ion says with genuine sympathy. "I am fully capable of-"

"Please let us, God," one of the struggling carriers cry with admiration. "It is an honour merely to be in your presence!"

Ion floats out of the chair and levitates before the carriers. He gestures for them to lower his throne, which they do. He looks somberly upon the awe-stricken people.

"I am no more important than you," Ion informs them genuinely. "If honour is what you seek, walk with me to the Hall of your Leaders."

And so it was. Like an obscure meeting of past and future, the giant metal man walks with the loin-clothed locals. Ion asks about their way of life, how well a hunter-gatherer lifestyle works on this forest moon. He learns a little bit about the flora and fauna within the region as he nears the entrance of the large wooden hall.

Though relatively primitive, the cave in which the Leaders of Terra Six are waiting has a mouth strewn with wooden carvings. A frieze containing images of Ion grace the perimeter of the cave mouth. Two massive wooden pillars give the area a somewhat spiritual and powerful atmosphere.

Inside the cave rests a massive clearing. Any signs of stalagmites and stalactites are gone. A square of flat, grey stone is lit by bio-fluorescent creatures. Blue and yellow light melds over the Council's massive table. It is made of one solid tree root, immense and able to fit undoubtedly 50 standard people.

The seats are formed from the branches themselves, and upon them rest the leaders; including Drake and Talia. One of Ion's oldest sayings is engraved along the edge of the root-table: *"The Planet Will Provide."*

"Welcome to Terra Six, Leader Ion," Drake says, expressionless. "How were your-"

"Leaders, let us get to the point here," Ion says, raising a hand to silence Drake. Drake's expression is one of extreme insult; the other Leaders are taken aback as well. "Your Representatives *foolishly* mentioned that you *think* you have omnipertium on this planet. I sat through your little – inaccurate by the way – play, out of respect for your people. You all, on the other hand, are not on my good side."

There is indecipherable chatter amongst the Terra Sixians. Fingers being pointed as to who may have said it from some, and quizzical glances as to why that would be a problem from others. Ion rolls his eyes impatiently.

"It doesn't really matter who said it," he informs the Council. "What matters is your planet now has a target on its metaphorical back. Omnipertium is the most rare and powerful metal in the known universe. You will now have entire civilizations coming to claim it. Don't believe me? Here is the leader of the Schleurghltings."

Ion opens his left hand, and the severed head of Aragorg appears floating above it. The council on Terra Six gasps in shock. One or two also vomit. Ion approaches their massive table and places the severed head in the middle of it, before them all.

"I found the Leader on their mother ship, which was making its way to your planet," Ion continues, floating back a few feet from the table, and yet above eye level of the Terra Six Council. "At first they threatened to fight me. When I refused, they threatened to destroy you. Hence, I had no choice but to take them all down."

"Praise be to God," is the response from the council. Ion rolls his eyes, yet again.

"Enough of that," he says to them assertively. "This is only the beginning of the attacks. I want to see what you seem to think is Omnipertium, so that I may prove to you that it is not. Then, I shall speak with the Centre Planet; informing them that I have taken down the Schleurghlting leader, and to have them inform the rest of the galaxy that you do not possess this precious metal."

"As you wish, Leader Ion," Talia responds to Ion with a nod. She makes a gesture, and a Terra Six Shaman brings out a small, ornate box. The gentleman is hunkered over as though carrying a great weight.

Ion floats down to the Shaman and picks up the box. He removes the lid, and lifts the piece of metal out with his right hand. His synthetic eyes look over it, examining its properties, density, and weight. After a moment, the baseball-sized chunk of metal glows red, then begins to melt in Ion's hands.

Ion peers at the melting, glowing piece of metal with a dissatisfied look. The Terra Sixians put their entire planet in jeopardy for this? What kind of resources did they use that led them to believe they had found omnipertium?

"Not omnipertium," he informs them. Ion closes his hand around the melting metal, and steam ejects from it. When he opens his hand again, the metal is in a perfect spherical shape. "If it were, it would have to withstand the heat of the star known as Eta Carinae. This barely made it past 1, 356 degrees Kelvin."

Ion's annoyed gaze is met with disappointed frowns. Despite feeling as though he had had his time wasted, Ion forces a smile upon them. He knows bringing them down any further would result in nothing positive.

"Fret not, Terra Sixians," Ion begins with a wave of a hand. He returns the metal to the box, and the Shaman takes it away again. "It is an honest mistake. And unfortunately, you do not have the resources Life-Admiral Crow and I have to test these sorts of things. But please, next time, make sure you tell me in person. *Never* bring something like this up in the Centre Planet Senate again, please."

"Of course, Leader Ion," Drake says with an ashamed head-nod. "We have one more thing to ask of you-"

"If it is about meeting the oracle," Ion interrupts, beginning to turn away. "I have no interest in meeting them. There are much more pressing matters on Ear-"

"Why, we have already met," Talia informs the Earth Leader. He turns to see her smiling coily. "Hello, Uncle."

"Uncle-?" Ion asks incredulously.

"Yes, I am your distant relative," Talia informs him. "A descendant of Life-Admiral Crow and Lady Nancy."

Ion's metal brow furrows. "I assure you, my dear, Nancy was no Lady. She was even less of an oracle."

"She is written in our history as the most accurate oracle in the known galaxy!" A council member barks.

"From what I saw from your people's little skit," Ion says emotionlessly. "It looks as though there are a great deal of 'facts' that need correcting."

"Talia is much more powerful than Nancy!" Drake insists. "She is the most powerful and prescient Oracle the universe has ever known!"

"Is that so?"

"We believe it to be true," the council says in unison.

"Perhaps I should be the judge of that," Ion says casually. "Talia, would you join me on my voyage back to Earth?"

XIII

Earth - 6-6-5-4-38's Dreamscape

"I am trying to beat the world record," 6-6-5-4-38 informs a programmer who represented Utopius within the Dreamscape. "I've always wanted to be recognized for something."

"Apologies for the intrusion, friend," the disembodied voice echoes throughout 6-6-5-4-38 virtual world. "There are merely some choices our citizens make that cause us to have concern for their mental health. Have you been feeling depressed lately?"

"No," lies 6-6-5-4-38. "Just want to try something new."

"All citizens are welcome to live whatever kind of existence brings them happiness," is the reply.

If that were true, 6-6-5-4-38 thinks, *this totalitarian regime wouldn't exist.*

"You have spent the majority of your time within the Dreamscape farming," the disembodied programmer's voice continues. "Why such a change of heart?"

"Once you perfect something, it is wise to seek other avenues," 6-6-5-4-38 answers. This is true; 6-6-5-4-38 has always had a passion for farming and gardening. For as long as they could remember, that is what they had done here in the Dreamscape. That was, in a way, what had caused them to think so radically. Alone in a virtual field with nothing but their thoughts. Realizing more and more that – although 6-6-5-4-38 had become skilled at it – farming does not, in fact, have any impact on the world around them. Not within the Dreamscspe.

"Very understandable," the disembodied voice answers jovially. "If, however, you do choose to go back to farming…know that we do offer citizens the opportunity to not enter the Dreamscsape. You are more than welcome to work in the field, instead."

"I…did not know that…" 6-6-5-4-38 replies thoughtfully. "Perhaps after this little endeavour, I may just do that."

"Know that you can, citizen 6-6-5-4-38! And have yourself a wonderful Dream."

The disembodied voice disengages from 6-6-5-4-38's Intersphere. With a sigh of relief, 6-6-5-4-38 enters the visual options screen within the Dreamscape. They browse through the scenario options and chose the setting they had chosen to have created for them.

The infinity room they had stood in moments ago begins to fill with colour. A replica of the anechoic chamber in South Minneapolis begins to take form around 6-6-5-4-38. The anechoic room is a places renowned for being [3]99.99% sound absorbent; so much so the longest reported time spent in it was merely 1 hour. People who stayed in longer than that had tended to suffer from hallucinations, eventually finding it unbearable. The room itself was said to be so soundproofed that one could hear their own heartbeat, and the blood flowing through their veins.

6-6-5-4-38 knows that the proud Crow had gone above and beyond to ensure the Dreamscape is as much like reality as possible. Sitting in this virtual room would be just like sitting in the real anechoic chamber. 6-6-5-4-38 would hear their own (virtual) heartbeat, their stomach, the whole nine yards.

They would also – in the condensed silence - be able to hear the pulsation of the Dreamscape. 6-6-5-4-38 would be able to make out the pulsations that the central processor sends out to people on the Intersphere, learn how it works, and communicate to it that way. Once 6-6-5-4-38 figured that out, they will be able to connect to the processor and send their brainwaves to others, hopefully enticing the citizens to begin a rebellion.

That is the hope, at least. The processor uses brainwaves to communicate with the citizens of Utopius. 6-6-5-4-38 believes that if their brainwaves can imitate the signal that the central processor sends, it would be indistinguishable by the processor; which would causing a meld between the two. Either science or fiction – this had to work.

---

[3]   https://www.dailymail.co.uk/sciencetech/article-2124581/The-worlds-quietest-place-chamber-Orfield-Laboratories.html

Freedom has become an illusion. It has become more of a word than an idea or state of being to 6-6-5-4-38. Ion and his crony brother Crow sure have done a bang-up job trying to make it seem otherwise, but 6-6-5-4-38 knows this must stop. 6-6-5-4-38 also believes that what Ion had done to make life this way was…so cruel, unrepentant. A true leader should have virtue!

6-6-5-4-38 further their certainty as they sit in the middle of the anechoic chamber. Thinking of all the deaths Ion has caused, the fear instilled in what few true-humans were left, the need for life the way it was 300 years ago. 6-6-5-4-38 closes their eyes and listens closely.

However within moments, the churning of their stomach becomes ear-shatteringly loud. The sound of their heartbeat echoes within their virtual ears. 6-6-5-4-38 gets the sensation of their blood running all throughout their body in a pure, concentrated and eerie way. Still, 6-6-5-4-38 tries to listen beyond that. Faintly, in the distance beyond all this, 6-6-5-4-38 can hear the central processor of the Intersphere. The sporadic pulsation seems to have no rhythm, but appears to have a distinct and complex pattern to it. The language 6-6-5-4-38 is hoping to imitate.

Then, suddenly…lucid visions consume 6-6-5-4-38. The constant beat of their heart becomes an overwhelming drumming that shook them to the very core. More than half an hour in, the chamber has become unbearable. 6-6-5-4-38 wants to scream to drown out the sound, but knows it would make it worse. They cover their ears in a feeble attempt to calm the ringing in them. Forcing themselves to focus, 6-6-5-4-38 brings up the Intersphere control panel.

With blurry vision, 6-6-5-4-38 chooses a new pre-programmed life scenario to enter. The deafening sounds of 6-6-5-4-38 insides at work stops, and the faint sound of a summer breeze reverberates within their digital ears. 6-6-5-4-38 opens their eyes and sees an all-too-familiar and calming corn field. They breathe a sigh of relief as the agonizing pulse that had just consumed them subsides.

Crow smiles gingerly as his plan begins to come to fruition.

XIV

The Planet Frosk – Crow's Laboratory

Crow awakes after many Froskian hours of work; planning, designing, and calculating how best to deal with the planet's pollution problem. He has just awoken from taking his last Uberman nap as the second sun was begins to rise. This is the Froskian's first call sign to be awake, alert, and ready to contribute to their planet before the third sun hits the horizon.

Crow lifts his head from his desk and looks out his work room window. The skyline is an array of dimmed colours brought on by the purple sun reaching the horizon. Higher up in the sky is a distinct orange through the smog clouding the view to the outer reaches of this planet.

Crow yawns, stretches, and begins to scan the room with his robotic eye. He is startled to find that two Frosks seem to be approaching his room door. His synthetic eye can whir about in any direction within the confines of his head. While doing an initial room search, he notices the duo moments from reaching the door with an x-ray enhancement. Approaching the door are the Voice of the People - Pyrrha, who is preparing to knock - and an unfamiliar Frosk directly behind him.

"Enter," Crow bellows as Pyrrha is raising his tarsel. The duo look confused, but do as instructed.

"Good morning Emissary Crow!" Pyrrha intones enthusiastically. He rubs his claw-like feelers together expectantly as he walks gradually toward the rising Crow. "I trust you had a restful evening.

"Oh my, yes," Crow answers with a light grin. "Got a full 30 Earth minutes. Your nights are long here on Frosk, Voice Pyrrha."

"I-that they are, I suppose," Pyrrha answers, clearly surprised. "From my understanding of Earth's rotation, it is about 75% longer than that of your planet."

"Evidently so!" Crow agrees. "I was able to lay out the majority of my plan already. Might I ask who your companion is?"

"Ah yes, this is Trius Avarus, he will- wait, did you say the *majority* of the plan?" Pyrrha appears to nearly fall over when he processes the statement.

"Indeed," Crow answers, grinning softly. "We will need a series of trial runs for them, just to make sure they work the way I think they should. Otherwise, a few more hours and we can begin the building stage."

Pyrrha's expression is blank for a moment. His left eyelids twitches involuntarily. "I will have Actias summoned to take a look then…ah…Now, Emissary Crow, as I was saying: This is Trius Avarus. He is a highly talented journalist. We would like for him to stay by your side, and log your progress; working alongside you and documenting your developments." Pyrrha's bug face curls into a grin, he claps his upper tarsal claws and his antennae convulse.

"Why?" Crow inquires flatly, his eyebrow raised.

"My, for documentations, dear Emissary!" Pyrrha answers. "The documentation of any and all developments on Froskian soil is not only tradition, but a necessary need for the betterment of our planet's future!"

"Of course," Crow answers, advancing casually toward Trius. "A pleasure to meet you, lad. I am Life-Admiral Crow."

Trius is what Earth would recognize as a giant firefly. He stands over six feet tall, with a spikey yellow touf of hair between his ever twitching antennae. His lower abdomen seems to be continuously glowing and ever-moving. Trius stands with his left arm outstretched, meeting the Earthly tradition of shaking hands/tarsi. The other tarsus holds an ornate staff. The top has a very intricate design of the three Forskian suns in eclipse over one another, and the staff itself seems to glow with their light.

"Trius has been chosen as the documenter for his exemplary journalistic skills and attention to detail," Pyrrha continues. "Speak with him at length, or act as though he is part of the background, the choice is yours Emmisary." Crow can tell by Pyrrha's tone that he would prefer that the Life-Admiral didn't communicate with Trius at all. Poor, foolish Pyrrha.

"You are as intimidating as my people promised you would be," Trius says casually and seemingly in a hurried tone. "I look forward to working with you and rue the day that I may upset you."

"Do you intend to upset me?" Crow asks flatly.

"No sir," Trius answers. "I hope only to observe and answer any inquiries you may have to the best of my capacity. Additionally I fully intend to send a detailed and truthful account to my superiors of your endeavours and advancements starting the second I am able to look over any and all work you have done thus far. Believe you me, Emissary, to the delight and surprise of us Frosks you claim to have a lot done already. Our planet is in dire need of-"

"That is, quite enough, Trius ahuh," Pyrrha interrupts, placing a tarsus on the Journalist's shoulder. "I believe the Earth Emissary understands your position during his working endeavours."

Trius nods to the Voice, then pulls a semi-holographic device from his pocket. The firefly enters a code or instruction to the device for a moment, then begins to scan Crow's work. It had all been placed in organized piles of Froskian paper on the Emissary's desk. Each labelled, categorized, and filed in a colour-coded fashion.

"Trius!" bellows Pyrrha. "Do you not think it respectful to ask the Life-Admiral *permission* before-?"

"It is quite alright, Voice," Crow interrupts with a care-free flick of his hand. "I have a very open policy in all my work. Anything your People need information on, feel free to take it. But do inform me before doing so, please."

"Understood," Trius answers, still in motion and moving Crow's physical files about. Crow rolls his eyes.

"Come here, Trius," Crow says, mildly impatiently.

The firefly pauses for a moment, looks almost longingly at the files, then saunters toward Crow. The Life-Admiral looks emotionlessly at the Froskian journalist for a moment, then reaches his robotic hand out to the semi-holographic device. In a fraction of a second, all of the information the journalist had been taking his time scanning are in his device; just as organized as Crow had laid it out.

"I always run a digital back-up within my internal memory," Crow says casually, beginning to reorganize the physical copies of his work. "Now Pyrrha, why don't you lead me to your Head of Innovation."

"At once, Life-Admiral!" There is a glow of respect and admiration coming from the Voice of the People. Froskians were very seldom impressed by other's technology, but they could not help but show it when they are.

Pyrrha leads Crow down a series of hallways, with Trius on their coat tails. Pyrrha points out some of the notable locations and people as they walk by, whilst the firefly continues to take notes. All the while, Trius's lower abdomen glows in an indistinguishable pattern – as if it were an uncontrollable and chronic convulsion to the giant sentient insect.

The massive building in which the Froskians had placed Crow is pretty well like any other: built strictly for the purpose of industry. There are very few aesthetic designs, little to no statues or art work. They are a cold gray that clash with the greenish-brown smog, which covers the world outside. Architects must not have been needed on this planet, for most of the buildings are simple, rectangular, and uniform. When beginning to arrive on the planet, Crow was able to see some smaller buildings he assumed were the people's living quarters. Featureless, made from cheap and degrading metal.

The building that Crow, Pyrrha and Trius are currently walking through is the Innovation building. A straight-forward skyscraper where each floor deals with a specific subject. The higher the floor, the more important the job. The first floor is for security, the second for the pencil pushers. The third up to the fifth floors are designated to the accountants, and the sixth and seventh geared toward the Innovation Planners. So it went up to floor twenty five, where the (what earth would call) CEO's of the main industries sit at a desk, and either approve or turn down new concept ideas.

Crow has been shifted to the 23rd floor of this skyscraper for the duration of his time here. That is where the head innovators generally work on brainstormed ideas of the 24th floor scientists. They have given him a specially designed room – cordoned off from the pre-existing lab and sound proofed – that he may get to work as soon as he sees fit.

Pyrrha comes to a stop before the air tube system; a series of pipes that act as both elevators and secondary means of travel for the workers here. These large, cylindrical tubes use pressure to send its users in whichever direction they see fit. These were made necessary to avoid contact with the air outside. Currently, Pyrrha, Crow and Trius stand before the ten different tubes. Pyrrha begins to prepare the nearest one to send the trio up to the Political building.

"This is gonna suck," jests Trius, not looking up from his note-taking.

"We will have to move into the tubes in quick succession," the Voice informs casually. "I have it programed to take all three of us at once, but the time duration demands we do it quickly. There are a great many Frosks using the system in this building."

With that, Pyrrha steps within a foot of the tube. In the blink of an eye, the Voice is but a blur soaring upward. Without hesitation, Crow takes five paces forward and follows suit. Trius is mere centimeters behind him. A sensation of pressure riddles Crow for only a moment before he is standing upright on a completely different floor, in a completely different part of the Capital City.

"Not so bad is it, emissary?" Pyrrha asks.

"Definitely different," Crow admits. "Earth used to use a sort of levee system to move floors. We even had some machines that were similar to flightless ships. Now we simply fly up with our artificial modifications…well, the majority of humanity anyway. This is quite an innovative form of travel though, Voice!"

"Mmmm...I miss flying," Trius says. "Now we are on the highest floor, political building, where the most important people on this planet sit and overlook the workings of the underlings. Always plotting for the betterment (mostly the betterment) of our species and societies. I assume we are here to see the Head of Innovation – Actias – Mr. Voice, sir?"

"Yes, Trius," the Voice answers in irritation. "Now stop talking. On another note, Emissary, the entirety of Froskian Leaders are currently overlooking some important matters as we speak. Perhaps later Actias will take you to get a quick look at other Froskian advancements."

"Excellent!" Crow exclaims enthusiastically. "Thank you for being so gracious as to have me a part of it."

"Our pleasure!" Pyrrha responds genuinely. "Right this way now."

The Voice leads his guests into a massive, heavily guarded and secure area. Immense doors, a series of cameras, a variety of fire-arms (attached to the walls), and a plethora of guards all observe the trio as they jaunt down the hallway. Pyrrha is in the lead, walking as if on a mission.

As the trio approach their destination, a series of robots float around the Voice, scanning him and making inquiries. Seemingly, there are a series of questions that must be answered for the security systems to not totally obliterate any non-authorized personnel.

"They're with me," the Voice says to the robots, one of his wings gesturing toward Crow and Trius. "Code Epsilon, Frezckleur, Zelch."

"Ah-pproved" is the robotic reply.

All security systems seem to disarm as they finally near the door; save for the live guards in heavy duty armor surrounding the walls and in front of the giant door. Crow feels as though the Froskian armor presented here shows a great deal of design flaws. It is very bulky, and does not conform to the natural shape of the variety of bug species that wear them. These had clearly been produced strictly to withstand blunt-force and explosions, not designed for optimal efficiency.

"Voice, please state business, duration of stay, and give both names and species of your entourage," bellows a large wasp-like guard. She is not only the largest security officer there, but she is also clearly the most decorated. A large assembly of badges, medals, and awards hang from the boxey chest of her armour. Evidently Earth wasn't the only planet to give out recognition in the form of medals and ribbons.

Pyrrha answers all inquiries made by the security guard in exact order. The officer nods, enters the information on the vision screen, and then gestures for other security officers to open the doors for the trio. Beyond the doors, in an octagon shaped room, rest the head members of the planet Frosk.

"Ah, I see you have made it!" says Shickles jovially. "Please, join us!"

The room Crow enters features a large, metal desk with all the Froskian representatives sitting on one side of it in a row to his right. On Crow's left is a giant holographic screen, currently projecting the planet's ecological status in a variety of statistical numbers and graphs. As Shickles gestures for Crow and his accompaniment to sit, three chairs seem to appear from thin air at the end closest to the entrance where they are standing. Pyrrha, Trius, and Crow all take a seat and gaze upon the projected image.

"Our Head of Torture was just about to speak with the Centre Planet about the Perusak attack," Actias informs Crow without looking at him. The bug is clearly still upset over Crow's comments from yesterday.

"After this brief conference, we will be looking at what you have developed thus far, emissary Crow," Kato says with a nod of respect.

"I am most pleased to hear of the progress you have made thus far," Dissosteria says to Crow, his old voice wavering slightly. "Let us begin the transmission."

In the seconds a signal is sent to speak with members of the Centre Planet, Crow cannot help but feel appalled. It had not been more than ten minutes since he had told Pyrrha the amount of progress he had made; how it had made it all the way to the Froskian Leaders in such a short time causes Crow to wonder if he is being watched more than he had anticipated.

"Greetings from Centre Planet!" echoes the jovial tones of the hippopotamus-like Centre Planet Representative. "My name is [4]Potur, how can I help the lovely people of Frosk today?"

[4] belua hippopotamus editur – latin for hippo

"We have called to clear our name," the Head of Torture bellows. Even when translated for Crow, he could tell this Frosk's voice is what many people would affiliate with the sound of death. "Provided for you and all those at the Centre Planet is evidence that the Great Planet of Frosk would never be so foolish or arrogant as to try and do harm to the Legendary Centre Planet."

"Magnificent!" Potur exclaims blithely. "Please, send the evidence to us, and our board will overview it as soon as- Oh! Earth Representative Crow, I see your aid with the Froskians has begun!"

"Yes, Officer Potur," Crow answers respectfully. "I have already made a fair amount of progress in our endeavour."

"Wonderful to hear," Potur grins. "And might I add, Leader Ion recently sent his news about the Schleurghltings. Dreadful scenario, but fortunately Centre Planet has already taken measures to remedy the chaos that might have been on the Schleurghlting planet."

"I am most glad to hear Officer!" Crow answers happily. "Please keep me informed on whatever measures you take, and let Earth know if we may be of any aid as well."

"Of course, Life-Admiral," Potur answers with a bow. "Now, to Dissosteria and the other Leaders of the Froskian people, we will be in touch again shortly. Thank you for your prompt action on such a volatile situation. Farewell to you all!"

With that the face of Potur disappears from the holographic screen. The previous image of the Froskian planet and its ecological statistics replace it. The Head of Torture takes his seat back down among the other leaders, and Crow leans forward to be within view of him.

"Excuse me, Head of Torture," Crow intones, trying to sound as polite as possible. "May I ask what evidence you provided to the Centre Planet?"

"Of course, of course," Shickles chimes in. "The Head of Torture himself was able to get ahold of a few Perusak shortly after the Centre Planet attack. With some help from Actias, he was able to extract a confession from multiple Perusak pirates."

"And their families, aheh!" adds the Head of Torture.

"So I see…" Crow says grimly, understanding the not-so-subtle implication. "Ah…would you all like to see my proposal concepts for the ecology crisis now?"

"You have more than one?" Actias and Kato ask, both in shock and in unison.

"But of course!" Crow answers, trying to sound humble. "I have three concepts, the science behind them, statistical success percentages, and required resources needed to have the projects done."

A buzzing surrounds the Life-Admiral. This was a sign of respect from the Froskian people; should they become very impressed, their wings flap in short, quick bursts. Such happens by all at the table…save for the Head of Torture. It seems this Representative is trying to remain nonchalant, or perhaps did not understand the very depth and detail that Crow had gone to in order to save this planet.

"Trius, would you mind showing the Froskian Leaders my work?" Crow asks. "Files 'Dyson Sphere', 'Frosk II', and 'Density' please"

With a nod from Dissosteria, Trius rises and walks up to Kato. The duo make eye contact for a short moment (to transfer the digital files Crow had sent to him), then Trius returns to his seat. Kato works on his vision screen briefly before the digital models Crow had created within his internal memory are displayed up on the giant screen before the group.

"Now," Crow begins, rising from the table and standing in front of the Froskians. "As mentioned, I offer you three separate potential remedies to your current crisis."

Crow turns to the massive screen behind him and alters the projection. The model of the planet Frosk zooms out to show the three suns which Frosk orbits. Using a projection from his own vision screen, Crow sends the hologram of a hollow sphere, slightly bigger than the second sun, toward the holographic stars.

"In previous scientific ideologies on Earth, the concept of the 'kardashev scale' was developed. With it, there are seven different levels. Where you rest on this scale is dictated by how you harness the energy of your planet, solar system, galaxy, and the universe. Currently, [5]Earth is a type I on the Kardashev scale. We use the entirety of our planet's energy to our benefit (some from the sun as well, but generally from the planet itself). We also do this in a way that is both ecologically moral, and ethical.

"However, we only have one sun in our solar system. The planet Frosk has three at your disposal. I propose you exceed even my own planet on this scale; I suggest the planet Frosk harnesses the power of the closest sun to you for your own benefit. Considering there aren't any other planets with sentient life within your solar system, you would cause no harm, and gain a 'greener' method of obtaining your energy."

Life-Admiral Crow smiles widely at his audience. However, the audience does not smile back. Dissosteria glares at Crow with an almost murderous gaze.

"We did tell you yesterday that we are not looking to change the way we produce energy, yes?" Schreik asks Crow, seemingly mildly irritated.

"Yes but-"

"Life-Admiral, please do not waste our time," Dissosteria wheezes. "We gave you our guidleines, all you have to do is follow them."

---

[5] https://www.youtube.com/watch?v=sNhhvQGsMEc

"This is only my first suggestion, Leader Dissosteria," Crow says somberly. "I just wanted to show you that you do indeed have options. And the ability to surpass Earth – and even Technicorum II scientifically!"

There are a few mumbles, some murmuring, and a great deal of talk among the Froskians. Schreik seems to be the prominent voice within the murmuring, undoubtedly advocating for the Froskian "clients and donors" that truly run the planet. Money is still the master of this race. *Such a shame* Crow thinks to himself. *They have all the power to do what is best, and yet they refuse to do it.*

"Tell me, Life-Admiral," Orthaug says with curiosity, leaning back in his chair and peering at Crow from between his claws. "How costly would this process be?"

"Well," Crow begins, bringing up the numbers he had gone over the previous evening. "Depending on your available resources, it could cost more or less. You would need to acquire these materials (he gestures to a list on the hologram that shows how to build a solar power receiver, and an energy transfer device) either from your own planet, or one nearby. If you are unable to acquire them that way, reaching out to the Galactic Senate is your best opti-"

"I have a better question," Schreik interrupts, leaning toward the Earthling. "How much money could it make *us*?"

"Ah…" Crow feels a bit uneasy at this, he did not figure this is the route the Frosks would go. Poor foresight on his part. "Well, considering the size of your second sun and how much energy it can produce…if you are able to store the energy somewhere…you could sell it to other planets for the next several hundred thousand years."

Buzzing again from the Froskians. Crow feels a bit foolish for bringing this concept up now, but did hold on to the hope that they may one day change their minds. He clears his throat, then changes the hologram to show the second option.

"Now, this one is the most costly, and would take the most time," Crow admits. "Option two: relocate to a nearby habitable pla-"

"Absolutely not," Dissosteria barks.

"Undertsood," Crow answers with a nod. He figured the Frosks would be unwilling to relocate. Imagine…their poor rich 1% having to start over! Oh, the nerve. "Then I have one more option, I think you will like this one best."

"I truly hope so, emissary," hisses the Head of Torture. "Thus far, we are unimpressed."

"Option *three*," Crow bellows, glaring threateningly at the Head of Torture. Without missing a beat, however, Crow manipulates the holograms to illustrate his points. "Is a density filter. We send several thousand of these within the planet's atmosphere. Then, using pre-programmed algorithms, the devices will pull all toxic contents from the air, reprogramming their molecular structure, and sending it back out as breathable air. It will generate some waste with left over atoms and molecules though, I recommend you look into a dump site for-"

"We have a garbage planet not far, Life-Admiral," Dissosteria says, gradually and seemingly painfully rising from his seat. "Send a blueprint for the machine and a timeline for when our skies should be cleansed to me, personally. Then, you may go. We will have our slaves begin construction as soon as possible."

Life-Admiral Crow gasps then instinctively. That must have been what the smaller, dingier houses were made for; to store the slaves of the Frosks. Slavery is a concept he and Ion had condemned entirely, and the duo did their best to avoid any culture that used it. However, it was not Centre Planet legislature that a planet must share whether they use slavery or not.

Admittedly this is not a surprise to Crow. The Frosks greatest interest outside of science is money. A civilization did not have to add an extra expense if the labour is being done for free, right? This sort of hoop is jumped on Earth, but the autonomous droids do not feel at all. No harm or suffering can be felt, and it gives an immense boost in progress to have an army of robots make sure the planet is running at peak efficiency 24/7.

"You did not know we use slaves here on Frosk, Earthling?" The Head of Torture inquires in a mocking tone. "Does that go against your so-called 'morals?'"

"If it is any consolation, Life-Admiral," Actias says while rising with the rest of the Froskian leaders. "The slaves are essentially brain-dead. Still-borns that have a chip implanted in their skulls that give them just enough brain function to perform whatever tasks are needed of them. That was an innovation *I personally* came up with myself. Kindly bring the Emissary back to his room, Trius."

With that, the Froskians exit the room, and Trius walks up to Crow. The firefly looks as though he is already preparing a report on the goings-on of today. The holographic vision screen looks as though it could explode from incoming information before Trius's compound eyes.

"How long have your people used slaves for profit?" Crow asks, striding back toward the transportation tubes. Trius walks alongside the clearly irate leader.

"As far as we have had documented history," Trius says, still typing away on the vision screen. "It started in small cultures, and as – what you could call – Capitalism became the dominant method of government and economy, it was adopted all over the planet."

"Is it at least true that they do not feel anything?" Crow inquires as they near the Tube system.

"Oh my, yes," Trius answers honestly. "They are not stillborn, though. A specific breed's litter is taken, then has brain death forced on them as the Control Chip is implemented within their brain. Pretty gruesome stuff, but the people of Frosk are happy, fat, and over-privileged (for the most part). They have a 'better us than them' mentality, and are grateful they were not the unfortunately chosen."

"Interesting..." Crow says thoughtfully as Trius programs the Tube for them. "Your people feel a sense of gratitude rather than revulsion when they see the slaves. Do they not know there is a better way – especially in a technocracy – for the same results to be achieved?"

"We have never known otherwise, we have been told for centuries this is the best method," Trius admits as he steps into the Tube. His speech carries on even as he and Crow are transported back to Crow's building. "We stick with what we know, for science is a no-nonesense business my friend. Plus, we have one of the richest economies in the known galaxy. How bad could it be?"

"Bad enough for me to want to leave this rock and get back to my own people," Crow answers coldly.

Chapter XV

Earth 2105 – Ion and Crow's Base

"I believe...that no living creature should have to suffer. You should not have to struggle to survive, and you should not have to answer to anyone for your dreams to be realized. Artists should be able to make their art. Starvation should not be a constant issue. Disease should be non-existent. We have not evolved to fall prey to the same trivial garbage that has plagued our species since the dawn of time. Regardless of your creed, beliefs, origins, orientations or perspectives, I believe this is a value anyone should hold and have made true. My friends... Science is the new answer, and through science we will find our salvation. We can finally have what humanity has sought after since we became sentient; we can be truly free."
Ion's Inauguration speech, 2050

"Why did it have to take this long?!" Ion demands impatiently to his brother. "We could have taken the *whole planet* by now, not just Canada."

"We agreed not to do this all by force!" Crow screams at Ion.

The fully autonomous body of Ion looms over his still fully human brother. Despite being almost 110 years old, Crow does not look a day over 25. The future is a bright place for humans looking to kill the curse of aging! Scientists had begun using stem cells and specific proteins and enzymes to target decaying cells. The still youthful face of Crow looks stern and angered.

"What else can we do?!" Ion demands aggressively. "We are running out of room on the floating city! Too many refugees looking to convert to our way of life a-"

"Is that not a good problem to have?!" Crow fires back, slamming his fists on a desk. "Isn't that what we hoped for? To have the Dreamscape demanded for by the people?"

"Not to this degree!" Ion exclaims, falling into a chair and putting his head into his hands. "Not when we aren't equipped for them...not without the proper *resources*, brother! We have taken enough from this planet!"

"Oh the planet, the planet, always about the fucking planet!" Crow spits, slamming his now empty glass all over the floor. "This isn't about the planet is it? This is about being a damned tyrant! You've already killed too many people. I made it disappear, but this is too much! I can't stop the planet from knowing this time, Ion. You are asking too much!"

"Just form the omnipertium you gathered, and it won't matter!" Ion yells back, his new synthetic eyes turning red. "There are dozens of ways they can stop me right now, but with that metal...with that metal we can make all those greedy bastards pay, and save this planet and its people."

"Is that what it's really about?!"

"Of cour-!"

"No, no, don't you lie to me." Crow interrupts, glaring sternly at Ion, pointing his finger. "Tell me, your brother – your best friend and the one who made *everything* possible for you – the truth."

"Little brother…" Ion begins, floating over to Crow and lightly placing a hand on his shoulder. "Remember when we were kids and…and that one time I caught you dissecting a bunch of frogs…remember how I had panicked?"

"I wanted to understand their physiology…" Crow says, looking down with a hint of embarrassment.

"I know that now, but I didn't then, remember how angry I was?"

"Yes."

"Do you know why?"

"You told me…that life is sacred. And next time, if I really want to know about an animal, make sure it is already dead."

"That sentiment hasn't changed to me, little brother," Ion almost whispers, his hand still on Crow's shoulder. "Life *is* sacred. It should not be taken away from the innocent. The people I have killed, they were not innocent. They may have been breathing, but they were already dead inside. They were hoarding money that could have fed a lot of people. They sent assassins after *both* of us. There is no doubt in my mind that was not the first occurrence for them, either. They need to be stopped, the people need to be saved, and Earth needs to be fixed."

Crow looks to his brother with sorrow in his eyes. He knows that Ion is right, but he does not want to have this much blood on his hands. Ion had promised to try and reason with these billionaires and leaders, but Crow knows he is going to wind up killing all of them.

"This is exactly what Nancy tried to warn me about," Crow sighs, leaning against a wall sullenly. "She predicted you would get violent, she knew-"

"Oh, Nancy this, Nancy that! She's *Dead!*" Ion screams, advancing on his strong-standing brother. "She's fucking dead, and she left you! Was she able to predict those things happening? Huh little brother?! Did her leaving *magically* make her prediction happen? No, she was a crazy bitch and you are better off without her. It's been 50 years! Move on, and help me fix the world, damn it!"

"You know what? Fuck you!" Crow bellows, looking up at his brother's robotic face. He thrusts his brother's hand off his shoulder and begins to walk toward the exit. "I didn't give you this synthetic body for you to become a murderer! You used to be such a great person, now you're just a monster! You swore never to be like this, you swore you wouldn't end up like th-"

There is a grotesque crunching sound. Crows eyes open wide as pain sears the entire left side of his body. The agony is so intense he cannot even let out a scream. He turns and looks down to see the source of the pain, only to witness his severed arm in the hands of his robotic brother. As fast as he could blink, Ion had moved from across the room to in front of him. Crow goes to fall to his knees, but Ion holds him and gently lays him down.

"These nano-bots were another one of your great ideas," Ion says, with a bit of spite in his voice. "I usually use them to infiltrate security or paralyze an enemy. Now, they'll save your life. They will keep you from bleeding out while I build you a better, metal arm with the omnipertium I am about to bring them…and *then* they will paralyze you. You can thank me when I get back from saving the world, little brother. You don't have to forgive me right away, but you can thank me for at least that."

With that, the current Leader of Canada exits their secret base at a speed undetectable to the eye. Within moments, Ion is walking through the doors of Crow Corp, just as a group of scientists are about to leave. The scientists gaze in awe at their cyborg Leader, unsure of how to react to his presence.

"I need to see Dr. Fraser," Ion says them, as they come to their senses and bow before the metal man.

"He is still in his lab," one of the citizens answer shakily. "Great leader, is everything-"

"Come with me, now," Ion answers hurriedly. "We don't have a lot of time!"

As fast as their new robotic legs could carry them, the still in-the-field scientists rush Leader Ion to Dr. Fraser, up on the fifth floor. Ion pushes the large metal doors open with ease, and looks upon the only person who could save his brother's arm with a purpose. Dr. Fraser's metal body almost short-circuits in fear, seeing the Canadian Leader for the first time in person.

"Dr. Fraser," Ion begins. "I am to understand you are the most accomplished bio-tech creator in this establishment."

"Next to Dr. Crow, y-yes sir!" Fraser answers, trying to look professional as he rises to shake Ion's hand. He stumbles over a trash can, only to have Ion kindly re-adjust him.

"Good. Because I need your help, and I need it now," Ion replies authoritatively, giving the doctor a quick hand shake. He begins to stride to where he knows the omnipertium is stored. "I have two tasks I need done by you, my friend."

"Name it, great Leader!" Dr. Fraser exclaims, hurrying to follow Ion alongside the other scientists.

"I need you to prep my upgrade," Ion says, preparing to stop outside of the door which holds the omnipertium. "And, I need you to make me a third arm."

"A third arm, sir? Why-?"

"No questions, only solutions."

"With all do respect, great Leader," one of the scientists say nervously through their holographic vision screen. A series of charts are visible to the group. "We will not have the required amount of metal to have all of the weapons you requested, then. There just simply isn't enough of that metal you found in there."

"With all do respect, doctor-?"

"Dr. Chen, sir,"

"Dr. Chen…my lovely young lass…you are the most highly regarded scientists on this planet. The best in bio-technology and otherwise. I am sure you can think of something, we do not have a lot of time."

"We could remove the cannon from your arsenal, sir," Dr. Fraser says. "The Centre Planet just made them illegal, anyway."

"Excellent thinking, Doctor!" Ion says, giving a friendly pat on their shoulder. "Now…I need a fully functioning robotic arm made as fast as possible. No extra gizmos, just the arm. Think you can handle that?"

"Well, great Leader, sir," another one of the scientists intones. "We need the supervision of Dr. Crow to-"

"My dear, brilliant doctor-?"

"Rodriguez"

"Doctor Rodriguez…who do you think I need the arm for?"

There is a silence within the group for a moment, now. Ion's synthetic eyebrows raise in anticipation, while the scientists merely stare blankly back at him. Ion then stands fully straight and crosses his arms.

"Get working on that arm *NOW!*" Ion screams so loudly, some windows break.

"Yes sir!" they all shout back in unison. It would not be long before this group of talented individuals had completed Crows arm, following the very specific instructions Crow himself had laid out (the moment omnipertium cools, it solidifies and never returns to liquid form again). After that was done, Ion would take on his true body. Soon, he would bring freedom to the entire Earth.

The United Earth Coalition – Meeting Centre of Earthling Leaders

They sit in a line before the nine-foot-tall metallic man. The once sacred gathering place of the United Earth Coalition has been sullied by Ion, the tyrant. The "top 1%" – billionaires, trillionaires, drug lords, and politicians alike – have all been kidnapped from their homes, paralyzed (by use of nanobots) and gathered here to hear Ion's speech.

"So it is that simple," Ion's voice says unyieldingly, projected into the minds of each person before him. The nanobots are translating Ion's thoughts into the native language of each of his captives. "You willingly sign over your wealth, countries, properties, and livelihoods to me. Or you die."

Laughter begins to erupt from the captives. Slowly and hesitantly at first, then collectively, they become hysteric. Ion's synthetic eyes narrow in disgust.

"You expect us to just *hand* you everything?!" laughs one leader of a nearby country.

"Or you will kill *us?!*" inquires a foreign drug lord. "Hahaha! You dumb, egomaniacal douchebag! If we don't kill you, the thousands that are behind us will!"

The large group of corrupt and selfish people continue to laugh at the robotic leader. Before this, Ion had felt so powerful. God-like even! The cyborg had a countless arsenal of extremely lethal weapons (banned by the galactic council or otherwise), an indestructible exoskeleton, and had managed to single-handedly collect the most corrupt people on the planet in less than an hour. Now, they have the absolute gall to mock *him*?!

Ion gives a robotic sigh and looks at the lineup. He approaches the drug lord that had spoken out earlier, smiles, then watches as their eyes roll back in their head. The drug lord begins to sign the papers – seemingly willingly – exactly where they needed to be signed before handing the documents to Ion.

The 1% cease laughing, and watch uneasily as the drug lord falls over onto their small desk. Ion had placed the entire group into their own individual desks, so they might have a surface to write on. The bionic man looms over the shaking and frightened drug lord, and gives out a sarcastic "ha, ha." Then, inexplicably, the drug lord gets up and walks about twelve feet behind Ion. They stop for a moment before quickly whirling around, now facing the other hoarders of wealth.

There is a cold silence as the Leader then proceeds to walk behind the drug lord. Ion stares dauntingly at the group of animalistic true criminals that he has gathered. So much fear in most of their eyes…they have no Earthly idea what is going to happen next. Ion couldn't help but feel amused as some of the more violent people here wet themselves in utter fear. Still looming over the group and standing behind the drug lord, Ion places his left hand on their head. Moments later, their head starts to steam. A liquid begins to pour out of their ears, and they let out an agonizing scream of pain.

The 1% watch in horror as the metallic captor literally melts the drug lords brain from within their skull. Leader Ion does not look away from his captives as he then crushes the drug lord's skull in his hand. The sickening crunch and final "hheurgh!" from the villain seems to echo for ages as the body is dropped to the floor. Not unlike their murderous life had been, the drug lord was struck down to appear like nothing more than a morsel of revolting trash on the ground. This seems like divine intervention, in a strange way.

"I've never been good at comedy," Ion admits through the nanobots, floating back toward the group slowly. "So I am rather confused about what you all thought was funny."

The group simply stare at Ion in horror...well, the ones less prone to *directly* commit murder do. The gang leaders, assassins and other more-than-well-off folk used to violence look angrily at him. One of the stuck up looking billionaires pukes all down her chest (because the nanobots are preventing any movement from the neck down).

"You...you sick bastard..." one of the politicians says, clearly in shock and staring blankly straight ahead of them. "You think just because you have that robotic body, you can do whatever you want. You think you can't be stopped. You think you're above morality-"

"I AM unstoppable, I CAN do whatever I want, and morality is the reason why you are here!" Ion bellows in their face. "Don't think I don't know about your little weekend getaways with *children*, you monster! And none of you better dare even *consider* yourselves 'good people.' You are the reason suffering continues to perpetuate in our species. Your selfishness has left billions to starve, and countless others to *die*. Your damned egos, and the egos of our ancestors, have made humanity into a parasite. But no more.

"I will not allow you selfish wretches to kill your people any more. I will not let there be another war, another reason for you to profit from the pain of others. This ends now. Whether you like it or not, you are going to sign those documents. You are going to go back home, and live your normal lives until this is all implemented. Granted I do not have to do to you what I did to that putrid drug pusher over there." Ion points over his shoulder with his thumb. "If you live long enough to see me turn this world into a Utopia, you will thank me. Most of you won't live that long, I'm sure, with the mindset you have now. But you will come around. You will apologize, and you will thank me for saving the human race."

Many of the 1% had tears rolling down their faces at this point. Some because they finally understood why Ion had done this, most because they knew they would not have their yachts any more. They sign then, all but a small handful willingly.

Once they are done, Ion gathers the documents and places them on a table. A humanesque robot appears from the shadows, takes the documents, then exits the room without incident. Ion hovers in front of the group, arms crossed and a look of revulsion placed on his robotic face.

"Some of you have made your first step at redemption," Ion says to them telepathically, his projected voice filled with venom. "You have now begun a path that could lead to prosperity for our entire species. I have recently spoken with the Head Representative of the Centre Planet...do you know what she told me?"

Ion glares at the group, still paralyzed from the neck down. Some shake their heads, no, others glare back angrily. No matter, Ion knows which ones would be leaving here alive and which ones would be made an example of.

"The head of the Centre Planet told me that we were still looked at as 'primitive' within the senate. Despite our contributions to the galaxy, and the advancements my brother and I have shared with them at no cost...we are still viewed as primitive. The reason being; we are a planet divided. We are an ouroboros that isn't stopping at the tail; self-consuming, self-indulgent, and destined to die. My vision, if you wish to be a part of it, ensures that humanity will live for aeons to come.

"Those of you that signed willingly, you are free to go. Return to whatever families you may have, and prepare for a new world order. Outside those doors are a group of autonomous robots who will escort you onto a safe ship home. As for the rest of you, you will be staying and getting what you have deserved for so long."

With that, those who had signed willingly were released from the nanobot control. Much like the now very dead drug pusher, they all fall forward aggressively. They had all been trying to move this entire time, it would seem. One billionaire from the Orient looks up at Ion almost blankly as the group starts rising and prepares to run out of the building.

"How do your actions against us make you any better?" the billionaire asks in his language. Those who were about to run for their lives stop to listened. "How is killing us any better than what we have done?"

"What all you have done, collectively, has killed and or harmed millions." Ion answers without remorse. "By *willingly* signing those documents, you are letting an era of peace begin."

Then Ion continues telepathically to them all (in their respective languages): "*By killing even one of you, I am preventing nearly countless lives from being destroyed. I am ensuring the planet can heal. By doing this, I am saving countless others. Your sacrifice is what will make this world both better, and viewed as legitimate throughout the known universe. Now go.*"

The individuals who had willingly signed the contracts begin to rise. Some stare at the door nervously before running as fast as they can away from the cyborg. A small group walk out guiltily, as if Ion's words had actually taken some effect on them. A fair group, however, rise slowly. They leer at the new leader of the planet.

This group begins to circle Ion with murderous intent. Like a volt of vultures, they eye their prey as if waiting for the right moment to dive in. Ion laughs internally – what did they think they were going to do to this indestructible robot-man?! Ion floats slowly to the ground. He merely leers back confidently at his former captives in response to their pitiful ensemble.

"Nothing is completely indestructible!" one shouts. They grab a chair and fling it at Ion. It breaks apart as Ion stands, unmoved.

A barrage of foreign objects, fists (which break upon contact), and entire bodies fly at the world leader. This annoys Ion. How petty and foolish they are. Even if they were to use bullets, lasers, atomics – whatever – they would never make a dent on him. Had he not made that clear?

"You all need to stop," Ion says out loud, frustrated. "You really are wasting your time."

Every object and body flung at him does not cause him to move. Despite trying to make it very apparent that this is a fruitless endeavour, the group carries on without relent. The few leaders and billionaires who did not sign their contracts voluntarily now sit in stupefied, immobile wonder – what would happen next?

"Seriously, stop!" Ion bellows in anger. They do not listen, and continue to attack. Ion's eyes glow red. "You absolute imbeciles, cut it out! Get away…get the *hell* away! You're starting to piss me off!"

Ion can feel the core temperature of his robotic body begin to rise. He begins to feel incapable of controlling his rage and exasperation. Instinct begins to overtake him, and he feels the overwhelming need to make them stop at any cost.

"…you're starting to PISS ME OFF!!!"

With that the Leader of the new world loses all control. Giving into his lesser instincts, Ion begins an absolute rampage on his would-be attackers. He turns to the nearest assailant (who happens to be the oriental billionaire) and punches a perfectly circular whole through their entire torso.

He then proceeds to slap another so hard in the face their head comes clean off, then pancakes onto a far wall. Ion then picks up another politician, lifts them over his head and tears them in half. The rest of the group begin to run as he takes another drug dealer and a billionaire and smashed them into each other, causing them to explode; thus turning the immobile would-be victims into a grotesque Jackson Pollock painting made of blood, guts and bone.

As the others near the door, Ion appears suddenly in front of them, as if he had teleported there. His arms turn into laser rifles, and he shoots each of the attempting escapees point blank, right between the eyes. Still in an uncontrollable rage, he looks over to the still paralyzed prisoners. He had intended to kill them…but now he wanted only to take down the truly vile ones.

The child sex traffickers, the corrupt politicians, the members of religious sectors that abused their image of "god-like" innocence. He lifts each of them off the ground at once – as if using telekinesis, when in actuality it is done with the aid of the nanobots – then smashes them all together.

Even as they scream in agony and beg for forgiveness, Ion slowly squishes the collective of literal monsters together, closer and closer. Before long, nothing remains of them; all that can be seen is a sphere of human flesh and bone. The blood that will now forever stain the once peaceful floor (at least metaphorically) beneath the new Earth Leader's synthetic feet flows in rivers. Pools of blood hither and thither gather whilst some drain out the exit door to what was supposed to be the former leader's get away ship.

Finally, when this is done, Ion stops and looks at the ground. The room is mostly silent for a moment, save for the sounds of steaming flesh. Ion looks at his remaining captives with remorse. The realization of this absolute atrocity hit the still human mind of Ion like a million painful needles. He had killed before – but never as if for sport. What had just transpired is…not becoming of a Utopian Leader.

"I took…I took this one a bit too far," He admits. "Your funds and ownership of both land and material things have now been processed…I own the world…as an apology, however, I will revoke my ownership for you four. I deeply regret my actions here…I-…The ship is waiting outside to take you home."

With that, the Great Leader of the majority of the world flies through the doors, and back toward the main capitol of Canada. Some automatons remain behind and begin cleaning the abrasive massacre (as instructed by Ion through brain waves), to ensure not a trace will be left behind. The four remaining prisoners – who moments ago thought that they would be killed by this tyrant – regain control of their bodies and scream with glee. But only for a moment.

"We have to take him down," the Leader of Ukraine says.

"How?" asks the leader of Brazil incredulously. "He had over two dozen people attacking him, and he doesn't even have a *dent*!"

"They also didn't have nukes," adds the leader of Russia. "We will have our revenge!"

"At what cost?" asks the leader of China. "He has killed…so many…so so many…"

"Together, we could! I truly believe it!" exclaims the leader of Ukraine.

Three leaders look at each other with hope in their eyes. Something was brewing with each of them. A concept of hope, a fear of losing humanity, and a pride from the legacy their respective countries had created bring them an inner strength. The fourth, however, begins walking toward the freedom of the outside world after what had felt like years of traumatizing imprisonment.

"You all may do whatever you like," the leader of Brazil says. "But my people will have nothing to do with this. We will never forget, and we will never bow, but we will *never* go to fight a war that cannot be won."

Earth's Floating City – The Office of the Wise Life-Admiral Crow

Crow had not seen Ion in almost two weeks. He currently sits in his main office at Crow Corp. The office is large, with Crow's immense metal desk resting before a massive window overlooking the edge of the Floating City. On both sides of the room sit two magnificent paintings, with a small sitting area to Crow's left, and a fireplace with a mini bar on his right.

Currently, Crow is overlooking the change from working in the physical world, to converting research to be done within the Dreamscape exclusively. This would diminish the current use of resources, and give scientists and other great minds the chance to do their work without affecting the still healing planet.

The now Life-Admiral (of the majority of Earth) had pretty well let go of the anger he had been feeling toward his brother. His new arm is vastly superior to his older one, granting him the ability to get work done much more efficiently. Still, Crow wishes that Ion had not been so impulsive. His abrasiveness had nearly destroyed everything they had worked for.

It was fortunate that Ion had filmed the entire "Day of the Great Signing" – as it had come to be known – for very few questioned the authority of their new Leaders. On the contrary; the majority of the people had been waiting for this day for quite some time! Some had even been trying to immigrate to the Floating City in Canada. Now, the conversion from full biology to pre-binary (or being a brain in a robot exoskeleton) is in effect, and the new floating cities are under construction. No one had any idea – save for those who were in the room and lived to tell the tale – the horror that had happened that day. Some grieved for those in the…ahem…plane crash that had occurred during their leader's return back home. Such tragedies can happen.

Crow is finishing his preliminary programming for the day, transmitting his thoughts and brainwaves to his computer that it may go faster than if he were to type it (even with his new arm). He looks blankly at the screen as he does so, using a different part of his brain to worry about what might have happened to Ion.

He had seen the new True Leader all over the globe through the news, giving speeches and instructing individuals on how to adapt to the new way of life. But that had been all Crow had seen of him. A mere figurehead in the ocean of political gambits and tasks that needed to be done. Crow hopes his brother will come and apologize for his truly insane actions. He wants to know that going forward, they will be wiser...if not for each other, for the fate of the Earth.

Then, seemingly as quickly as Crow could blink, Ion stands behind him in the doorway. Crow can see his brother's reflection on the massive window to the ocean outside. He turns slowly to the cyborg, placing a look of disappointment on his face – despite his feeling of relief.

"Well, look who it is," Crow says as Ion gradually walks to a chair in front of his brother's desk. "The man of the hour...well – ahuh - cyborg. The All Powerful Leader of We, the Truly Free, hm? Thought you might grace me with your presence, or are you thinking about taking my other arm?"

Ion stares at Crow for a moment, a look of sadness and regret written all over his robotic face. He looks at his synthetic hands for a moment before burying his face in them. It seems as if he were crying, or would if he could. Alas, omnipertium does not come with tear ducts.

"I am *so* sorry, little brother," Ion's robotic voice bursts, seemingly vibrating with sorrow. "I never...I never wanted to hurt you, or take this so far...sweet science, I have become everything I swore to you I would never be!"

"Aw, I wish you would have thought of that," Crow says, initially somberly before rising from his chair and shouting: "Before you *TORE MY ARM OFF.*"

"Well..." Ion says, sitting up in his chair. "You have to admit...you look pretty awesome."

Crow looks at his brother angrily for a moment. He leans on the desk with his hands and glares at his brother. Ion forces a smile on his synthetic face nervously. But Crow cannot hold back any longer, he tilts his head back and laughs.

"True, true!" Crow hollers. He sits next to his brother, placing a compassionate hand on his back. "I really can't believe you got away with all that, though. Great job doctoring the footage, one can hardly tell...and this new arm does help a lot, I may add a few more modifications to myself..."

The duo sit in uneasy silence for a moment, not looking at each other. Ion still feels a heavy weight on his figurative heart over everything that had happened. Crow can tell his brother meant well, and truly believes he did not mean to go so far.

"I am truly...truly sorry..." Ion says, finally turning to look at his brother. "I really am...and I've put a lot of thought into how to prevent this sort of thing from happening again...I want you to remove some parts of my brain."

"WHAT?!" Crow bellows, eyes wide as he stands up and looks at Ion, shocked. "You...you can't mean that?!"

"I do," is the casual answer. "I don't want to be able to feel anger, fear, or hatred again. I need to be more logical, like you. That is the only way I see myself being able to do that."

"But...you're hardly human as it is!" Crow exclaims incredulously. "Taking that away...you *need* to feel those emotions, brother. It is part of being alive – part of being human!"

"Human's aren't perfect," Ion says with a casual shrug. "If we are going to make the world a Utopia, we cannot repeat the mistakes I have made. Please...do this for me?"

Chapter XVI

Technicorum II – Planet Capitol's Hall of Elders

"My Great Elders, I fear some of the Perusaks were captured by the Froskians," Titus informs the Council from a bowing position before them. "Some of our spies fear that their Head of Torture may have gathered damning evidence against us."

"Do you believe the Frosks would take this to the Centre Planet?" Sephia asks the room with a tone of fear. "This plan was supposed to be bullet-proof, Elder Conyx!"

"Mind your tongue, Sephia!" Conyx spits back. "The Perusak are a barbaric, yet proud people…it was our deepest belief that even when tortured they would not give out any information!"

"It matters not," the Elder Basilis hisses at the others. "Whether the Centre Planet believes this or not, they now know their defenses aren't as strong as they'd been led to believe. Earth Leader Ion may have saved them, but it was the creations of his brother that had been made standard there. Now, their inventions will be left in question. Ion cannot protect the Centre Planet every time there is a crisis!"

"Mmmm! Thus…their focus may be on Earth's insufficient technology?" Titus asks.

"Indeed," wheezes Elder Helod. "They will need new, more efficient defences. Frosks specialty is in the for-profit sectors of commerce and trade. *We* however…have the upper hand. We will be forgiven, and take the monkey's place as Defense Advisor."

"So is the hope," admits Elder Calo.

The group look through their Xeroph-optimized Vision Screens and each use simulations to predict potential outcomes of their situation. The five Elders and the Interplanetary Representative hiss in excitement; evidently the simulations provide positive outcomes in their favour.

Their sounds of joy echo throughout their dark chamber. The bloodstone den is dimly lit by heating lamps; a necessity to keep the cold-blooded reptilians at a more than comfortable temperature. Standing in a semi-circle atop the stone risers, the five Elders loom over their pawn - contemplating their next moves. The group then change their Vision Screens to the next topic of discussion.

"Now…*cough*" begins Helod, one eye shut and a grimace of pain made with their cough. "Speaking of the 'great' Earth monkey and his pitiful planet…are we ready?"

"Nearly prepared, great Elders!" exclaims Titus excitedly. "The proper arrangements have been made. The Life-Admiral should have experienced an...unfortunate incident by now, for example. Many things have been set in motion, and this false God and his monkey brother are none-the-wiser of our progress!"

"This is NOT happening fast enough, Titus!" Elder Sephia bellows, slamming a massive, scaley fist onto the circular table before them. "We wanted this done *before* the Colosseum! How much longer must we wait?"

"The youth fears what he must tell us," Conyx informs the rest of the council. Conyx's forked tongue shoots in and out of their mouth, as if using it as a tool to confirm their statement. "The answer is much longer than we'd hoped."

"Spit it out, don't just stare at us like a hatchling!" Calo spits at the Interplanetary Representative. Titus gulps in fear, shaking while looking up at their wise and powerful Elder Council.

"Mmmmmmmm! Well....G-Great El-...Elders..." Titus stammers. "You s-see...we may ha- have to execute this p-plan...while the Colosseum Games are....going"

The Elders glare down to their underling. Some let out expressions and sounds of disgust. Others turn their heads in disbelief. Helod, however, grins a massive toothy grin. Venom drips from their teeth, onto their table and begins to sizzle.

"This...may be better" Helod says, speaking more still and distinctly than the Ancient Elder had within memory.

Meanwhile, on Ion's Modified Stealth Ship:

"Are you going to ask me why we have stopped before Technicorum II?" Ion asks his apparently distant niece.

"No, Great Leader," Talia answers, seemingly awe-struck. *The Terra Sixians take this whole 'God' thing much too seriously*, Ion thinks to himself. "I have already foresee-

"Foreseen why we are here, I'm sure," Ion interrupts, rolling his metal eyes uncaringly. "Then you know my brother just informed me that he had just been attacked on Frosk, and now it is-"

"'*my duty to set the Xerophs straight*,' yes, I know."

Ion looks at his guest with a raised metal eyebrow adjacent to a squinting synthetic eye. He can see Talia's feeling of admiration still apparent, yet is even more bothered by her arrogance. The great Leader knows that what he is about to do could be dangerous, down there on Technicorum II. His thoughts now turn as to whether or not it would be wise to take her with him.

"You should go without me, Great Leader," Talia says, as if reading Ion's mind. "There are millions of potential futures where I die, and a small handful where I survive with minor wounds. All of them, however, have them detecting your entrance into their atmosphere – if you are to do so using this ship. However...if you are to use your own method of flight, your mass is not large enough for their systems to detect you."

What first started to seem like a terrible decision to Ion is slowly appearing to have been a good one. Whether Talia would have been with him or not, his initial plan was to enter Technicorum II with the stealth ship. Now he *may* know (if this oracle malarkey has any merit at all) that he can get in undetected. This could be a tremendous asset for him.

"Well then..." Ion says, preparing the craft for himself to make a safe exit without getting Talia sucked into the vacuum of space. "If I make it there undetected, then a lot of metaphorical points will go toward me thinking you aren't as full of shit as I thought. Sit tight, friend. This shouldn't take too long."

Back With the Elder Council...

"And after that, my dear fellow Elders, the Earth shall-"

There is a massive BOOM! As the ceiling of the Elder's Chamber began to be torn off like an aluminum can lid. The Elders and Titus duck for cover from falling debris, as Ion lifts the entire roof with on hand, and tosses it into the nearby forest (in an area he had detected did not house any significant life). There is a moment where Sephia is sure that the ceiling emits a sheen similar to the colour of Ion's robotic body.

The Great Earth Leader floats down to where Titus stands in awe of the spectacle they are seeing. He drifts next to the Interplanetary Representative and gives them a look of contempt. Ion then proceeds to hack into the Xeroph security system with his brainwaves, locking himself into the room with the giant reptiles, and creating a protective shield for them where the ceiling used to be. This is in case the Xeroph military decides they want to step in and try to take the Earth Leader down.

"Oh, sweet Xerophs," Ion sighs, looking into Helod's eye slits. "How you disappoint me."

Instinctively, Titus swings as hard as they can at Ion with their upper right arm. Upon impact, Titus' bones are fractured and shattered. The very tough, scaley skin of the Xeroph shreds itself as the arm becomes mangled. The claw on their arm carries through unintentionally, and suffers a great deal as well. The claws themselves rip from the hand as they go to scrape along Ion's metal back. Blood shoots out in all directions as Titus screams in agony.

Titus recoils and seeks shelter behind a nearby scientific tool. The Elders look down disapprovingly to their Interplanetary Representative. Ion sighs, then heats his body to the point the blood he is now mostly covered in burns away. He then sends nanobots to repair the damage Titus had honestly done to itself.

The giant lizard gazes in awe as their arm begins to be repaired. Ion presses forward with his purpose nonetheless. He knows Titus does not deserve to be healed – especially after attacking a Planetary Leader – but this is business. Ion straightens, then glares at the Xeroph Elders.

"I'm going to pretend that didn't happen," Ion says, squinting sternly at the reptilian Elders. "And, I'm going to pretend a few other very foolish things didn't happen as well…under certain conditions."

"Great Earth Leader!" Sephia intones, trying to convey confusion and terror. "What could you possibly be-"

"I have had quite enough of your games, cold-blood," Ion expresses, his voice sending tones of seriousness and anger. "I am now here on business. Business that your incompetent Interplanetary Representative didn't finish, and business that could lead to your demise, should I bring it to the Centre Planet."

There is a tense silence now. The Xerophs do not know the extent of Ion's intelligence toward their goals. Had the Earth Leader heard their plan to bring his planet down?

"What are you after, *cough* Leader Ion?" Elder Basilis asks.

"Honestly, I'd be mildly satisfied leaving this planet with each of your heads," Ion answers, looking at his hands as if he were looking for dirt under his once existent nails. He begins to float about the room slowly, enunciating certain words with a fast move forward toward one Elder or another. "Considering you tried to destroy the Centre Planet, using the Perusak's as decoys. Oh yes, the Frosks and Earth have this knowledge, and undeniable proof, as well. You also tried to kill my brother…which is, ahuh, *unacceptable!*

"You're quite lucky he had a Froskian bodyguard," Ion continues, his synthetic eyes turning red. "Because if you *had* succeeded, we wouldn't be having this conversation. No, you would all die slowly, in front of the entire Galactic Imperium – as to be made an example of – and then I would have scorched this planet until it was nothing but a glass surface.

"But, I digress," Ion sighs, his tone conveying both authority and unmoving seriousness. "All can be forgiven, and even forgotten…if you do as I ask. Do you think you could maybe…work *with* us, instead of against us?"

"What is it you require, Leader Ion?" Conyx asks. Their tongue zipping in and out of their mouth again. However, the lizard only looked confused; as if whatever information it was trying to pull from the air is unable to be found.

"I can make the Perusak race appear solely responsible for the Centre Planet attack," Ion begins stoicly. His body begins to emit an angelic light as he goes on. "And I can forget your people tried to assassinate my brother-"

"Well, Leader Ion, we didn't-"

In very swift movements, Ion produces a beam of energy from his hands. He fashions it into a rope, then jumps onto the shoulders of Calo (the Elder who had just been speaking). He ties their snout shut, then returns to his place before the Council to stare at the silenced Elder. After a brief moment, Calo begins to scream in anguish as their snout begins to smoke. Ion simply watches as the giant lizard claws at their face, trying to remove the beam of energy: alas, their claws are merely burned as well – not as severely as their now sealed snout, however.

"Leader Ion!" Helod wheezes. "Please!"

With that, Ion lifts his arm, and the energy beam flies to his hand, and off the mouth of Calo. He looks very seriously about the room, though he feels pure disgust, at this point. He thinks he has made his point to these hyper-intelligent lizards.

"Don't lie to me," Ion orders sternly. "Not only will I know, but I will punish you for it. Calo will never be able to tell lies again…Now," Ion clasps his hands together and smiles at the Elders. "Where was I?"

"Mmmm! Our…assassination attempt…on Life-Admiral Crow," the nearly healed Titus answers.

"Yes, right!" Ion exclaims jovially. "Your assassination attempt on the most intelligent living thing in the known galaxy. Well, in case you have not heard yet, you failed."

Brief glances are shared among the Council Members and the healing Titus. Sephia and Basilis turn from Calo – as they are trying to comfort the burned lizard – only for a moment. Ion knew they do not want to give away how absolutely astonishing this revelation is to them. The Earth Leader does not know what else they are planning (yet), and feels a sense of pride, thinking there wouldn't be any more trouble from them. As long as they choose to do as Ion commands.

"Try not to mask your disdain too much, Elders." Ion tones casually, gliding slowly about the room again and smiling at the Xerophs. "The Life-Admiral and I are willing to let this little fiasco go forgotten - as are the Frosks – if you swear never to attack, blackmail, or any other form of inconvenience against our planets ever again."

There is a shocked pause for a moment. The now whimpering Calo goes to speak, then whines in despair. Conyx continues to lick at the air only to have a grimace placed on their face. Finally, Helod steps forward with narrowed eyes.

"Is that all you and the Froskian people ask of us?"

"Oh my sweet Elder Helod!" Ion exclaims, again jovial. He claps his robotic hands together and rests them under his chin. "Abso-*lutely* not! You see, I have a very lovely garden to finish – Titus knows all about it, don't you Representative Titus?"

Titus, beginning to rise from the ground now fully healed, looks to Ion. The lizard then looks around at the Council, sending a consoling look to Calo for a moment, only to return their gaze to Ion. Somberly – almost reluctantly – Titus nods in agreement.

"It does our planet a great deal of justice…" Titus admits, looking at their scaley feet.

"Wonderful, so you will hand over the nice potted one you have in the corner here then?" Ion asks, a facetious grin rising upon his face.

"Do as you wish, Earth Leader," Sephia says, bowing their head.

"So I shall," Ion says, throwing a threatening glance at the Council.

Ion telepathically has his nanobots coat a protective shield around the plant. He gradually saunters to the TDC, acts as if he is looking it over (he had discreetly scanned it earlier) and gives a thumbs up to the Council. Some of the members roll their eyes, Helod simply glares with murderous intent. Ion then has the nanobots float the plant up to his ship, and turns to the elders, still grinning.

"What of the Frosks?" Titus asks.

"Hm?"

"What do the Frosks demand of us?"

"Oh, nothing actually!" Ion answers gleefully. "They are staying quiet as a favour to us. Seems like Technicorum II owes a lot of favours to Earth, right now."

"Arrogant monkey," Basilis mutters.

"Arrogant, you say?" Ion inquires, still maintaining a happy demeanour. He rises to the opened roof, looking down upon the Elders with his arms crossed. "Arrogance is thinking you can frame one of the three – of which we are the other two – galactic super powers for terrorism. Arrogance is thinking you can lie, *to me*. Make no mistake, my cold-blooded friends, you are a very brute war force. Incomparable to almost any other military entity in our known universe. However, if I wanted to, or if the Centre Planet wanted to, we would wipe your existence from the face of the galaxy. So, no more games, Elders. Act as wise as everyone seems to think you are, and stick to what you are good at. And more importantly, stay away from Earth and the Centre Planet…anything you would like to add? Basilis? Helod?"

"Get off our planet, ape," Helod wheezes almost inaudibly.

"Gladly!" Ion answers, rising beyond the shield he had hacked to replace the ceiling. "I look forward to a more professional meeting in the future, my friends!"

With that, Ion departs. Settling a score for his brother, his planet, and the majority of the known galaxy. He soars at sonic speed back to his ship, where he is sure Talia is waiting to tell him she has "already seen what had come to pass" or something to that effect. In the meantime, Ion speaks with his brother about finally attaining the death cure.

Chapter XVII

Frosk – Twenty [Earth] Hours Earlier

"I suppose I will be leaving tomorrow, then," Crow says to Trius solemnly.

"So it would appear, Life-Admiral," Trius responds, equally somber.

The duo had overseen the first steps of the development of the "Pollu-Magnet" (as Crow had titled it) over the past couple days. Crow had solidified a very specific, step-by-step process for its creation and implementation for the Frosks shortly after presenting it to their Leaders. The manufacturing had just begun, and up until now, the Life-Admiral had avoided directly watching it being put together by the slaves of the planet. He did not feel comfortable watching what had been abolished so long ago on Earth be continued on a much older, arguably more established planet. He feels it unthinkable that the Frosks could use such an abhorrent practice.

Outside of this, Trius and Crow had developed quite a bond. They had spoken at length about interplanetary politics, shared some views in regards to economic structures, and equally felt contempt toward the ongoing slavery occurring on Frosk. Not only was Trius an excellent journalist and individual, he happened to also be a very skilled artist. Crow found himself consistently mesmerized by his quick hands and attention to detail. The Life-Admiral knew he would miss their interactions, and hoped that next time they met that they both would be able to breath in the air without the aid of a facemask.

"Would you…would you like to see something great before you depart?" Trius inquires.

"I am always looking for an excuse to learn something new, and see something extravagant!" Crow exclaims. "What do you have in mind?"

"I know we both hold a fair amount of contempt toward the slavery on this planet, but would you be willing to view the Queen Frosk's Birthing Sanctum? It's regarded as one of the most astonishing places in the galaxy. The Queen has also been known to give blessings to those worthy."

"I haven't even heard of this!" Crow expresses, appalled. "My word, are you sure I have clearance?"

"I have clearance!" Trius informs. "And I would be honoured to show you. Such a highly regarded individual as yourself should see our Queen at least once."

"Then I am honoured," Crow replies, bowing his head in respect.

The two depart, taking a series of tubes to reach their destination. They pass through security – some of which try to get Crow to remove his mechanical enhancements. Fortunately, they eventually realize that they are part of his body, and can not be removed. When they finally arrive at the Sanctum, Crow can hardly believe what he sees.

It is unlike any other part of Frosk. Within a dome, there is a massive and luxurious garden filled with unthinkable plant life. Creatures (that seemingly were abundant on the planet before all the pollution had taken over) float about. Flying cephalopods, obscure birds singing mystic songs, things that appear to simply be fluffs with eyes, and a variety of others parade around without a care. In the centre of it all, surrounded by (what appears to be) a sacred stone enclosure, rest three very large insects.

One appears as if it were a mix of mosquitos, horse flies, fireflies and perhaps a few different other types of insects that can be found on Earth. The second looks to be a hybrid of bees, wasps, and hornets. The final almost looks decrepit. The species is indistinguishable, and it appears as if a light breeze might blow them into dust. Behind the Royal Trio is a series of tubes that lead out of the dome. Every few seconds, it looks as if something is being pulled from it. As Crow goes on to observe the (mostly) majestic Queens, he notices that the start of this end of the tube system connects to the Royal Trios (respective) reproductive systems.

"Amazing, isn't it?" Trius asks Crow, leaning upon his staff earnestly. For the first time since they had met, Trius had turned off his Vision Screen.

"I...thought there was only one of them?"

"There was," Trius admits with a nod. "Queen Peripa was chosen centuries ago - for her wisdom and beauty - to birth our People. As she grew older, her eggs became less desirable. So, now she gives birth to the slaves, while Queen Vespa and Pyridae create our most deadly warriors and most brilliant scientists respectively. The one the rest of the galaxy has seen - as a tourist attraction - is a hologram of Queen Peripa from two centuries ago. Back when she looked much more graceful and elegant."

Crow feels a heavy weight on his chest. Admittedly, this was quite a disturbing sight. It reminded him of videos he had seen in his youth - back in high school science - of a Queen tick giving birth. However, he felt the utmost respect and admiration for the three sole creators of life on this planet.

"They are..." Crow began, having to find his breath. "...Extravagant."

"Our thanks, Wise Crow!" croaks Queen Peripa. Crow bows on one knee in respect, while Trius reels back in awe before following suit.

"Thank you for permitting me to be in your presence, my Humble Queens!" Crow bellows, still bowing before them. "Might I add you have an exquisite Sanctum! It's beauty is unmatched!"

"You flatter us," buzzes Queen Vespa.

"We wanted to thank you," adds Queen Pyridae. "For making sure our species may thrive for centuries to come!"

"We have heard of your works," Queen Peripa continues, her voice nearly an aged whisper. "You put our species to shame, in many ways."

"Not at all, my Queens!" Crow rebuts. "I simply do what your species has done centuries longer than I; seek greater scientific advancements for a better future, for all."

"So humble," the Trio of Queens buzz in unison. Crow blushes lightly at their flattery.

"We would like to bestow upon you a blessing" Queen Pyride hums.

"One to show our thanks, and appreciation from our people," Queen Vespa joins.

"Take this blessing, and may it bring you some of the fortune that you have brought our planet," Queen Peripa tones.

As if from nowhere, a figure floats above the Queens and over to Crow's arms. The Life-Admiral gasps as a glisteningly golden, seemingly sentient cephalopods glides over to him. It affectionately wrapping itself around Crow's shoulder.

"This is Nila," Queen Vespa informs. "The 'Golden Child' – ironically so – of our gene splicing program. An apex predator, with the capabilities of relationship building, affection, and even prescience."

"Using genetics from throughout the Imperium, we have spliced the most intelligent, beautiful, and deadly cephalopod imaginable," Queen Pyridae continues. "Adaptive to any environment, and a beauty to behold."

"May she be your greatest companion, dearest treasure, and a caring bringer of luck," Queen Peripa finishes.

With the blessing given, it was time for Trius and Crow to depart. They give their thanks for the Queens' graciousness, then carry on their way with other matters Crow had to attend to before departing back to Earth. Crow smiles joyously as Nila floats about his head. The cephalopod, though apparently deadly, seemed to grow an immediate attachment to the Earthling. She whizzes about even as Crow has some microbots create a (seemingly) invisible barrier around her – protecting her from the harmful air of Frosk.

"She's a playful one, eh Life-Admiral?" Trius comments, grinning.

"That she is, dear friend," Crow chuckles. Nila rests for a moment on his hand, wrapping her tentacles between his fingers. She could not have been bigger than an Earth football (as extremely similar sports were enjoyed throughout the galaxy), and she chatters her beak in a sign of affection as she rests on him. "Quite the blessing to receive from your Queens! I feel truly honoured! Have you ever gotten a blessing, Trius?"

"Oh my, yes!" Trius answers, once again locked into his Vision Screen, his tail flickering sporadically once again. "Where do you think I got this staff?"

---

13 Hours Prior To Obtaining TDC

"Life-Admiral!" the Head of Torture bellows from over his tools. "I did not expect to see you in my quarters! Come to tell me that you are going to miss me? Or perhaps you wanted to witness my incomparable skills at work?"

"Head of Torture" Crow says with a nod of respect. Nila seems a bit nervous around the Head of Torture, and clings a bit more tightly to Crows hand. "Apologies for not informing you I would come by, I am merely trying to make sure all is said and done before I depart tomorrow."

"Of course, of course," The Head of Torture nods, placing down a variety of sharp instruments he had just finished cleaning.

The Head of Torture's "office" (if you really could call it that) is large, dark, and has a variety of sharp tools strewn about. The floor is permanently stained in a rainbow of blood. The smell of countless lost souls is etched into every surface of the room. Holographic projectors, medical reading tools, and things such as restraints (in a variety of sizes) are hidden within niches in the room, which Crow could only detect with his synthetic body modifications.

"Now," the daunting Frosk says, turning his attention away from his tools to the Life-Admiral. "What is it you need to discuss with me?"

"Well, there are a couple things that I must speak with you about," Crow admits, approaching the giant insect slowly, creating a hologram from his Vision Screen. "I want to make it clear I fully believe Frosk had nothing to do with the Centre Planet attack. As you can see here, the Centre Planet themselves sent out a report today. I had made my own report as well, using samples I retrieved from when Ion had stopped the Perusaks. We are fully on your side, just so you know."

"Hmph. It seems my methods did provide the Centre Planet with the information they needed to know we were innocent," the Head of Torture says smugly, reading through the report. "This is why a job like mine must be done. You can never fully trust another entity until they have nothing to live for."

"So it would seem," Crow replies somberly, removing the report. "I would like to also speak to you about Dissosteria's sudden need for me to depart-"

"Don't let that bother you too much, Life-Admiral," is the reply. The Head of Torture walks about the room, as if prepping for work in the near future. "Leader Dissosteria prides himself in science...seeing you think up your method simply made him feel foolish for not thinking of it first. I assure you, the bond between Frosk and Earth has never been stronger."

"Is that why your Queens gifted me with this cephalopod as a blessing?"

"Oh my, yes," is the answer. "Nila there is a greater gift than most have received. Do be sure to take good care of her. She is the last of her specific breed."

"Believe me, I shall!" Crow promises. "Look, Head of Torture...you have assured me that our planet's bond has never been stronger...however, you very specifically have seemed confrontational to me since I got here, may I ask why?"

"You Earthlings sure think emotionally," the Frosk chortles. "Life-Admiral, it is my *job* to be intimidating and confrontational. Diplomatic situations or not, I am tasked with keeping people in line and – granted circumstances – safe."

"Should I have been…worried about anything while I've been here?"

"Not about anything from the planet itself…aside from our air haha, for now. However we believe whatever threat may have been heading our way is gone. Additionally, you are in my dojo now, I feel more comfortable talking to you entity to entity than when we had to be so formal. Is there anything else you wanted to discuss, Life-Admiral? I have a couple Xeroph's en route to-"

"Funny you should mention that," Crow says, standing straight and putting on his most diplomatic voice. "Remember how Earth asked not to be paid *financially* for our work with you?"

"Yes, I do."

"Well, Leader Ion and I have thought of another way that may be beneficial toward both of us…"

___

45 Minutes Before Obtaining TDC

After a few more farewells and well wishes, Life-Admiral Crow returns to his quarters and prepares to travel back home. Crow has missed his people the entire time he has been gone, and looks forward to personally updating them in the Intersphere. Nila floats about the room – as if scanning it – as the Earthling sets the cephalopod out some food and drink, gathers his things and prepares for slumber.

He looks over the Pollu-Magnet blueprints for a while, making sure he had not missed anything in the design or calculations. After all is ready to be brought aboard his ship, and Crow feels satisfied that all should go as planned, he dawns his night clothes and crawls into bed.

As he slips under the covers, Nila floats from her food dish and lands on Crow's stomach. Even through the sheet, he can feel the cephalopods tentacle pads as they laid gently up to his neck. He finds this oddly comforting, and begins to allow himself to fall into his regulated 30 minute interval of slumber.

Just as he begins to feel sleep take him, Crow hears a noise. A subtle noise. One that most would consider benign and, in turn, disregard. However…there was something sinister in it. Faint as it was, the "plock" he had heard from the ceiling above him causes a feeling of concern.

Laying completely still yet ready to rise and fight, Crow uses his synthetic eye to look through the ceiling above him. Everything appears standard; air systems, filtration systems, and the floor above all look clear. It was not until Crow turns on his thermal sight that he notices their outline.

Imperceivable to the standard eye by use of an organic cloaking device, the giant chameleon-like entities rest between the ceiling of Crow's room, and the floor of the room above. It looks to the Life-Admiral as though the duo are bickering about something using hand signals. Crow recognized them to be of Xeroph origin immediately. One holds a standard and legal (within the galactic imperium) blade in their hand, whilst the other has a vial dangling from a string in their mouth.

Evidently the two Xerophs were deciding how to murder the Earth Leader. One was making the point (using their hand signals) that Life-Admiral Crow clearly still has flesh, and no doubt would be able to die from a stab wound or well-calculated cut. The other argued that the excessively corrosive sap from a tree (which evidently was rare even on their planet) would be the most effective. Crow decides this "sap" was what resided within the vial. Besides, "Elder Conyx had given it to [them] for a reason!" the one with the poison seems to shout in their symbolic language.

Growing weary of the non-verbal argument, the Xeroph with the stabbing utensil moves through the air filtration system ducts both with quickness and agility. The other sighs angrily, then follows suit – situating themselves on the opposite side of Crow's bed to where the other had landed.

Just as the Life-Admiral is about to use his element of surprise and move to the offence against these reptiles, Trius walks through a wall – clearly using a density modifier. The Frosk moves even faster than the Xeroph on Crows right, extending his wings and leaping toward it with a fierce look on his face. He lets out a warcry as his wings dice the Xeroph; sending blood splatters all over both Crow and the walls.

The warcry is sharp enough to alert Nila, who uses the cephalopod ability to change form. She propels herself from Crow's stomach straight into a vital artery on the other Xeroph, spraying more blood all over the room and leaving the potential assassin in a state of slow death.

Crow rises slowly from his bed, a relatively blank expression on his face. Nila hovers back over to his shoulder and rests affectionately. The Earthling gives her an affectionate pat.

"Hello Trius," Crow says, forcing a grin. "I see you have been expecting me to have company."

"We thought we'd captured the potential threat," Trius admits, his tail flickering madly once again and face going through his Visionscreeen. "Evidently some have slipped through. Greatest apologies, Life-Admiral."

"I think just Crow will do, at this point," he replies, wiping alien blood from his face. "Thank you for stepping in…though you should know I have a great deal of defensive modifications, I could have managed."

"That's not the point, my friend," Trius says. "You have done this planet a great service. The least we can do is keep you safe…I've summoned a cleaning crew to come and fix this all up for you…what do we do about Technicorum II now, though? Will there be a war?"

"I have a better idea, Trius," Crow says, fully risen from his bed and a brilliant concept in his mind. "I think I know what Technicorum II will be doing as payment for Earth's services now…"

Chapter XVIII

Planet Earth – The Utopian Research Facility

"What is this?" Talia asks incredulously.

Surrounding the Oracle and the Earth Leader are a variety of scientific instruments beyond description. Lights behind glass walls flicker from their devices, holograms of Dreamscape code and a variety of parts of Earth hover along the wall. Large, seemingly indestructible metal doors come sporadically along the walls and the silver room is lit brightly in a seemingly neon green tone. All the doors in this underground research lab are labelled in a language that no doubt only Life-Admiral Crow and Ion understand.

"Not even in my visions has this place been done justice!" she exclaims, looking over at the unimpressed Leader. He stands before a wall-sized Visionscreen, going through the programs that had been broadcasting to their people during Crow and Ion's absence.

"Mhm, visions," Ion says facetiously, not looking away from the Visionscreen and rolling his eyes. "I'm sure you know every part of our underground research facility. Considering it is the most protected and secret place in the known Universe. Even more well-guarded and encrypted than the Centre Planet Archives."

"And you should know," Talia says, not looking away from the holographic image of a slowly rotating Earth. "You and Life-Admiral Crow designed them."

"Right again, kid," Ion says, finishing up his inspection. "I should have brought you stickers."

"A nice thought, but not necessary," she jests. "So, where will you take me first? The Dreamscape programming center? Your collection of rare otherworldly plantlife? The cloning facility? OOouhh! Maybe you'll stumble on Crow's shrine to-"

"How do you know about the clone lab?" Ion inquires, standing before a door and gesturing Talia to follow.

"I told you, I've been here already," she answers, gradually pulling away from the Visionscreens. "Not physically but-"

"I don't believe you," Ion says flatly as she finally stands before him. He is further frustrated as his truth detecting programs show that she is indeed, telling her truth.

"You didn't believe in Nancy's abilities either, but you will," Talia answers with a grin. "In a couple hours, I'm sure. We are dropping off the Sessienna for Crow to inspect when he returns, correct?"

"Stop doing that," Ion demands, moving his hands in obscure patterns and using his synthetic eye to open the door. "But yes, now please be quiet."

They enter what can only be described as an underground greenhouse; more accurately a series of greenhouses. The entire (to porperly describe its size) stadium was broken into cordoned off sections of plant life. Some are in specific houses to ensure they were at the optimal temperature; others appear dangerous, and many are placed into planet-specific sanctions. It looks as though Ion had collected plants from every planet in the known galaxy.

There are beautiful flowers of every shape and colour you could imagine, and carnivorous ones that are feeding on meat that had been shot through a chute before them. Green leaves, pink ones, and some in colours that couldn't be processed by the human brain. Ion traces his metal finger gently against the plastic outer shells of the fixtures as he walks toward the section marked *Technicorum II*.

"I have never seen…so much beauty in my life," Talia says, a gentle tear running down her cheek.

"The universe has gifted us sentient creatures with immeasurable beauty," Ion agrees with a nod. He stops and turns to Talia just outside of the Technicorum II greenhouse. "And we don't even remotely deserve it. Not a single thinking thing properly appreciates this divine beauty. Now, you may wish to stay here for a moment."

"I would love to see some of the plant life from Technicorum II!"

"And they would love to see you, I'm sure. Most of their plants are carnivorous. Now, please wait, this will only take a moment." Ion turns from her, has his identity verified by the mechanical door, and then enters the greenhouse.

Talia can see the Earth Leader as he walks gracefully straight down to where a shrine appears to be. While walking, he produces the Sessienna plant seemingly out of thin air. He gently pets a particularly aggressive looking plant to his right before reaching the ornate desk, on which is engraved *Salvation*. He places the Sessienna gently onto the desk, admires it for a moment then returns to Talia.

"What is so important about that plant anyway?" Talia asks as Ion begins to exit back into the main atrium.

"I thought you've seen all of this already," Ion says, a slight mocking tone in his underlying speech.

"I have seen many, many futures…many potential to be, some unavoidable. However I cannot pick and choose what visions I get. I have not seen this part of my life yet, but-"

"Then you may die down here," Ion says blankly.

"What makes you think that? Do you intend to cause me harm?"

"Absolutely not!" Ion states seriously as they return to the atrium and walk toward another door. "I just know Nancy could not predict her own death, and you only – apparently – see what *could* be, not what *will*…So I have my suspicions. Especially considering the scanning and procedures you are about to undergo could lead to death."

"Scanning?"

"You think I brought you here for my own amusement?"

"Do you mean to discover whether or not Oracles are something that can actually exist using a brain scan and some 'procedures?'"

"Basically…but this will be more intrusive than a regular brain scan, Talia. I will have to monitor you for days. And when my brother gets back, he will do in depth research on your brain itself. I am simply doing the preliminary research."

"Do what you must," Talia says calmly. "I didn't come here to be amused by *you*, either. There is something I must warn you about, but you being the skeptic that you are, it would be a waste to tell you. So, God, do what you must to believe in me, as I believe in you."

The duo enter what appears to Talia to be a research ward. A variety of medical tools, scanning apparatuses, and monitoring systems lay before them. Directly ahead is a chair – an uncomfortable looking one, Talia thinks – with a desk next to it. Without being prompted, Talia sits in the chair. She busies herself with the holographic controls on it, changing the incline and such as Ion meanders about the room.

Within moments, Ion is floating in a full lotus position next to her, setting up an IV and preparing a needle. Seemingly levitating next to him is some sort of brain scanning device that clearly will be placed on her head. Ion prepares a needle as Talia feels herself tense up somewhat.

"This will put you to sleep for a while," Ion begins, not looking away from the syringe. "While you are under, I will use this to monitor your brain function. Any questions or inquiries before I continue?"

"Why do you consistently say that Nancy could not predict her own death?" Talia asks, looking up at the ceiling as Ion injects the needle.

"I meant more toward the upcoming procedures, but alright I will humor you. I say that, my dear Talia, because she seemed very frightened when I witnessed her death. Frightened, confused, and seemingly unable to prevent it from happening."

Before Talia could retort to this seemingly ominous statement, whatever Ion had injected into her arm causes her to pass out. Ion lets out a robotic sigh as he places the brain scanning device on her head. He looks at the human with pity, and feels sorry that when she wakes up he will be giving her the news that oracles don't exist.

It is true, Ion and Crow had encountered numerous entities that claimed to have prescience in the past. To the very farthest reaches of the Galaxy they had been led, with promises to be told what the future would look like. Not a single one had been legitimate. Ion questioned if another regular human could possibly break this trend. His doubts are very high. As he contemplates this, the voice of Life-Admiral Crow enters his consciousness.

"Brother, I am departing Frosk presently and should arrive home in moments. How were your missions on Terra Six and Technicorum II?"

"Excellent brother," Ion mentally replies confidently. As he converses via brainwave, he begins the scans on Talia. *"I retrieved the Sessienna, made the deal with the Xerophs, and even have…a bit of a surprise for you. A new project to undergo. I'll explain when you get here"*

"Oh…kay…anything I should worry about?"

"Not worry so much as get excited for. I-…wait a minute…"

"What is it?"

As Ion was reviewing the scans, a notice appears on his Visionscreen. Evidently, one of their projects they had been working on for decades had finally reached the point they had anticipated. Ion's synthetic lips curl into a smile.

"The alien Project…I believe it is time we have a word with Citizen 6-6-5-4-38"

Chapter XIX

The DreamScape - 6-6-5-4-38's Dreamscape

It had begun to feel like it would never end. 6-6-5-4-38 spent several consecutive sessions in the anecho chamber, pushing for as long as they could to "beat the world record." More importantly, 6-6-5-4-38 listened to the metaphorical voice of the Dreamscape server. It was a sound without pattern, lacking any true defining features. It had felt more like a brainwave than the vibrations and inner workings of an advanced form of technology.

With every listen, the citizen feels they are one step closer to finding their solution. One step closer to mentally connecting to the server and communicating with the other Earth citizens. Freedom is so close to 6-6-5-4-38, they would have felt it in their bones – were they not taken away as part of Ion's psychotic control over the people of Earth.

Presently, the Earth citizen is in the Dreamscape. The matrix they inhabit makes it feel as though they are sitting in a wicker chair, on the deck of an old style farm home. The barn is hiding the harsh sun from their eyes to their right, and on their left is an immeasurably long plain of fields. The smell of corn, wheat, carrots, and a variety of other agriculture waft into the fabricated senses of 6-6-5-4-38, giving them a feeling of peace and a job well done. In the faint air, 6-6-5-4-38 can hear the soft pulsation of the Intersphere server.

"Tomorrow," they think, "I will finally crack the code."

After exiting the Dreamscape and returning to their mechanical body's living quarters, 6-6-5-4-38 flops themselves into a chair. As per the usual, they begin to look into the world news. Without their usual unbiased outlet, the citizen switches aimlessly between a series of them.

There are the usual highlights of art, fashion, and scientific advancements made in the Dreamscape. The Earth leaders permit everyone from artists to zoologists to show their work all throughout the Intersphere. Clothing designers even "sell" their designs within the Dreamscape. Admittedly this is an admirable thing the Earth leaders do. Nonetheless, 6-5-4-38 looks forward to finding the massive blunders Crow and Ion laid upon "their" people.

A broadcast shows Earth Leader Ion shaking hands with the final, non-Utopius colonized civilization's leader. The last of the pure-human race did not agree with the ideals of Ion's extreme measures, but seem to have come to peace with the rest of the world converting. The final pure-humans live a nomadic life, travelling around their relatively small country and engaging in trade.

Once, a long time ago, they used to meander about the planet regardless of where it was on the map. However, with the Earth reclaiming itself and the developing surplus of animals, the travel became more treacherous. Additionally, Leader Ion had previously condemned them for trying to convert some of his people that had chosen to work in the field to their way of life (apparently).

Thus, the pure-humans generally stick to themselves, and engage in some trade with Ion and Crow. Their population has begun to rise again – given they began to work with Ion to have medicine that would elongate the lives of their citizens. Many of them had succumb to plagues within the past couple hundred years, and Ion and Crow's help had become a necessity.

Currently, the pure-humans and Leader Ion are working on an agreement that would grant them better land access, and the resources necessary to survive. How long that would last, 6-6-5-4-38 is unsure. Crow and Ion seem to bring down the hammer once even the most minuscule of negativity surfaces.

6-6-5-4-38 moved on to see that the Life-Admiral has returned to Earth after a short visit with the Froskians. There are no details outlined as to what he had contributed to the giant insect's bottom line during that particular news segment. But 6-6-5-4-38 figures Crow had done nothing but waste time and find another way to oppress the Utopian citizens.

Not once had a citizen been asked to embark on an interplanetary mission with either of the Earth leaders. There were a great deal of individuals – perhaps not 6-6-5-4-38, but undoubtedly a great deal – who would have loved to see a different planet. The so called "Leaders" only brought robotic sentries with them, if anything at all. Citizens were told to "experience space in the Dreamscape" if space travel was a desire. As if doing so made any kind of difference. Annoyed, 6-6-5-4-38 exits the news on their vision screen, and further plots their endeavour to begin their rebellion.

So it was, the moment 6-6-5-4-38 enters the Intersphere, they waste no time the following day within the Dreamscape. They pull up the synthetic projection of the anecho chamber. They close their digital eyes in the middle of the room – sitting in a meditative position – and do their damndest to have their brainwaves echo with the Dreamscape itself. Before they know it, they are back in the physical matrix: the all-blue series of data and projections of other Dreamscapes. Below them, they see the Intersphere server, which connects all the citizens of Utopius in this one area.

The projected vessel of 6-6-5-4-38 glides over to the server, where they place their digital hand. Manipulating their own brainwaves, the Earth citizen sends them out to the same frequency and pulsation. They begin to feel as though they are merging with the Intersphere itself. An overwhelming sensation of joy and anticipation wash over them, as they maintain the link and run over their speech to the potential recruits in their mind. A rush washes over them, and all they can see is white. Only for a moment before they can feel themselves becoming one with the digital streaming, entering the citizens of Earth's collective consciousness.

They open their eyes, and they are in a seemingly neon-green lit room. It takes a moment for them to adjust, for some reason – as if they were in their robotic body. Blurry human-esque figures lie before them, seemingly floating and encased in something. As their eyes adjust more and more, they see a tall figure to their left. When their eyes finish adjusting, 6-6-5-4-38 realizes they are looking at Earth Leader Ion.

He is before a holographic projection, looking through dark blue-lit analytics. 6-6-5-4-38 is extremely confused, unable to fully grasp what is happening. Is this part of one of the other citizen's Dreamscape? Had he booted them out of the Intersphere and taken their place? And why could they no longer hear the pulsation of the Dreamscape server?

"No 6-6-5-4-38, you are no longer in the simulation," Leader Ion says, not turning away from the holographic charts. "You are currently in reality, your brain has been placed into a special tank with synthetic eyes attached."

"I-...how-?"

"Don't bother talking," Ion states calmly. "You don't have a synthetic voice box anyway. Regardless, you have spoken volumes over the past decade...much longer than last time, interesting..."

Ion continues to go through holographic charts and inputs information sporadically. In the semi-silence, 6-6-5-4-38 asks themselves a million questions: what does this tyrant mean by "last time?" How did he know of their plans? And why are there *humans in tubes*. The blurry figures 6-6-5-4-38 had noticed before are indeed human beings, floating in stasis within some kind of giant petri dish. Had this maniac been cloning people this entire time?!

"I will answer your questions in a moment," Ion informs, finishing a few details within the holographic charts. "You usually have the same ones. I see a couple new inquiries this time, though. It would appear our enhancement serum has been working. You are thinking faster and more adeptly than when we first brought you here."

How long has this been going on? And what does he mean? 6-6-5-4-38 is whirring in a frenzy of anger mixed with confusion. The sensation of a headache begins to build in them, and they cannot seem to calm themselves.

"I'm going to give something to you to calm you down," Ion informs sympathetically. "It will make it easier for you to take all this information in anyway."

The Earth citizen watches as Leader Ion does something on the holographic screen. Moments after he does so, 6-6-5-4-38 feels their headache pass, and a sense of calm wash over them. As if sedated, 6-6-5-4-38 brain lapses into an undeniably catatonic state. Leader Ion glides over to them, floats in a full lotus position, and places a calm, synthetic smile upon his face.

"6-6-5-4-38, you are part of an Earth brain experiment where we have taken a series of off-world species, and placed them in our Dreamscape. You consented to do this 104 years, six days, and fourteen hours ago. With permission from the Centre Planet, we have been seeking to discover the hidden strength of every species' brain within the Galactic Imperium. This is to help speed the process of evolution, create a better understanding of our genetic mappings, and find a means to connect each and every entity in our known universe. I will now send you the forms you signed, proving this case."

Before 6-6-5-4-38 eyes appears a holographic set of forms. It shows the essence of this program, signatures from Centre Planet Representatives, signatures from Ion and Life-Admiral Crow, and the signature of 6-6-5-4-38 themselves, revealing their true name. Honestly, the Earth citizen feels, that doesn't much matter anymore. According to this form, this experiment was a one way ticket - 6-6-5-4-38 had essentially donated their body and brain to science.

"The only thing not covered in there…is *why* we have chosen to begin this experiment. You see, we have a plan to expand the Dreamscape for every individual in the galaxy. Not every species has the same interests as humans – far from it really. So, we have created a better understanding of each planet's culture, and have begun programming new Dreamscapes for the other worlds. To do so, and to prevent any rebellions like you had planned, we needed preventative measures."

Ion produces a hologram from his hands. Floating between them is a human brain on the right, and what undoubtedly had to be the brain of 6-6-5-4-38 (as it was much larger and complex). Still being sedated, 6-6-5-4-38 merely stares through synthetic eyes.

"We have speculated for quite a while that the Centre Planet species - your species - has the ability to read brain waves," Ion continues, highlighting a specific part of the Centre Planet alien brain. "You have receptors here, which most if not all other species do not. This is why you were able to hack into our servers – a feat no human would be able to do. The server communicates using very similar patterns to that of brainwaves, thus – with your species capabilities - you were able to hack it. We need to keep the security of the Dreamscape air tight. Hence, you becoming part of our project not only proves our theory, but shows us how we can prevent further rebellion."

"That is also where the clones come in, my friend. You are not the first to grow weary of the Dreamscape and feel oppressed. Some citizens have chosen to move off world, others have asked to die. Many however, like you had agreed to in your contract, have asked to have their memory erased and start fresh in the Dreamscape. That is why we have cloned humans. Think of them as "reset" buttons for our citizens. With the additional back up in the case the synthetic bodies no longer serve as a necessary method of housing our people."

6-6-5-4-38 soaks this all in. Everything Crow and Ion have done, good or bad, has been to perpetuate their concept of a Utopia. No true consideration for their people, or by the sounds of it the other species within the galaxy. 6-6-5-4-38 would have been enraged if they were not sedated.

"Now, I would like to thank you for all you have done for this galaxy," Ion says, clapping his metal hands together and floating back to the holographic control panel. "You have done the Imperium a great service, even when you were trying to overthrow the two people trying to bring peace to it. I will now erase your memory, have you start fresh, and leave you to take on whatever life you wish to live. Thank you again."

Unable to move, protest, scream or do anything, 6-6-5-4-38 sits in their vat feeling helpless. All they can do is watch as their vision becomes darker, and succumb to the will of Leader Ion. They only hoped that this feeling of defiance and need for freedom will stick within them when they begin their essentially new existence.

Earth – The Great Plains of Alberta, Canada

Helios had just finished their shift tending the wildlife. Since the Great Leader Ion had taken over Earth, there was so much more peace and prosperity. Feeling the want to give more recently, they had asked Life-Admiral Crow himself for the opportunity to spend time that could have been spent in the Dreamscape to work in the field. With a jovial grin, the Life-Admiral had agreed!

The Earth citizen had spent most of their time within the Dreamscape farming anyway. They began to realize that applying their developed skills to benefit the wonderful planet they had been born in was preferable to staying in the Dreamscape. Thus far, Helios had begun the rejuvenation of a large part of land for the so called "pure-humans" to occupy. Evidently their population had grown too large for the land Leader Ion had already donated them centuries ago. Helios felt the term "pure-human" was insensitive to the equally important cyborgs that currently held the majority of this planet's population.

Nonetheless, Helios was glad to help. After all, ask anything and the planet shall provide. As the Earth continues to reclaim itself, It still provides ample space for respectful human beings to occupy. Thus Helios laboured for the benefit of others, and in the name of the Great Leaders Ion and Crow.

Presently, Helios is preparing to be transported back to their living quarters at the Planetary Capitol – the floating city of incomparable beauty. Helios felt fortunate to be able to work in the field, and even more fortunate that they could go back halfway across their country in the same day. As was standard, the Earth citizen had a view over the horizon of the floating city. They never grew weary of watching a sunset on the Great Utopian Capitol.

Upon arrival to their living quarters, Helios looks up intergalactic news. Evidently the Perusaks had indeed been behind the Centre Planet attack. Punitive measures were taking place. Additionally, the Xerophs of Technicorum II had been tasked with taking over the leadership role in the Schleurghlting planet. Evidently, Earth Leader Ion had bravely stepped in on the giant arachnid leader's ship attempting to attack Terra Six! Was there any end to the Ruler's benevolence?

Helios lays back with a great sense of pride in their synthetic heart. The life that Leaders Crow and Ion provide to their people is unique to them. No other race in the galaxy receive this sort of bliss, abundance of freedom, or joy. Helios is certain of it. Just prior to looking away from the evening intergalactic news and doing some botany research, Helios' Visionscreen begins to receive a call. Oh my, it's Life-Admiral Crow!

"Good evening, Life-Admiral!" Helios answers excitedly. "What a pleasant surprise!"

"Hello Helios," Crow smiles back at his citizen. "Thank you for taking the time to speak with me, friend!"

"Any time, sir!" Helios answers. "How can I help you?"

"I was just hoping to see how you felt the field work has been treating you."

"Oh my, wonderfully Life-Admiral!" Helios answers enthusiastically. "The crops I have been working on over the past few months have begun to grow marvellously. Additionally, a great deal of the fauna seem to have recognized that humans will soon inhabit the area. They appear to have moved their homes further within the forests. Truly splendid...I am quite surprised more citizens do not choose to do field work, it is so rewarding!"

"I am so happy you think so, Helios!" Crow answers, looking as if he were working on something in the background. "How long are you willing to work in the fiel-"

"As long as I can, Great Leader!"

"Oh my lad, 'friend' will do, no need for the formalities...perhaps it is time we remove your citizen number, and have your name as your official title in the database."

"That would make me most joyous, si-ah...friend!"

"Consider it done!" Crow says. "Say farewell to 6-6-5-4-38...and hello to friend Helios!"

"Thank you so much, friend!"

"Any time! Now, I am very glad you are having such a great experience. However, I must continue on with my duties."

"Of course! Of course! But...Life-Admiral-?"

"Yes, Helios?"

"Would you…would you mind reciting the words of Leader Ion with me before you depart?"

"I would be honoured, my friend."

In unison, the duo recite:
Freedom from fear,
Pardon from pain,
Independence from ION!

Chapter XX

Earth 2125 – The First Office of the Floating City

If you are looking for purpose, you need look no further than yourself. To be is to be, what more do you need? A tree does not have an existential crisis when the fall comes; its leaves changing colour and falling off. No – if the tree is able to think at all, it understands that it is going through a cycle. By the end of the winter, things will return to being full, green, and fruit-bearing. Why then, have we humans wasted so much time worrying about making money? Everything we need comes cyclically, without thought and the way nature intended. We have foolishly created barriers for no reason other than to fulfill our need for a feeling of superiority. In the DreamScape, you can experience it. Do it all you wish. Become the leader of your own planet and run it into decay. Leave our real living, breathing one out of it.

Early DreamScape message from Leader Ion

"So the premise is simple," Mrs. Vena says. "We turn these reclaimed areas into tourist super stations, invite off-worlders, and turn an immeasurable profit!"

The business mogul smiles one of the over dramatic smiles all corrupt capitalists make. Crow rolls his eyes equally dramatically. Leader Ion sits, arms crossed and clearly unimpressed. Vena had brought a very intricate holographic presentation, and seems so confident in her skills that she does not notice the clear discontent in the Earth leaders.

"Why would we do that?" Ion asks baldly.

"For revenue!" is the confident response. "And to further our place in the Galactic Imp-"

"We are highly regarded throughout the galaxy, Mrs. Vena," Crow interrupts, sipping at some tea. "Any further, and we may be asked to take on the role of the Centre Planet."

"What, are you two afraid of making a little money?" Vena inquires incredulously, sitting her still-human self in front of Ion and Crows massive metal desk. "If it is your image you are worried about, this would only strengthen it! Showcasing the natural beauty of Earth would make species like the Xerophs respect us more, and having a better economy would make the Frosks look at us wi-"

"The Frosks would look at us as competition," Ion dictates. "They are the most advanced *capitalists* in the known galaxy. We are viewed as the most advanced utilitarians. I can see how *you* – a capitalist - feel about that, but my brother and I – the *Leaders* of this planet – prefer the planet the way it is currently run."

"Well, what if I told you not every Earth citizen feels this way?"

"We know how our people feel," Crow assertively assures Vena. "That is why so many have not been forced to convert to their cyborg bodies."

"This is ridiculous!" Vena shouts, rising from her seat and leaning on their desk with her hands. "Do you not think we could use the income for resources? At the very least to give us a leg up in trade?"

"The planet shall provide," Ion says flatly. "With the majority of the population, we no longer require food or medicine. Work is done by the cyborg bodies while our citizens joyfully experience the Dreamscape. What you are asking us to do is perpetuate the very thing we have fought so hard to move away from. Our species is not meant to devolve, Mrs. Vena, we are meant to progress."

The mogul glares at the two Leaders with venom. The duo can tell that their little guest here is brewing something within her mind, but they know that it is something they can handle. Shortly, they will have to deal with a much bigger threat.

"Your people won't like this," the businesswoman insists to them. "I know many individuals that would spit in your faces if they knew what you are turning down."

"And we spit in the face of unnecessary greed," Crow assures her sincerely. "You may go now, friend. Thank you for coming to see us."

Mrs. Vena exits their office with an angered stride. Crow heaves a tired sigh, and looks at the seemingly emotionless Ion. Once again, the cyborg wonders if going through with what Ion had asked him to do was truly worth taking away his humanity.

"Now we must deal with the rebels, brother," Ion says somewhat robotically. "Do you have the transmission ready?"

"Of course, brother," Crow answers, using his Visionscreen to prepare for their next item on the agenda. "Are you ready to make some history?"

"We were born for nothing less."

Earth 2125 – Underground Rebel Base

"They're in a damned city in the sky!" bellows the Head of National Security. "You don't think a nuke shot at the right place won't send it plummeting into the ocean?"

"The citizen death doll could be astronomical," retorts the Secretary of Homeland Security. "Millions of people live in their Capital alone, could we really have that much blood on our hands?"

"Fer Christ sake! They're damned robots! It's not like we haven't done much worse fer a lot less."

"It doesn't really matter" interjects the Head of Finance. "The Centre Planet regulates the use of atomics; furthermore an attack isn't within our budget. With Ion being the true ruler of our country, any and all funding we use toward this is regulated by his government."

"This is *bullshit*" shouts the Attorney General. "How could we let this country fall so far and not do anything about it? I say, we gather as many rebels as we can find, fly to their city - under the guise of a 'peace treaty' - and blow that place up from the inside; Star Wars style!"

"Mr. President," the Vice President (technically former, at this point) says. "We need to know what to do. We are at a loss."

The pure-human President is visibly sweating. All eyes are on him as he adjusts his tie and gulps down furiously. This bunker – which was designed to house these cabinet members in the case of nuclear threat – was not very well ventilated. The President and his group of anti-progression (as Ion and Crow would put it) leaders sit in a circle, with a massive screen overlooking their still mostly human citizens.

The President looks up at this screen, as if hoping there would be answers there. Their country's resources have been minimized. Their land sanctioned off for the Earth to reclaim itself under the new laws of Ion. Their people are not suffering, but they are becoming sedentary and complacent. The Dreamscape has become a part of their everyday life. Could a group of catatonic citizens create a rebellion, even with the help of their formerly elected leader?

"I-…I ah" the President stammers. The glares of his peers intensify. "M-Mrs. Vice President ah…I don't know." There is a sad pause within the room

"You can't just…not know, sir," the Secretary of Interior blurts. "You're the leader of this country! Lead!"

"What do you want me to tell you?" is the dismissive, nearly whispered reply. "We have nothing now…The dream this country once had in principal is now their reality. They don't need people like us anymore - and if they did - I don't think they would have any faith left in-"

"How could they not have any faith in us?!" the Secretary of State nearly screams in desperation.

"Because *I* DON'T!" is the admitting statement. Another silent pause, many of the members look down at their hands in despair. "You all didn't see what I saw that day…in the U.E.C when he – when *it* slaughtered….all those people. You don't know what that monster is capable of, and I hope you never have to know.

"What I do know is that….in times like these the President is usually supposed to stand on the table and shout 'THERE IS HOPE! THERE IS ALWAYS HOPE AND WE CAN BAND TOGETHER AND DEFEAT THIS ENEMY…!

"…The sad truth is that there is no 'defeating' this enemy. There is no magic solution to a non-magnetic metal man…there is no changing the mind of a psychopath with all the power. My dear friends, I am so sorry but…our only true hope is to…let go of hope altogether…"

So much is said in the silence. Flames are extinguished in many that are there. Tears are shed both in fear and sadness. Some, however, grimace and find their rage building. How could the one person - who's *only job* is to lead and advocate hope for their people - believe the sole solution to their dilemma is to bend over for an oppressor?

"I say again, *bullshit*," the Attorney General snarls. "If you won't help us, we'll help ourselves. Secretary of Defense, forget this Centre Planet horse-shit and point some nukes at the damned Capital!"

"I wouldn't if I were you," the voice of Ion echoes about the room.

The terrified gaze of the President becomes shockingly apparent to his peers. He closes his eyes after looking at the television screen – which evidently Crow and Ion had hacked. Prominently visible to all in this small room is the face of Utpoius Leader Ion; a look of distaste upon his synthetic face. All others present either sit quietly in fear, or glare in rage.

"It is something quite special, you know," Ion continues. "For so many 'leaders' to collectively be so stupid. We've known about your pathetic little rebellion since it was merely an idea within the mind of the Vice President."

Stunned silence for a moment. The collective former country leaders seem at a loss for words to this knowledge. They knew this so called "Life-Admiral" had superhuman levels of scientific knowledge – did it truly extend into computer hacking?

"You don' scurr us!" bellows the Secretary of Defense. "You ain't even here to do nuthin!"

Abruptly, the door beneath the screen opens. In saunters Leader Ion, expressionless and with crossed arms. His synthetic eyes glare forebodingly into the very soul of the Defense Secretary.

"You don't say…now tell me, what should be the punishment for conspiracy of genocide and treason?"

None seem to have an answer.

"The President mentioned a much more savage me – one who 'allegedly' butchered a great deal of people. Something you had all been speaking of doing only moments ago. Not only do I have actual evidence proving that you are all responsible for this, I have been live streaming your entire meeting to the people of Utopius. What do you think, friends?"

The screen replaces the image of Ion's face with a crowd of both pure-humans and the citizens within robotic bodies. Many carry signs of protest to their former leaders, others chant aggressively for their demise.

"You – you can't do this!" exclaims the Secretary of Interior. "We still have rights!"

"I suppose it is your right to conspire against your government," Ion sighs, brushing some dust off his left shoulder. "It is the right of the people – of whom you claim to represent – to express outrage. Now…what to do…what to do…Mr. President, you seem to have a pretty good grasp on my thoughts as a person. What do you think I would do, if you were me?"

"W-well, ah…" the President stammers, sweating even more heavily. "The…old laws of our country state…death…but you…L-leader Ion-"

"Am merciful," Ion interrupts with a humble tone, lightly placing a hand over where his heart would be. "Even though you wish death on *so* many…I don't think you would learn much from being granted that fate yourself. No – perhaps exile…yes, exile is more suiting for individuals of your caliber. What do you think, friends?"

Cheering from the masses. From most, that is. Others wish to see blood, and make it blatantly clear that is what they seek. Leader Ion, however, remains stoic.

"You MONSTER!" the Vice President bellows. Her brow furrows as she rises and points an accusing finger at Ion. "You invade our privacy without our knowledge and share it with the world? And to top it off, you claim to be a *person?!* You are no person! You're a fuckin' machine that only knows how to kill!"

Panting from her rant, the Vice President forces herself to keep a stern expression on her face. Some jeers come from her co-conspirators, whilst the citizens watching holler in outrage on the screen above Ion's head. The Leader raises an eyebrow at the disbarred VP.

"A killing machine you say?" Ion jests, signalling for a squad of cyborgs to enter the bunker and apprehend the conspirators. "You honestly have no idea what you are talking about. So hypocritical for you to insult my methods of espionage on violent conspirators, when you yourselves were doing the same on innocent civilians for *decades* before you signed control over to me. I have heard enough from all of you. You and this laughable rebellion can go cry into the reclaiming Earth I took back from you. Enjoy your exile. May I be rid of your arrogance forever."

Chapter XXI

Planet Earth – Utopian Research Facility
Medical Wing

"They 'blessed' you with a cephalopod?" Ion inquires, seemingly confused.

"Yes, her name is Nila, isn't she beautiful?" Crow asks, petting the flying squid affectionately.

Nila, glides over to Ion with a look of joy in her eyes. She seems to dance her way over to the Earth Leader before she rests sweetly on his metal shoulder. Ion doesn't seem overly bothered as he continues to work on the holographic charts before him, whilst Nila nuzzles right in.

"What purpose does a pet have to our planet, exactly?"

"Well for one, she saved my life the night of the assassination," Crow says, looking at Talia as she rests on a medical table. "Why did you bring a Terra Sixian into my lab?"

"We both know 'save' is an exaggeration. They couldn't have hurt you if they blew up the whole planet," Ion continues, finishing up the chart. "To answer your question: I brought the so-called 'oracle' here for examination. I want to prove the concept is a lie once and for all. Additionally...you may want to sit down for this..."

Crow looks at his brother, puzzled. As requested, Crow summons a chair telepathically and sits. Ion, finally turning away from the charts, gently brushes Nila off. Her eyes seem to glow for a moment before she floats over to the Life-Admiral.

"This Terra Sixian's name is Talia...she is your distant granddaughter."

Crows brow furrows for a moment before his eyes go wide. His mouth moves as if to speak, but no words escape. Tears begin to form in his eyes, and Ion rises to place a consoling hand on his brother's shoulder.

"Did-did you know anything about this?" Crow finally asks, somewhat hoarse.

"Not until she told me," Ion says, sincere tones added to his synthetic voice. "She claims to be prescient as well. Even more so than N-...she was. I brought her back as a favour to you. We can see if this whole 'oracle' business is legitimate."

Crow sits again in silence, soaking in that he had been a father and never known. So many questions, so few answers. Had Ion known? Could he have been there for his child? Why would Nancy have left and never told him she was carrying his offspring?

"Did you test her DNA for-"

"Yes, she is indeed our relative…very distantly at this point, but she does have our blood in her veins."

"Did you know about Nancy?"

"I knew she left you abruptly, and very little else," Ion admits, moving to where Talia is lying. "She will awake soon, and my tests have only furthered my belief. As far as I can tell, her brain is no different from that of an average human."

"Did you have her sedated the entire time you did the tests?"

"I had to."

"How are you supposed to detect when a prediction is being made, when her brain is barely functioning?" Crow demands, rising from his feet and beginning some work on the holographic charts. "We must monitor while she is having an episode."

"As you wish, brother," Ion says with a nod of respect.

The metal titan begins to gather the appropriate materials for a brain scan, whilst Crow looks over the charts and begins writing a lab for the upcoming research. As they move quickly, Talia gradually regains her consciousness.

"Am I…am I alive God?" she asks looking at Ion. She turns her head and notices Crow standing before the charts. She raises an eyebrow, still feeling sedated. "Grandfather?" Crow simply stops for a moment, frozen.

"Hello, Talia," he replies, finally coming to his senses. "Thank you for volunteering for this research...ah...Yes, we will go through pleasantries later, I suppose. You and I have to prove to my stubborn brother that oracles aren't just a bunch of crazy people."

"Haha, yeah," Talia chuckles, still sedated. "God doesn't understand what He Himself created."

"I did not *create* you," Ion insists, placing the brain scanning mechanism onto his relative. "I was born several billion years after the big bang."

"You inspired the cultural norms of many societies – specifically my own," Talia continues. "Our civilization wouldn't exist without both of your ideologies, and no doubt would have perished long ago. Therefore, in a way: God."

"Whatever you say, child," Ion sighs, done setting up the brain scanning mechanism.

"My dear, I am going to need you to do something for me," Crow requests, taking a seat once again next to the young lass. "Might you be able to conjure up a prediction for me?"

"I am sorry, Grandfather," Talia answers somberly. "Prescience is unpredictable. I cannot conjure a vision at will."

"Of course you can't" Ion scoffs.

"Enough out of you!" Crow bellows.

"Me, brother? We have a planet to run. We have a meeting with the Centre Planet to go through with the Frosks and the Xerophs. I brought her here for you, and to disprove the concept of oracles. I have done that."

"So you *think*. Why don't you go and focus on our planet and prepare for the meeting then, yes?"

Crow looks dismissively at his brother, who places a sad gaze upon his synthetic face. Without further word, he places the instruments he had been preparing down and exits the room. Crow sighs sadly. He does not want to be so rude to his brother, but this had been an argument for many centuries now. The Life-Admiral makes a mental note to apologize later, and returns his focus on Talia. He takes up the mechanisms Ion had been setting up and finishes the preparations.

"Now, my dear…" Crow says, finalizing the brain-wave reading set up. "Is there anything I could do to perhaps instigate a vision?"

"I always found focusing on a particular matter helps bring my predictions into fruition," she admits. She now seems less groggy; as if the sedation she had been under is wearing off. "What is it that You and God seek to know?"

"Perhaps something about the Colosseum?"

"I have had visions of this already, Earth wins by a landslide."

"Yes but how?" Crow inquires, pulling up a Centre Planet advertisement for the games on the VisionScreen. "Is the Earth safe while we are gone? And does the rest of the galaxy find out that we stole the Centre Planet's omnipertium?"

"You stole omnipertium?!" Talia asks, flabbergasted. Crow looks mildly worried, but only for a moment. Talia bursts into laughter after maintaining a look of shock for a moment. "I of course am joking, this is something I knew already. God is indestructible because of this metal. He tells me after his first round in the Colosseum. This is a question I must ask him for the other aspects to fall into place."

"I see…well, for the time being, my dear, focus on this, please?"

An hour of strict observation passes as Talia watches promotions and clips of the Colosseum. Crow has barely begun commuting with Dreamscape programmers when the Terra Sixian's eyes roll back. Crow cuts a written, encoded message short as he turns to look at her chart. Talia's [6]temporal and parietal lobes seem to be lighting up.

They do not light up in a fashion that Crow had seen by other stimuli, no; they seem to vibrate and move in a kaleidoscope fashion. It moves in waves, a motion that could be linked in a similar pattern to that of the fibonaci sequence. Just as abruptly as it began, it stops. Crow cannot help but feel glad he had been recording the entire time.

"God will walk through the door in 30 seconds" Talia says, visibly lucid and determined. "Good thing, too. He will want to hear this."

---

[6] https://mayfieldclinic.com/pe-anatbrain.htm

Crow looks at Talia and sets a timer to test her prediction. Sure as she had said, the Earth Leader walks through the doors, looking morose. The Life-Admiral can tell that how he had spoken to his brother earlier still bothers the robotic man.

"If you are quite done entertaining the thoughts of a delusional young girl," Ion begins assertively. "I would very much like an apology, and your aide in some diplomatic matters."

"Entertaining a delusional girl, eh?" Crow asks, walking over to Ion and pulling up a holographic display of Talia's recent brain scan from the palm of his hand. "Kindly explain this."

Ion looks over the hologram, changing between the scans, and comparing some others through his own Visionscreen. With a reluctant expression, Ion nods. He removes the look on his face and returns his standard stoic one, then floats over to the charts.

"That is…promising," Ion admits. "I still feel an apology is in order."

"Of course, I am sorry for being so aggressive, brother."

"Do you believe in oracles now, God?" Talia asks sheepishly.

"One circumstance hardly gives definitive proof," Ion says flatly. "Still, I will look at these in depth with my brother. What was this vision of yours about anyway, lass?"

"A malicious Xeroph plot," Talia says, rising from the bed and removing the brain scan gear. "Kindly get me a drink…yes a plot, one intended to seek vengeance for the last one you foiled."

"Those damned Xerophs!" Crow bellows, having a drink brought to Talia by a droid. "They are so full of hubris! What happens, my dear?"

"Before I give you any more details, I do have a few questions that I would like answered."

Ion looks over at the Life-Admiral. Crow himself looks a bit uneasily at the cyborg.

Could she be a spy? Perhaps a shapeshifter? Ion asks telepathically.

The odds are slim, Crow admits. *Any and all alien recording devices are useless within this facility. Even if she were, she couldn't share the information. Plus, our nanobots are keeping track of any verbal communications she may perform.*

Those nanobots will stop her from sharing the wrong information with the wrong people, yes?

Of course

"Very good," Ion says out loud, both as an answer to Crow and Talia. "What is it you wish to know?"

Talia furrows her brow, seemingly referencing previous visions – or at least hoping to do so. Evidently what she asks can have a great effect on their near future. She sits upright in her medical bed now, looking from Ion to Crow methodically.

"Why did you permit the founders of Terra Two to go off-planet?"

"They were becoming a great nuisance," Ion answers blankly. "Constantly trying to start pitiful revolutions, and threatening the lives of other citizens. Plus, they were so unhappy here, no matter what we did. We gave them the chance to prove their ideologies were better."

"Okay…" Talia takes another moment to conjure up another question. "Why do you have an underground base?"

"A number of reasons," Crow answers. "We conduct a great deal of experiments to benefit the galaxy. There is no need for anyone to steal our ideas."

"And what if I were a spy seeking to share what I have se-"

"We would have figured that out already, and you would be dead," Ion answers coldly.

"So I see…" Talia answers, looking mildly proud. "Glad to find out you have some trust in me…okay, I may have other inquiries later, but this one is the most important: when Earth has been fully reclaimed, and you have won the colosseum, what do you plan to do next?"

She asks a dangerous question, Ion thinks to Crow.

"Continue to be an example of what great planets and civilizations could be," Crow answers with a smile. "We set a high standard, but if the Imperium could come together, we could collectively make something great."

"Plus, we seek life outside of our own galaxy," Ion adds. "Our planet once thought we were alone in this universe. With the Life-Admirals advancement, we have discovered this to be untrue at least on a *galactic* level. We seek to find answers on a universal one."

"Is there space travel methods that would make that possible within our lifetime?" Talia asks, genuinely curious. "You have made it possible within the galaxy, but the universe is vast, and ever-expanding."

"We believe we can find a way," Crow assures her. "Even if we have to seek help to find a way."

"Now," Ion says. "We have more scans to get from you, and I have a meeting at the Centre Planet to attend. Brother, have you made the preparations ready for the Xerophs and Frosks?"

"Almost done that, Ion," Crow replies, going back to the holographic wall system. "I will prep Talia for another scan, then we should let her rest for the day."

"As you wish. Please have the preparations ready for when I get back to the floating city."

"Of course," Crow says with a nod.

Crow busies himself with physically prepping Talia for further scans, as well as sending messages through his brainwave technology to ensure Ion will have the preparations he needs ready for when he arrives at the Capital. Through his robotic eye, the Life-Admiral can see Talia gazing at him. She has an expression that seems to imply she has yet another question for him.

"What is it child?" Crow asks softly. "What else do you seek to know?"

"It's...it's nothing really..." Talia answers. "I mean – it's more a question for God but...you may know that answer."

"Ask away!"

"Why did He…sacrifice His human form? I mean…we know it was for the betterment of the planet and all of us but…beyond that, we've never had an answer."

Crow stops again, thinking deeply on how to properly answer this question. It was a much more complicated answer than "because it's cool" or "he wanted to be a God." Ion never did want to be a God, he wanted to finally have a species fully at peace, and a planet not trying to destroy itself – among other things. The Life-Admiral doesn't turn from what he is doing, but looks at Talia seriously with his still human eye.

"My dear, Leader Ion chose to become less human, in order to be more human than the rest of us. He has always had a bleeding heart for humanity and this planet, and with my help he wanted to make it perfect. He knew, though, that a lot of people would not be willing to give up such things as wealth. They would stop us by any means necessary…"

"…So we figured the only way to ensure our vision could be made a reality would essentially be to sacrifice ourselves. Our pride, and in a way our humanity. We were seeking to salvage something greater than ourselves, because for centuries no one else seemed to care to. So, Ion chose to become indestructible, that he may take down anyone that wished to perpetuate the insane ideology of selfish destruction. It was the only way for us to finally bring peace."

"…was that why you left Nancy?" Talia asks, seemingly ashamed for even bringing it up. "To make all that possible?"

"I didn't leave her," Crow answers with a frown. "I came home one day and…she wasn't there. She'd had a prediction a couple days before that she had refused to talk to me about…I always thought she had left to try and prevent something awful from happening." The cyborg seemed to force back a tear swelling in his one still human eye.

"And God never took a mate?"

"He never seemed interested," Crow admits, finalizing his work and approaching the Terra Sixian. "I think that made his decision much easier for him. His only forms of attachment were his principals, and his care for my own personal well-being."

"I see."

"May I…ask you a question, young one?"

"Of course, Life-Admiral," Talia responds with a sincere grin.

"Do-….do your people know what became of Nancy?" Crow asks, fearing what the response might be.

"You really loved her, didn't you?" Talia asks, tilting her head slightly.

"She was the only one who saw me as a person," Crow answers somberly. "Not some kind of genius freak of nature…it was nice to be looked at by someone with love, rather than awe."

There is a silence for a moment as Crow thinks back to his times with Nancy. Getting their first house together, planning on a future that could have lasted as long as Crow has lived thus far. Finding beauty in the smallest of things, and sparking hope throughout the galaxy. She had been his inspiration to create the engine that made interplanetary travel possible to begin with. So much lost, it weighed heavy on the brilliant man's heart to this day. Talia, seeing this pain, places a consoling hand on her (distant) grandfather's arm.

"We know she had moved off of the floating city, and wound up with the exiles. How she managed that, we are unsure. It was her daughter who went off-planet to New Terra – or Terra Two, depending on who you ask. Anyway, every child after, to this day, has had an ever-expanding and more powerful level of prescience. As for her ultimate fate, that seems to be lost to time."

The Life-Admiral seems to stare through Talia for a while. Mulling over what this could mean in his head, even the great Crow couldn't seem to make sense of the whole thing. Unfortunately, he knows there are more pressing matters at hand. He finishes up what needs to be done to read Talia's brain activity, and shows her more material on the Colosseum.

Chapter XXII

Planet Frosk – The Great Meeting Hall:
Froskian Capital

Trius walks into the meeting hall, staff in hand, and a look of determination upon his insect face. The sporadically glowing tail Life-Admiral Crow had gotten used to now emits zero light, and sits irregullarly still as it trails behind him. Upon entering, the eyes of Schreik, Orthaug, Actias, Pyrrha, Kato, Shickles, Leader Dissosteria and the Head of Torture all fall upon him.

"Good morning, Leaders," Trius states with a traditional Froskian bow. "I have the full report you had requested on the Earth Life-Admiral."

"Excellent!" Shickles bellows joyously. "Thank you for taking lead on this, Trius. Please, give us the full report."

Trius sends a holographic projection from his Optic Visionscreen, displaying a written rundown of the Earth Representative's stay on Frosk; with video alongside it as support. The group look up at the image with satisfied expressions as they read along to what Trius tells them.

"The Earthling presented himself as relatively apprehensive to me at first. Fully willing to share his findings on our project, however hesitant to speak his mind. By the end of his endeavour here, he and I had become friendly. He was more open about his perspectives, and was vocal about his opinion of our planet."

"And his views-?" Dissosteria breaths, seemingly weary in his old age.

"He feels our 'capitalistic' – as they on earth call it – ways of economy are outdated, and that our use of slaves could be done differently. I had asked him how he felt with our ongoing technological competition with the Xerophs. He responded with 'I do not believe in competition.' When I asked what he did believe in, his answer was: 'Prosperity. For my people and my planet.' Which I found an interesting comment."

"However, he was consistently amazed by our technological advancements, transportation methods, and systems of running the various departments of science and commerce. Overall, the Life-Admiral found his time here both educational and enjoyable. He took the blessing from the Queens in a respectful manner, and treated everyone he encountered with kindness. Even after the failed Xeroph assassination attempt – of which the Blessing and I stopped – he seemed to continue to hold his high respect for our planet."

"I found it most interesting that the Queens gifted the Earthling with a pet," the Head of Torture comments. "More interesting is how quickly the cephalopod and the human seemed to bond. I spoke to the Earth Representative myself…absolutely a brilliant entity. I cannot speak for the Leader Ion, but I know working with Life-Admiral Crow in any capacity would greatly benefit our planet."

There is a stirring amongst the Leaders. Some questioning Trius' assessment whilst looking through the holographic material provided, most nodding in agreement. Trius had accomplished what the Leaders had wanted: find out if Earth could be a permanent ally with the Frosks. Indeed, the concept had been discussed for quite some time, however the Froskian pride had prevented them from moving forward with any kind of partnership from a young race like the humans.

"This is more than satisfactory, I think," Orthaug says once the talk dies down. "I feel a partnership with Leader Ion and Life-Admiral Crow would prove to be mutually beneficial."

"Let us not forget that they asked us to cover up for the Xerophs in order to get a *plant*," Actias says aggressively. Evidently his initial interactions with Crow still stung the sentient bug.

"I am sure they had their reasons," Schriek responds, brushing Actias off. "More importantly…if the payment they seek isn't economic, we can stand to make an immense profit."

Dissoteria's antennae begin to writhe enthusiastically. Were Crow and Ion present, they would have frowned at such a reaction, though they would have expected it. Where the Xerophs seek superiority and power over all other planets, the Frosks look to be the wealthiest and most envied.

However, Dissosteria understands that the Earth Leaders would tolerate greed over the threat of violence any day. And the work Frosk is looking to do would take years of research, and benefit the galaxy as a whole. This task would also, of course, line the pockets of all those involved to a bursting limit. Fortunately, only these two scientific super powers would be necessary to achieve it.

"Trius, your work shall be commended throughout Frosk!" Dissosteria bellows, a fire burning in his belly unlike any other had in decades. "See to it that a proposal for our partnership is ready for the next Centre Planet meeting."

"As you wish, Great Leader," Trius says, bowing again and removing the Visionscreen projection as he prepares to depart.

"Well, I am not so sure it is the greatest of ideas," Actias adds defiantly. "We know so little of their planet, or even the two Leaders themselves. They are shrouded in secrecy."

"And yet they are entirely transparent," the Head of Torture adds, his wings buzzing in annoyance. "They are highly regarded throughout the Imperium for a reason, Actias. They play no games, show no offences, and have only done us a great benefit. Already we have seen improvement in our atmosphere thanks to Crow's invention."

"I'm just trying to say to you all that we ought to be at least a little cautious," Actias asserts, rising from his chair and leaning against the table. "Every planet wears a mask within this galaxy. We had to defend our names because of those damned lizards, for science sake! I say we build the relationship a little more here, before we walk into a very serious project and wind up having half our planet eaten by Leader Ion."

"Ahah, Leader Ion is known for his respect for planets, not destruction of them Secretary Actias," Shickles laughs.

"He may have a point, though," Pyrrha says, sitting back thoughtfully. "Perhaps we should learn a bit more about their planet. Then - after the Colosseum - we will solidify our partnership, and begin our work."

"To vote, then?" Kato asks, seemingly feeling as though this whole would be a waste of their time.

"Aye?" Dissosteria asks.

Six green lights emit from the center of the table. This anonymous voting system had actually been inspired by Earth shortly after the planet had joined the Galactic Imperium. Forms of democracy could arguably be found throughout the galaxy, however the Frosks enjoyed the anonymity this particular fashion of voting provided them.

"Opposed?" Actias sighs, knowing that he would lose. Three red lights emit from the middle of the table.

"It is done then," Dissosteria rasps with a nod of finality.

"Then Pyrrha and I will begin relationship-building visits before the Colosseum begins," Shickles announces. "And I will prepare to embark for our meeting with the Centre Planet post-haste."

"May we find a new galaxy, then" Orthaug says jovially, even as Actias storms out of the Great Meeting Hall.

Chapter XXIII

Centre Planet – Just Outside the Citadel

Ion stands in silence alongside Titus and Crombolus Shickles outside the Centre Planet Citadel. Shickles has what appears to be a smile on his insect face, whereas Titus wears a grimace as he side gazes at the Froskian representative. Prior to arriving on the planet, the trio had met at a remote part of space, so Ion could bestow a gift upon them.

Placed on each of their heads is a specially designed helmet, created by the Life-Admiral. Each fit perfectly to the forms of their individual heads, making it both seamless and undetectable. With the recent discovery of the Centre Planet inhabitants being telepathic, the Earth Leaders knew they could not take any chances. The helmets emit each Representative's brainwaves at two specific frequencies. One – which links the trio's thoughts together – allows each of them to communicate telepathically to one another. The other brainwave is set at a frequency to which only the Centre Planet Representatives could detect (which Crow verified while reviewing 6-6-5-4-38's thought reading capabilities). Now, any member of the Centre Planet will only be able to read what the trio are about to say.

Leader Ion did not share the information about the Centre Planet Representative's ability to read minds to Titus or Shickles. It is information they do not require, and hence he had simply told them it would be so they could communicate between themselves without being detected. Considering they are currently covering up Technicorum II's attack on the Centre Planet *and* the assassination attempt of Life-Admiral Crow, the Frosk and Xeroph both consented to this without hesitation.

The trio knows what they had been summoned to the Centre Planet for: further development of the Planet's security, the official apology to the Frosks for even considering them culprits in the Centre Planet attack, and what would be happening to the Schleurghlting's planet. With addition to the uploading of non-biased software to help in the Colosseum. The Centre Planet updated their programs every event, and seek to ensure whomever wins this terms' Colosseum will win with dignity and integrity.

Are we ready? Ion asks the two telepathically.

Most certainly, yes! Shickles replies gleefully.

You must tell me how the Life-Admiral created these, Titus says, keeping his stride even as they walk toward the main doors of the Citadel. *This could be extremely useful to us Xerophs during a planetary take-over.*

We shall see, Ion answers. *Your people still aren't exactly in Earth's 'good books.' Considering you tried to assassinate one of the most brilliant entities in the known Universe.*

Titus grunts angrily at this as he waits for the other two Representatives to be verified by Centre Planet Security. The large, hippopotamus-like Centre Planet guard leers at the Xeroph in response, without missing a beat in the security clearance. After all three have been given the okay, they enter the Citadel. It seems eerie to them, having only really seen it as countless planetary representatives filled the dome in preparations for the galactic meeting. Currently, it is nearly empty of anybody; save for our trio and one other.

At the centre of the citadel – as always – sits the Head Representative. She does not look up from the work she is doing as they enter and bow respectfully. The Centre Planet Head Representative toils on with what looks like a communication with a Schleurghlting ambassador.

"Welcome, all," she says gleefully. "My apologies for the slight delay, I am simply finalizing a task with the Schleughrltings. You are all earlier than expected."

"Greetings, Head Representative!" Shickles says. "We are most excited to discuss the proceedings of the Colosseum."

"Of course, of course," she replies, rising from the elaborate chair and approaching the trio. "Now, we have a number of items on the agenda. Please, avert your attention here."

A hyperrealistic series of images appear before them all throughout the dome, split into three screens. On the left side, a group of Centre Planet Representatives appear. In the middle, the vivid image of a Schleughrlting is displayed as if paused in time. On the far right, an eagle's eye image of this year's Colosseum arena rests. The left image appears to come alive as the sound of Centre Planet Representative's voices fill the room.

"From We here at the Authoritative Centre Planet, We give our humblest apologies to the Planet of Frosk. Having delved deeper into the subject, and working with the Perusak race, we have found you innocent of any charges.

"The Perusak's have admitted to stealing your ships in an attempt to commit genocide, and take down highly regarded members within the Galactic Imperium. All those found guilty of conspiracy have been dealt with, and probationary measures have been laid on their planet. Representative Shickles, know the Centre Planet thanks you for your ongoing support and graciousness throughout our galaxy."

"Thank you," is Shickles gracious response as he bows.

The paused and realistic image of the Centre Planet apology fades. Now, the Schleurghlting video seems to come alive. The giant spider in the video sounds sincere and apologetic as it begins. It grabs both the attention of Ion and Titus.

"The Schleurghlting people formally and officially apologize to Earth Leader Ion for our former Leaders' hubris and contempt. We would like it to be known throughout the Imperium that no bad blood is to be had between our planets, and we are currently developing once again. We hope to rise to a commendable level of greatness and respect in our Galaxy.

"That said, we are reaching out to the Representatives of Technicorum II for aid. Given that the Xeroph people are one of the most commended within the Imperium, we ask that they help us rebuild our government, replenish our planet, and aid us become wiser and stronger than ever."

Once again the image fades, leaving only the massive overview of this term's Colosseum filling the room. The Head Representative turns to Titus with a stoic look, hands folded, and smiles. Titus forces a blank expression on their face.

"Would your people be willing to help the Schleurghltings rebuild their societies?" she asks.

"I can assemble a task force at the earliest convenience," Titus informs the Head Representative. "We would be honoured to share some of our knowledge, and help rebuild a fellow species' planet for the better."

"Very good. Now, the task of this years' programming…We at the Centre Planet would like all three of your civilizations to contribute to the final coding. We have yet to experience a bastardized game or a break in the system. However, with the recent attack on our planet, we do not wish to take any chances."

"Earth will always stand by you, Head Representative." Ion says.

"Agreed," Shickles and Titus say in unison. Titus raises their lip menacingly as their eyes are directed at Schickles. Schickles merely smiles, almost mockingly.

"So it is done, then," The Head Representative smiles, removing the vivid image from the room and approaching the three Planetary Representatives. "Now is only the task of re-coding the security here, Leader Ion, and we shall not meet again until the Colosseum."

"As you wish, Head Representative," Ion says, floating over to her with two devices in his hand. "Here are programs designed by our top programmers and security enforcers – including Life-Admiral Crow. Both are labelled; one for the Centre Planet security, the other a completely unique, self-correcting program to heighten the security of the Colosseum."

"I- my word, Leader Ion!" the Head Representative bellows, shocked. "I hadn't even inquired about the task, and yet you have both done?"

"Earth is always looking to better itself, as well as the rest of the galaxy," he informs. "We anticipated the contribution to security for both venues, and felt making you wait would be inconvenient."

Suck up Titus sneers through their communication device.

You didn't think of this yourselves? Shickles asks telepathically. *We Frosks have done the same for the Colosseum already as well.* Strange *your people had not thought of it.*

"The same can be said of Frosk," Shickles informs, also approaching the Centre Planet Representative with a program. "We too anticipated this need, especially with the Perusak attack."

"Marvellous!" the Head Representative exclaims. "When might we anticipate the contribution of Technicorum II?"

"Even sooner than you can expect our aid with the Schleurghltings," Titus assures.

"Tremendous. Now – Leader Ion and Representative Shickles…are your planets able to contribute to our defence systems?"

"Earth can send blueprints to whomever has the appropriate resources to build weapons, Head Representative."

"And we Frosks are more than willing to provide those resources!"

Don't overstep, insect! Titus hisses telepathically. Shickles merely grins at the Lizard.

"I am sure the Xerophs will have their hands full re-establishing a planet."

"I agree, Titus," Ion adds, soothing tones being emitted within his voice. "We wouldn't want the Centre Planet to suffer by dipping our hands into too many pots, as it were."

Bastards! The both of you!

You owe us, Ion reminds the giant lizard baldly.

Finally Titus grunts in agreement with Shickles. The Head Representative claps for joy and smiles at the trio. A massive grin on their hippopotamus like face.

"Marvellous, truly marvellous! How thoughtful of you all. It is so nice to see three of our greatest super powers finally coming together!"

"Mmmyes," Titus spits. "Thank you for your time, Head Representative. I really must prepare Technicorum II for our new task, though. I will see you at the Colosseum."

"That is all I need of any of you now, anyway," the Head Representative assures. "Unless I find, oh I don't know…a secret someone may be hiding. We will not convene again until the Colosseum, indeed. Farewell to you all."

The trio leave on that cryptic note with a sense of loathing within them. Ion however brushes this off. There are greater matters to deal with, and new fears to anticipate. Primarily dealing with the apparent oracle waiting with the Life-Admiral back on Earth. Not to mention preparing security measures to be set in place while he is gone fighting in the Colosseum.

The meeting had gone well, and as far as Ion can tell no unwanted information reached the Head Representative. That is all that mattered for now. The Xerophs could make an attempt at another ploy if they wanted. But with the Colosseum approaching, Crow and Ion figure that the chances of that are slim. With the additional placement of Xerophs on the Schleurghlting's planet, they would indeed have their hands full.

Ion arrives back at Earth, prepared to look into Crow's new findings and pre-planing an apology for his crassness toward Talia. His mind is on another additional thought though – another time really. The Colosseum would bring Ion a battle the likes of which he hadn't experienced in centuries. Not being able to feel many emotions, the Earth Leader does long for a good battle from time to time. And one had not been experienced since the Pure-Human Revolution.

Chapter XXIV

Earth 2130 – Exile Island

I will grant those unwilling to see my views the freedom to establish a planet of their own. Things should not have to happen by force, and often when they are taken by such means - the results are less than you desired. It is not the fault of the Leader if the People cannot see their own greed and foolishness taking priority over the greater good. It is the duty of the Leader to make sure that good always triumphs. Please know that every decision I make is not for a lack of caring; but for caring too much.
Leader Ion on the release of the "Pure Human" exiles

Ion exits his modest ship, with a sentry of guards close at his heals. He smiles at the literal army before him; showing no signs of fear, anxiety, or concern for this massive group of individuals. Roughly three percent of the world's population had either been exiled to this island, or chosen to move there as part of the "Pure-Human" Movement. Ion scoffs internally at the very thought of it. The rebellion had cleared strenuously re-terraformed land in anticipation of Ion's arrival. A flattened, grassy sphere in the centre of this forest island made these "Pure Humans" look very out of place.

Standing strong is a massive army led by none other than Mrs. Vena. Evidently she had taken Life-Admiral Crow and Leader Ion's rejection so personally, she had decided to sacrifice her freedom in order to create a rebellion. She stands evidently stoic, her torn pants suit waving lazily in the wind. She had tied her hair back in a sky blue bandana – the colour of her "fearsome" rebellion. Ion approaches her gradually, as she and two attendants do the same.

"Hello Mrs. Vena," Ion says casually, delicately propelling a fallen leaf through the air with his hand as he speaks to her. The Island that the exiles had been sent to – once a cesspool of human idiocy – is now a lush forest (outside of the area these "Pure-Humans" had demolished). Ion had made it so where the exiles had been sent would still be an area which could provide adequate resources for any number of humans to thrive there. "Nice to see you again. Tell me…why are you so thankless?"

"Thankless?!" Vena blurts, appalled. "You've taken away our humanity, our individuality, and in many ways our freedom! How *dare* you even insinuate that-"

"Does your little rebellion know that you were looking to exploit *this very island* for profit?" Ion booms over her. The rebellion behind her begins to stir, and the two guards next to her glance with a mild distaste on their faces. "Are you all even aware of the zero percent crime rate in our floating cities? Or how our planet is regarded in the Intergalactic Senate? Or how liberties are multiplied tenfold within the Dreamscape? I imagine not, or you would not be trying to kill my citizens."

"Anything to take you down!" hollers a member of the crowd. Ion floats toward the individual and looks them dead in the eyes.

"Anything you say? Even…at the cost of other human being's lives?" the member of the crowd looks at their feet nervously. Ion's tall stature is quite intimidating. The Earth Leader bellows loud onto the army, walking up and down the line and leering at each of them. "Because we made *very* certain that specific loopholes would be discovered by your little troupe here. We had information leak of secret tunnels directly to my office, and I even flew *by myself* in an aircraft for half a day – giving you ample opportunity to strike me down. You did not. Instead, you took my other bait: the location of Centre Planet-banned weapons. Indeed, I orchestrated this knowledge to you, and you chose the most barbaric and destructive route.

"So despite being aware that I - the evident 'oppressor' of you people – would be vulnerable to your delightful gang…you chose to acquire illegal firearms and use them against my people. DID ANY OF YOU KNOW ABOUT THAT?"

There is a silence among the crowd. A few shuffle uneasily, a few more cough. Ion floats back in front of Vena, a disappointed look on his face. She leers at him with pure hate. The Earth Leader appears undeterred by this, though.

"So you knew and did nothing then? What kind of-"

"There have been zero casualties on my end," Ion interrupts matter-of-factly. "I cannot say the same for the kamikaze pilots you sent to my cities though. Brilliant move, by the way. It really worked in your favour. I applaud watching you do your due diligence to make sure we didn't have…oh, I don't know…an invisible shield around our cities. Your people didn't die *effectively* for nothing, did they? I haven't even sent a single one of my citizens to battle, either. What a tyrannical bastard I am.

"Now," Ion claps his hands together with an assertive *clunk*. "Why don't you all just hand over the weapons you stole, and make the most of the land my brother and I *gave* you? Then I can be on my merry way, and we need never cross paths again?"

There is a roar of defiance from the "Pure-Human" army. Evidently they do not see the fault in their ways. Ion looks grimly at them, while Mrs. Vena goes on a rather droll monologue.

"We will never stand down!" she hollers, impassioned. "History has taught us that 'the only thing necessary for the triumph of evil is for good – people – to do nothing'! And I refuse to let humanity die in your metal, inhuman hands!"

"Apparently you and your band here do not understand irony," Ion sighs. "At least you know Edmund Burke…regardless, this foolishness has gone on long enough. Life-Admiral Crow and I have a proposition for you-"

"PROPOSITION *THIS!*" shouts a gunner from far away.

A sudden volley of gunfire strikes Ion and his small group of automatons. They whiz and zip, either bouncing off the ship or meeting their autonomous marks and falling to the ground. Vena and her entourage fall back, running to their troupe as artillery and other such weapons tear up the ground around Ion.

The damage is immediate, massive, and done without mercy to Leader Ion's ship, entourage, and person. The few seconds in which the strikes decimate the earth feel longer than they play out, as massive chunks of earth erupt from the explosion. Immense pieces of ship are strewn through the forest behind Ion's group as his modest ship is destroyed. Some debris flies into the group of "Pure-Humans" as well, harming a small handful. Dust billows, shadowing the indestructible man in a thick wall of Earth.

The Earth Leader floats right where he had stood before the gunfire, along with the autonomous droid group. The ground beneath them now sunken in from the Pure-Human attack. Ion and his droids had not been effected by any of it. As the "Pure-Humans" call a cease fire. As the dust settles, Ion glares at them with a frown. First he looks to the ground, where lush and magnificent green grass rested just moments before. He then turns his head to see the forest behind him. Debris is strewn about, trees knocked over and a handful of poor, unsuspecting creatures lay dead. Were Ion still able, he would have lashed out in fury. Now, however, all he can do is frown.

"Look at what your hubris and arrogance have done," the unscathed Ion says sadly. The revolutionaries stare in awe at the seemingly untouched (albeit dusty) Earth Leader and his robotic entourage. "First you try and take the lives of my innocent civilians, and now you have laid waste to the land I provided you...you've slaughtered rare animals I had just brought back from extinction...why? I ask...why?"

None could speak as the "Pure-Human's" mouths are agape in shame. Some drop their weapons to the ground in defeat, others tear up in pure regret. Mrs. Vena, however, only feels greater anger.

"WHY WON'T YOU DIE?!" she hollers, charging Ion. He remains still as she races over, striking him with a rifle. Upon contact, the weapon breaks in half. Still flustered, she moves to strike him with her bare hands. Ion catches it, and she struggles to get loose. He looks at her with sadness in his synthetic eyes.

"Yet you fight on," he says sadly. Vena continues to struggle as he speaks on. "Are there any more among you who still wish to fight?"

A shockingly large number of individuals still roar in defiance of the robotic man. Those many still with fight in them begin to charge Ion and his guard, weapons in hand. Laser blades, hand-to-hand weapon adaptors (essentially giant metal boxing gloves) and a variety of other illegal weaponry surge toward the Leader. He releases Vena, watching as some of the rebellion retreat. Ion sighs a morose sigh, and engages his non-lethal defense weapons.

As the masses close in on him and the relentless Vena continues her attack, Ion closes his eyes. A surge of concentrated, none lethal electricity emanates from his body, releasing onto the oncoming rebellion. A blue sphere engulfs the front lines, surging through their bodies.

Those within range fall to their knees, gyrating on the ground as the electricity shocks them into unconsciousness. Rebellious members overly determined choose to continue their charge, while others farther back stop in their tracks. The unconscious people nearly create a mound before Ion, which he flies over to reach those still aiming for the kill. Ion mentally commands his robotic entourage to head back to the Capital to inform Crow of the current situation, and to acquire a vessel to bring him back home.

Once again he stands before the crazed "Pure-Humans," firing non-lethal orbs of electricity at them from the palms of his hands. He bobs and weaves around his attackers at break-neck speeds; a green-tinted blur among his fleshy adversaries. The Leader begins speaking, if not for himself but for any still conscious who may stop by hearing his words.

"This is why humanity had to change…we are admirably resilient, yes – but not always for the right reasons. I offered you all a life free from pain, with the ability to experience whatever your hearts desired. I found a way for you to do so in a way that would no longer harm our planet, or bring suffering to another. Yet, defiant you stand.

"Even with your defiance, I gave you your own land; that you might live the lives you seemed to long for. Selfishly, you spit in my metaphorical face and ask for more than I can give. You do not deserve this planet, and perhaps you do not even deserve my kindness…still, I wish you all well…"

So it went as the horde continue to climb upon the Great Leader. Neither a scratch nor an effective strike land upon him. Ion does not deliver his justice with malice, he does not use excessive force against his attackers – no smile can be found on his somber metal face. He simply subdues them and carries on with what the rebellion is making him do.

No matter how he tries to beg them to stop, or attempt to state him and his brother's offer, they continue. Weapon fragments line the now sandy crater where they stand as the attacker's weapons are destroyed against his indestructible body.

The Earth Leader is so bombarded by those within his own species, he fails to notice the ship of another resting above him. Without warning, an entity slams down several yards from where the fight rages on. The massive BOOM that echoes across the forest causes all those involved to stop and look upon the most peculiar species the "Pure-Humans" have ever seen. Leader Ion, however, recognizes them right away.

"Earth Leader Ion," the bacteriophage-looking entity hollers over the battle field. "Your species has been chosen for a purge."

Chapter XXV

Planet Earth – Crow's Underground Lab

"…and he threw up just – all over himself," Crow says, laughing. He and Talia are enjoying an old Earth classic: French fries, cheese and gravy. A Canadian culinary staple which Crow had said "must be tried by everyone in the universe, at least once." The Oracle had almost spit out her mouthful of the delicious delicacy with laughter at the thought of God having the capability to even become physically ill. "Yeah, Ion used to be a lot of fun…my word - that was over 300 years ago now. Back when he was still human."

"Great Ion that is funny," Talia rasps, finally finishing her laughing fit. She flung a piece of cheese in the air, which Nila swoops down and munches. The Cephalopod meanders over to Talia, landing on her shoulder and nuzzles lightly. "Why would he ever choose to give that all up?"

"What do you mean?"

"Well, being human for one," Talia begins, lightly petting Nila with one hand and munching on more poutine with the other. "But even being able to process real emotion like that for another."

"Leader Ion – my beloved brother – never really felt as though he fit in," Crow begins thoughtfully. "For most of his life, he was an average man. Never overly excelled in school, only caring for philosophy, environmental science and politics. We lived in a time where capitalism was beginning to eat itself. The rich only getting richer and hoarding their wealth, the middle-class becoming just as financially stable as the lowest class. Politicians lying on behalf of lobbyists, or changing stories in order to follow the conditions of bribes and blackmail.

"On top of all of it was degradation of our planet's ecosystem. Ion had always held an interest in the planet's well-being, and felt that if any of the Earth Gods were real, they would have stood up for their masterpiece and prevented humanity from being so malicious toward what was given to them.

"Despite constantly feeling like an outcast – or 'not of this world' as he had put it in his youth – he believed his separation from the people of this planet was what gave him the greatest potential. Hence, he believed he could do what no one else was willing to do. He created his purpose to be...well, saviour of the planet; a delegator of the new world. He's lucky I agreed with many of his ideologies...there is no way he could have accomplished all he has without my help."

"Does he still...feel-?"

"I gave him nerve censors, yes."

"No, I mean..." Talia leans forward, appearing nervous to even ask. "Emotions. Is he still human, as far as that goes?"

"He is...less angry now that his dreams are almost fully realized," Crow answers, omitting some facts. "So yes, he is still human, in that sense."

"The legend goes that in order to take over the planet…Leader Ion had killed numerous leaders, drug dealers, and corrupt business people…is this true?"

"Let's just say…" Crow begins, sipping some alien wine. "The road to heaven sometimes has to be paved in the blood of the damned."

"Well, were it not for the Pure Human Revolution, we may all have been dead anyway," Talia says, finishing her poutine. "This is actually insanely good. Terra Sixians only get whatever fruit falls from the trees!"

"That is because your people learned from Earth's former gluttony."

"We try, Grandfather, we really do," Talia says somberly. "Our entire civilization is based off of both you and your brothers' theses on politics and science. We aren't perfect, but we are only really starting…do you ever miss it? The old days?"

"Our world is far better off now than it ever had been," Crow answers.

"I meant in the context of you and God being Pure-Human."

        Crow thought over this for a moment. He often finds himself looking at his brother and seeing his old human form rather than his current metal one. However, he does not overly long for both he and Ion to be of pure flesh again. Truthfully, were they still Pure Human, they would have been assassinated centuries ago.

"Yes...and no," Crow answers truthfully. "Ion and I did not have the best upbringing, but we took everything in stride. We had – well, at least he had, I still have a few of mine – scars that would not let us forget our pasts. But we do not live there anymore. All there truly is in this existence is the current moment. And the current moment – the now, as Alan Watts had put it – defines what the future can hold. So I try not to look back, only focusing on where I am and where we will be. It is what has kept me alive this long. And - outside of stem cells and cell manipulation - what has kept me young."

The duo laugh lightly as Ion enters the lab's small dining area. The metal man stands seemingly emotionless in the doorway for a moment, seeing Crow's unfinished plate of poutine resting before him at the small metal table. The Earth Leader glides over to Talia, picks up her empty plate and silverware, placing them in the dishwasher. Within seconds it looks like brand dishware.

"Well hello to you too, brother," Crow says, going back to his meal. "How was the Centre Planet?"

"Suspicious," Ion admits. "But nothing to worry about now. They were very thrilled with our prompt work on the new programs. They now seek blueprints for updated security on their planet's defenses."

"More work for you, grandfather," Talia comments casually.

"And what of this oracle business?" Ion inquires, floating in a full lotus position between the duo around the table.

"All the scans I have done are proof enough for me," Crow answers, sending a hologram of the results to the centre of the table. Ion looks through them skeptically. "The readings are unlike anything I have seen in a normal human brain. Additionally, Talia has evidently had a rather vital prediction she would like to share with us."

"After I become an Earth Citizen," she adds, grinning at her God. Ion places a mildly unimpressed look on his metal face as he continues to go through her scans.

"And why would you want to do that?" Ion asks.

"To prove my loyalty to you, God," Talia answers flatly. "And to set important matters in motion for the future."

"So I see…" Ion sighs, focusing more on the scans and comparative notes. There is silence for a while as Talia maintains a hopeful look, and Crow tries to give her an expression of encouragement. "Well…it would appear I owe you an apology, young one. It would be impossible for you to get past Life-Admiral Crow's security to falsify this information. I humbly thank you for your patience with me."

"It's fine, Great Leader," Talia answers with a grin. "Now, when can we get back to Terra Six?"

"Your readiness to abandon your people concerns me," Ion admits, closing the hologram and looking timidly at Crow. "Why are you so ready to give up your Terra Sixian citizenship and become a citizen of Earth?"

"The best possible future involves me becoming an advisor," Talia answers matter-of-factly.

"Oh, and advisor now?" Ion mocks, looking at Crow with a mildly angered expression. "You certainly make a lot of assumptions about how our politics work. We are not really in need of an advisor."

"God, I need you to listen to me, very carefully," Talia says with finality. "By the time I am done telling you this, Grandfather will receive contact from the Frosks. They are going to ask for help with a new project. They hope to explore the next galaxy over, and begin colonization. After that, you and I will go to Terra Six and ask for me to transfer as a full Earth Citizen. The Centre Planet will approve without hesitation, and after that we will return here. Then, I will prepare you for what the Xerophs intend to inflict upon this planet, hopefully preventing its destruction."

"I-"

Just as Ion was about to shoot this entire little narrative down, Trius from Frosk sends a transmission to the Life-Admiral. With a raised eyebrow to Ion, Crow rises from the table and walks to an area where Ion and Talia would not be viewed within the transmission. He answers the call, standing stoicly and with purpose before the hologram.

"Hello Life-Admiral, my friend!" Trius says, waving.

"Trius! What a surprise, is all going well with the Pollu-Magnet?"

"Oh my yes!" Trius answers gleefully. "The air is clearing at exactly the rate you predicted. We will soon be able to fly freely again!"

"Tremendous!" Crow bellows gleefully. "I am very glad to be of service to your amazing people."

"That is why I am calling actually, Life-Admiral," Trius says, turning serious. "Dissosteria sent you away before your term with Frosk was over for a reason. We are looking for your aide in a different – but much more serious – project. Would you be willing to return to Frosk in the near future and discuss it?"

"I- well, certainly!" Crow answers. "May I ask what this meeting will be about?"

"I cannot discuss this over the open airwaves," Trius answers. "However, I can say it will expand our concepts of space. And it cannot be accomplished without your intellect. Are you willing to meet before the Colosseum?"

"Give me a bit of time to set things in motion on Earth," Crow answers. "Then I will venture there once again."

"Many thanks, Life-Admiral," Trius says. "We anticipate your arrival!"

With that, the holographic image of Trius dissipates. Crow turns to Ion once again with a raised eyebrow. His glance is only met with a blank look from Ion.

"So the oracle made an accurate prediction," Ion says. "Quite a surprise. Very well, Talia. Let us go to Terra Six."

Chapter XXVI

Centre Planet – The Impenetrable Office of the Head Representative

The one known to the galaxy as the "Head Representative" currently floats within the centre of a suspended sphere of (what appears to be) water. On a nearby base created to house the Centre Planet race, the Head Representative is relaxing and rejuvenating her flesh after a long quarter of interplanetary politics.

Pamphias – the name her creators had given her – is beginning to feel the weight of century's long peace-making, political gambits, and foiled plots. Her ancient armour like skin is finally starting to age – despite the advancements in youth maintenance her species had created. The enriched water she currently floats in is soothing to the point of making her sleepy; however the anti-aging effects it once placed to her physical form are becoming less and less effective.

At one time, Pamphias had been a highly decorated war hero. Over a millennium ago, she had led her species to conquer most of the known galaxy. Being highly intelligent, the Centre Planet species felt their superior scientific and strategic minds were the only ones capable of running a functioning galaxy (not unlike the Xerophs of Technicorum II. And believe you me, the Centre Planet race was very glad they had not encountered them before ending their escapade). Hence, they surged many a planet; that they may enslave and recreate the species and political systems.

But no one remembers those times. For too many generations, the Centre Planet had been the cultural hub of peace. Keeping trade, egalitarianism, and hope as prominent components for any member of the galactic imperium. Indeed – for too long had they felt the intense regret that still pulsated in their psyche from the atrocities they had committed. All in the name of their pre-conceived superiority. Now, Pamphias believes that Earth Leader Ion and Life-Admiral Crow will be running down the same path.

The thing most intelligent species don't immediately understand is that there is no one specific right way to do anything. The needs, beliefs and ideologies of every planet differ. That is why there are monarchical planets, Empirical planets, democratic planets, anarchical planets, and other inconceivable political methods throughout this galaxy. And all concepts are allowed - given slavery and planet-on-planet war are avoided at all costs. The damned Schleurghltings certainly did not seem to understand this method.

But what works on the Schleurghlting planet could never work on Technicorum II, or Frosk, or Zephia or anywhere that housed sentient life. The Centre Planet had learned this the hard way, and they have been doing their damndest to make sure no other species would unknowingly make the same mistake.

Pamphias is not certain this is the case of the Earth Leaders, but there are definite signs. A tremendous feeling of pride in their planet's method of living, the stepping up to take down the Perusak's attack *and* the obliteration of the Schleurghlting Leader. So much damage, so many hoops to leap through in the hopes that things may go back to order. The Head Representative is honestly not surprised Ion's actions had not started an intergalactic uproar. He had indeed saved many lives during the Perusak kamikaze-spree – but how long could that favour levitate the Earthling into being (figuratively) bullet-proof?

There will come a time – and there is no telling when – that the cyborg will decide to unveil his true power. How much that is, even the Centre Planet does not know. And that is a frightening thought for any living creature in this galaxy. More importantly: a deep concern that should have been addressed the moment Ion sacrificed his flesh for machinery.

One can always see too clearly looking back. They can never seem to fully appreciate the potential danger in the moment. This is true of all sentient things. But now there are too many questions left unanswered – too much fear brimming for this honestly god-like political figure. There are whispers of his worship throughout the galaxy. There had been for quite some time, however more so since the Centre Planet attack.

During Ion's last visit to the Centre Planet, the Head Representative had been trying to read Ion's mind to delve deeper into what he was truly planning. However, all she could read was his good intentions, and solidified proof that he and the Life-Admiral only wished to perpetuate peace. Crow is one of the most brilliant minds in the known universe – could it be possible for him to create a method of cloaking their thoughts? For centuries now? The concept is unheard of, given any non-Centre Planet beings do not possess knowledge of their telepathy.

Too many questions, too little time. The Earthling's momentum is building in a smililar correlation to the anticipation of the Colosseum. Are they truly satisfied with their own planet's success? Is one planet enough for a powerful cyborg to have control of? Over centuries and centuries of mistakes and unnecessary violence, Pamphias has learned that letting these questions left unanswered can only lead to devastation.

Therefore, to the Head Representative there is clearly only one method that must take place in order for her intentions not to be predicted. To her, secrecy and careful movement is essential during any plot interruption and crisis aversion. The Colosseum will take place, and based on the Leader's success and observable vulnerability, certain actions will be taken.

Pamphias mentally commands the rejuvenating sphere to finish its process. The liquid globe shrinks – seemingly into the hippopotamus-like entity. She floats down to the ground below gradually, changing from a fetal position to a standing one. Inexplicably completely dry, the Head Representative dons her garments, and walks through the sanctum to the Communications Department.

Her golden garb flows fluidly as she moves on a mission through the halls. The grandiose architecture of the Sanctum is quiet at this time. Omnipertium beams formed in luxurious shapes reflect her as she passes. The imported [7]Alex andrite flooring appears a beautiful purple under the synthetic lights above her. Her massive strides echo in the metal and stone halls. Statues of fallen political and war heroes decorate the walls, with holographic images of the Centre Planet's original home displaying inconceivably beautiful landscapes. Memories of a long-forgotten planet.

Pamphias enters the Communications Department and is greeted by the slew of individuals operating it. The Centre Planet version of a salute is performed, which the Head Representative returns politely. She then approaches her friend within the department – a trusted worker whose reliability had prevented many a catastrophe over the centuries.

"Com Tech 776, how are you today?"

"Head Representative, I am well today. The usual communication tracking and such, you know?" the Com Tech replies.

"Luxuries of the job," she jests back. "Could you do me a service?"

"Anything for you, Head Representative!"

"I would like a secret transmission with the Xeroph known as Helod."

"Political quagmires, Head Representative?"

---

[7] https://www.gia.edu/alexandrite

"Prevention of potential threat."

"Are the Xerophs continuing to be a nuisance?" the Com Tech inquires, setting the communications up through the holographic screen.

"Not the Xerophs this time, no," she answers somberly. "I don't know if you'd believe me if I told you. But we will need a lot of help to avoid a disruption of peace."

Chapter XXVII

Aboard Ion's Modified Stealth Ship – Route to Terra Six

"So what happens after you become a citizen of my planet?" Ion inquires, mentally inputting the coordinates of their destination.

"We return to Earth, check in on the doctors overviewing the TDC project, and then I tell you about a Xeroph plot."

"I would appreciate it if you were to just tell me now."

"It won't work that way," Talia answers, crossing her arms. "If I do that, you will just leave me on Terra Six."

"And-?"

"And…if you do that, Earth will perish."

"You may have proven to be an oracle, child," Ion says assertively, putting the ship into gear. "But that does not mean I trust you."

"You will."

Ion rolls his synthetic, glowing eyes as they reach the meteor belt he had last encountered on his travels to Terra Six. Within view was the Schleurghlting ship. The Earth Leader tries not to take notice of it as he begins to bob and weave through the gauntlet of space rock.

"Is that the Schleurghlting ship you destroyed?"

"Yes, think nothing of it."

"It's just...Well, God, I know that you are powerful but...seeing it in person...you did that all by yourself?"

"Yes," Ion sighs, glad he is almost through the belt.

"And it doesn't bother you that you killed so many?"

"Does it bother you when you cut down a tree?"

"Yes," admits Talia sadly. "When I must, I realize that I am taking away the home of some rather adorable critters. Just so I can make a table!"

"You only make one table when you cut down a tree?" Ion inquires, sounding doubtful.

"Well...no," Talia admits. "A plethora of tables, dishware, spears. Many necessary things are made afterward."

"And then you plant three more trees to replace the one you took yes?"

"Yes, God."

"Well then, you needn't feel bad," Ion says passively. "You provided for your people, paid respect to your planet, and then replaced what you took. That is what happened with that ship. I took away – in this case – a bad and corrupt tree. With it, I provided safety for Terra Six. Now, the Centre Planet is replacing their leaders. It all balances, and in balancing the faults are corrected. We have arrived."

Upon landing on Terra Six, the duo are met by the Terra Sixian council. Other members of the village had also crowded upon their landing site; all of whom bearing gifts. Ion waves regally to them, and politely insists that their gifts would serve their people much better than they would serve him. Their offerings include natural foods – things that looked similar to beets, carrots and onions, among other things. All of which are unnecessary to the Cyborg. There are also adeptly crafted cutlery, dishware and other fine art delicacies.

The Earth Leader verbally admires their craftsmanship, and further insists that these wonderful things belong here on Terra Six. The crowd, mildly reluctant, do as their God commands. Some make use of the accessories immediately. While this goes on, Talia embraces an older woman - who appears to be her mother. Leader Ion moves on to speak with the Council.

"I trust you have found your time with Talia enlightening?" Drake inquires as the group are reaching the mouth of the Council Hall cave mouth. Drakes all white eyes seem to gleam in anticipation whilst he gazes up to speak with Ion.

"So it would seem," Ion admits baldly. "I must say I am surprised, and being surprised does not happen to me often."

"Is that why you have called us here, God?" one of the members of Council asks Ion. "To tell us we have done right by you?"

"Indeed," Ion says with a nod. The council (save for Talia, who appears to still be speaking with her mother) take their standard places upon their massive wooden table, whilst Ion levitates to just above their eye level. "I am quite content with my findings, having done some research to test the potential for prescience. I apologize for doubting you…all of you." The Earth Leader adds a nod of respect to Drake, who's eyes widen in appreciation.

"With that said," the Earth Leader continues. "Planet Earth is seeking to take Talia as a citizen of our planet – something I know is unheard of, in regards to you New-Terrans and Earth."

Meanwhile, on Earth

"Out for anuva adventcha a'e we, Loife-Adm'ral?" the lead botanist asks Crow.

"Yes, Professor Anderson I am afraid so," Crow answers somberly, preparing the *sessienna* for observation on a nearby table. "This solar cycle has been very politically demanding. I hope that after Leader Ion wins the Colosseum, we will be left to focus on ourselves for a while."

"Well, you 'ave the bes' moinds werkin' when yaur gone, tha's fer true," Anderson continues, looking over a sample of *sessienna* at a microscopic level with his synthetic eyes. "Qui' fussin' so much, lad. Keep i' up, I'll gi'e ye a skelpit lug, honest."

"I know I worry too much, Professor Anderson. How could I not, though? There's danger around every corner. It feels like humanity has finally got things figured out, it would be such a shame for it to crumble now."

"Tha's why i' won'!" Anderson assures, looking empathetically up from the *sessienna* and directly at the Life-Admiral. "You 'n' yer bruva 'ave werk'd so 'ard faur dis plane'. Made a lo' ah sacrifices. The people know it, and they's so fankful faur i'. Let yaur moind focus on savin da universe, an' le' us return your kin'ness by keepin' da people safe, ya?"

"Thank you Professor Anderson," Crow says with a grin. He places an appreciative hand on his shoulder for a moment. "It means a lot. Now, I'll have to fly – (gulps) again – to Frosk soon. But I need to know if the *sessienna* possesses these chemicals." The Life-Admiral sends a holographic list over to Anderson, which he immediately looks over thoroughly. "If they do, let me know what would happen to them over very long periods of time."

"'Ow long we talkin', guv?"

"Please start with a millennia," Crow answers seriously as he begins to depart the lab. "Then move on to eternity."

Back on Terra Six

"We knew this day would come," one of the Council Members say sorrowfully. "We had just hoped we would have more time with our Oracle."

"I respect that," Ion responds, nodding. "However she has warned us of a plot that could evidently effect the entire galaxy. I must do everything in my power to prevent it."

"Thank you for being our somber saviour, oh Great One."

"Praise be to God," they say in unison.

"Yes, yes. Well, I have prepared the required documents for Talia's citizenship. I simply need your signatures, and I can send the file off to the Centre Planet for approval."

The Council share some nervous glances amongst themselves. Ion's metallic brow furrows in confusion. He could read some very obvious resistance among the group; something he had not yet experienced from these people whom considered themselves his worshippers. Drake, sitting at the centre of their massive table, clears his throat nervously.

"I…I am afraid we cannot do that, Oh Lord," Drake admits, looking away from Ion for the first time.

"Oh?" Ion exclaims, raising an eyebrow. "I must admit, you Terra Sixians really have been keeping me on my metaphorical toes lately…please, enlighten me on why you 'cannot do that.'"

"Well…" begins one of the older Council members. "As I am sure you can tell, God, we Terra Sixians are quite devout to tradition."

"Yes," Ion glares, impatiently.

"Outside of our traditions of following Your word on planetary revival and appreciation, we take our Pure-Human forms very seriously. Were it not for the Pure-Human revolution, we would never have begun our civilization here."

"So you rely on the traditions of your ancestors?" Ion inquires.

"In a way," admits a younger Council member, their dark hair covering their eyes.

"You do realize your ancestors profusely shunned me as a living entity, let alone an individual to follow, yes?"

"Not all ideologies are meant to be followed!" Drake blurts in desperation. "We grow and adapt, much like your teachings have showed us."

"Very rustic of you," Ion breathes, looking at his hands is if he did not care. "Picking and choosing what parts of the past you follow. But fine, is there any way for us to rectify this situation?"

"Can you guarantee Talia will maintain her Pure-Human form?"

"Why would I take that away from her? Every citizen of Utopius chose whether or not to have cyborg bodies. This law has not changed."

"Not according to our histories!" shouts a tiny member of the Council.

"I have told you about a dozen times, wherever your sources are from, they are flawed."

"From the journals of Nancy herself!"

"I'll bet. Regardless, yes she may keep her Pure-Human form. Is there any other issues I can resolve?"

"She must purify herself," Drake answers.

"…Okay…how?"

"She must enter the forest and perform a ritual," the older Council member nods, their saggy skin rippling as they do so. Ion, still floating above the group, folds his arms and looks upon them impatiently.

"How long will that take?"
"Could be days, maybe weeks."

"I really, don't have time for that," Ion concedes, floating over to Talia with an outstretched hand. "Talia, if you are willing to put up with this, press this button when you are finished."

"Mother," Talia says, looking upon her creator and taking the device from Ion. "Do I have your blessing to partake in this ritual?"

"Of course, my child," Talia's mother says with a smile. Her strawberry blonde dreads weave in the wind from the cave mouth. She gently caresses her daughters' cheek affectionately. "If God wishes for you to return to the Home Planet, and if it will save our galaxy, I support it whole-heartedly."

"Great," Ion sighs impatiently. "I will go back to Earth then. Kindly do not take your time with this, Talia. And please inform me when the proper actions have been taken with the Centre Planet."

"Praise be to God," the group say in unison as the Earth Leader exits the cave.

"Ugh!" Ion's voice echoes as he takes his leave back to his ship. The TDC experiment would need some supervision, anyway.

Chapter XXVIII

Planet Frosk – The Great Meeting Hall

Crow pets Nila sweetly as he lands on Frosk. The poor scientist had done much more space travel than he was comfortable with as of late, and his legs feel more like jelly than the metal they are mostly made of. Oh, how the human condition can hinder even the brightest among us.

He heaves a great breath of relief through his breathing apparatus, hoping to find solace. With the exhalation, the breathing apparatus informs him that Frosk's air is nearly breathable. Indeed – the Pollu-Magnet™ certainly had been working hard since Crow's previous departure. The smog looks much more like a thin, green fog than a vast and nearly opaque thick wall of biohazardous toxins.

For the first time in what probably could not be measured, the hexagonal space pad is visible to him. The green-ish, Geiger-esque design of it is intricate, and the space in which he stands glows a navy blue in his outline. Several feet away, the Earthling can see Trius, Actias, and Shickles coming forward to greet him. Each possess massive insect grins on their faces. They are adorned in the traditional Frosk colours – quite formal, and fixed upon their exoskeletons. They look both regal and professional, the plates laced with intricate designs that showed whomever wore it is both intelligent and powerful.

"Hello friends!" Crow bellows, waving to the group as Nila nestles on his shoulder.

"Greetings, Life-Admiral!" Shickles buzzes, his language translated through Crow's internal device. "Thank you for returning so promptly.

"Of course! I am amazed at how well the Pollu-Magnet™ is working."

"We...innovated some aspects of it," Actias responds icily. "We upgraded a cooling system, so we could run it even stronger."

"Careful not to set it too high!" Crow exclaims, worry striking his face. "I had the settings programmed very specifically; so that the devices would not end up attracting particles within your species lungs and other internal organs. That could cause some issues of its own."

"I assure you, Life-Admiral, we know what we are doing," Actias chimes, suppressing aggression.

"I have no doubt about that," Crow answers, laying a light and compassionate hand upon the Head of Innovation's shoulder. "Now, let us begin! What is it you are looking to accomplish now?"

"All in time, Emissary Crow," Shickles says, gesturing for the group to walk forward. His antennae seem to writhe in anticipation.

The quartet march in unison along the finally visible pathways within Frosk. Plant life is once again beginning to grow, and Crow notes that many potent tree-like plants line the various walkways throughout the Capital. The once strictly industrious planet is beginning to look much more welcoming, albeit still dominantly metal. Surrounding each plant and basin is a barely visible ventilation system: presumably a condensed version or Crow's Pollu-Magnet™. The Life-Admiral deduces that the toxins within the air are still much too toxic for most living things to filter through. Nonetheless, he is impressed by their current dedication toward a cleaner environment.

After a series of tubes, questioning from the bumblebee-esque security, and familiar plain hallways, they arrive before the Froskian Council. In their traditional places rest Schriek, Orthaug, Pyrrha, Kato, The Head of Torture, and Dissosteria. Upon arrival, Actias and Shickles take their place. At the opposite end of the long table is a seat for the Earth Ambassador to occupy.

"That will be all, Trius," Dissosteria grumbles.

"You won't be sitting in?" Crow inquires, a sad tone in his voice.

"Unfortunately not, I am but a meager journalist. I just wanted to see you in. Do bid farewell before you depart again, friend."

Trius exits, his ornate staff glowing with the image of Frosks three suns is beaming in the room's dim light. Crow takes his place at the table, and looks at the hologram emanating from the centre of it. An image of our galaxy – known to the Earthling as the Milky Way – floats both majestic and careless. The group around Life-Admiral Crow seem to nod in unison, then Actias figuratively pushes a holographic button (presumably to shut out any potential in-listeners – you can never be too careful with security). Orthaug rises from his seat and (almost unbelievably to Crow) spreads his large mosquito-like wings. He flies up to the hologram, clears his throat, and begins his speech.

"Esteemed members of Council and the inconceivably wise Life-Admiral Crow…what I am about to share with you is not only top secret among us, but to be kept secret from the Centre Planet as well. What I am about to share *cannot* leave either this room, or our collective minds. Are we all in agreement?"

In unison, the group state "aye." Orthaug nods, then with a motion of his upper tarsus expands the image of our galaxy, breaking away from the closed-in image and revealing surrounding galaxies. Beautiful cosmic displays of potentially innumerable amounts of planet, all of which in an array of colours, shapes and densities.

"As I am sure you all know, we would be very foolish to believe we are the only Galaxy that has developed sentient life. However, the Centre Planet has forbidden us from creating technology that would allow us to reach out to surrounding galaxies – and hence other sentient life. The reason they have made this law is uncertain, however we Froskians have found a disturbance from this galaxy…here."

Orthaug gestures toward what Earth calls the "Spiral Galaxy." A tiny highlighted sphere goes around one particular spot, accentuating the area. Crow's brow furrows as he delivers his undivided attention.

"Though this spectrum is quite broad, we have surmised that the 'activity' is coming from somewhere around this area."

"And what sort of activity is it?" Crow inquires, curious.

"…Brain activity," Orthaug answers after a dramatic pause. "Brain activity so strong it has reached us, here. We believe that it is one massive creature, waiting to be found by other highly intellectual beings."

"How can you be sure it is a singular being?" Crow asks, feeling skeptical.

"Because, *Life-Admiral*," Actias spits. "It is a singular wave. If you would-"

"May I see the wave?"

Orthaug pulls up the image of the brainwave frequency. A massive, alpha brainwave image lies before the Froskian, which he uses his right upper tarsus to throw the hologram over to Crow. It rests before him, where the Life-Admiral analyses it and goes through his internal database to compare to others.

"This looks very similar to a human brainwave," Crow notes. "Odd...the only other humans outside of Earth are on Terra Six...which is practically the farthest planet from this Galaxy..."

Crow expands the hologram, and notes some finer ripples deep within the alpha pattern. It seems almost as if the wave had acted like a ripple in water – colliding with itself, and propelled by more than one frequency. Crow hypothesises that this could potentially be multiple waves moving in unison.

"This could be a collective wave from a multiple sources condensed in one area," Crow says. "But we cannot be sure until we get closer and find the source. What do you propose we do, friends?"

"Build a stealth ship," Dissosteria coughs. "Completely undetectable, and able to travel many thousand lightyears within a short time."

"I can already provide the stealth end," Crow begins. "What is your status on the travel speed?"

"We have indeed been working on faster engines, better hulls, and worm-hole simulating technology," Actias says confidently. "However...we could use some aid."

"Say no more, friends," Crow answers, rising confidently. "Collectively, we will find whatever is sending this signal."

Chapter XXIX

Terra Six – The Sacred Falls

The Terra Sixian Council had brought Talia to a place known as the Sacred Falls. In an ensemble, and chanting in their traditional method, the young Oracle was brought to a part of the forest moon many dared not go. For beyond the fact it was an enclosure that capsulated immense beauty, it had been ground zero for the first of the Terra Sixian's arrival.

Presently, Talia meditates at the foot of the lake bed. A near perfect circle of water, created by a massive, blue-green waterfall. She is encircled by trees, and though there are a great deal of additional fauna in the area, few break within the circle. It would seem the wise creatures knew just how profoundly sacred this area is.

The sun beams lightly above Talia's head, and fish (similar to coy) leap ever so slightly out of the water, as if to nip at her bare feet. She is wearing her usual "Oracle" garb: shin and arm guards made from beautifully crafted wood (a special wood that was both strong, yet able to move with the body as if made from cloth), cloth material made from the fibers of tree leaves covering her body, and regally designed (yet not overly large) shoulder guards. She had used the gift of the Labe Fruit (a common fruit on this forest moon, which is used both for traditional body art, tattooing, and dying clothes) to paint her face in red and white. Over her pineal gland, she had traced an all-seeing eye.

A luxurious breeze wafts over the Oracle, yet she is barely conscious of it. She is delving deeper and deeper into a meditative state, using the ancient mantras of *Om* and Earth's *Aum Gum Shreem Maha Lakshmiyei Namaha* ([8]Speaking to Lord Ganesh) to channel her cleanse and hence transformation into an Earth Citizen.

So it went in the serene and somewhat silent forest. The only notable noise – which at this point Talia had tuned out – that could be noticed is the never ending flow and crash of the waterfall. Yet, Talia had seen this all before in her prescient memories. She knew what was to come, and she knew what she must do to ensure the best results for the future.

---

[8]   https://www.yogiapproved.com/om/3-sanskrit-mantras-boost-meditation-practice/

Were it not for prior knowledge, Talia would have undoubtedly not noticed the entity rising from the water. Free from noise and without making a single ripple over the surface, this entity practically forms into existence several feet before Talia from the waterbed itself. The spectre is clearly of feminine physique (to a human's standard) and appears as if to be made of the planet itself. Skin of opaquely blue water, hair made of vines, and eyes made of indistinguishable flowers. This being looks at Talia in anticipation.

As if on cue, and without opening her eyes, Talia makes a series of hand movements without breaking from her chanting. The being before her looks knowingly and expectantly upon her, a smile curling upon her liquid lips. Talia pauses for a moment before rising herself and finally opening her eyes.

"You have seen this already?" the being asks, her voice the sound of space dust.

"I have."

"Then let us not waste time, you know what to do."

Without hesitation Talia places her shoeless feet onto the water. However, she does not sink. She glides over to the being from the water as if walking on any hard surface. Upon approaching her, the entity looks into Talia's eyes, speaks a long dead language, and seemingly summons a leaf from nowhere. The leaf itself is well curved, almost bowl-like, and very turgid.

The entity runs her hand along the side of it, opening what could only be compared to a wound within her palm. She then places her palm over the leaf, where her life-essence is poured. Talia looks to the entity with respect, nods her head, and gingerly takes the large leaf. She drinks from it, slowly at first, then quickly, being sure not to miss a drop.

The being looks to her knowingly, then leans into her ear. "It is time, Catalyst. Stop them, save the rest. You know what must be done." With that, she sinks back into the water. Talia is left standing before the great waterfall, still on the surface of the water.

The Oracle bends her arms and places the tips of her fingers onto her temples. Her eyes go a pure white as they roll back into her skull. Abruptly, just like the being that had been there but a moment ago, Talia sinks into the sacred waters.

She floats there in the same position from which she had been standing – eyes still open, mouth agape. Yet no water enters her lungs; she does not require to breath. The Oracle enters an intense state of prescient prediction, seeing countless futures in the optimal ways that they must progress. Such a journey and knowledge attained had only been documented during DMT trips from within the galaxy – though the experience is not psychedelic. This is pure, raw knowledge of all that will be, and what *could* be, if Talia is to fail.

After what felt like a millennia, Talia returns to her physical form and consciousness. She does not panic when she returns, but swims to the surface. She crawls onto the bank, starving for oxygen and feeling physically and mentally drained. The exhaustion is intense and incomparable.

The Oracle lays upon the water's edge, drying in the sun. For the first time in her life, Talia feels a complete purpose and understanding of her role within this universe. Though she does not feel as though she was any kind of saviour, it very quickly has become her duty to ensure Leader Ion carries forth his current intentions.

Feeling like Atlas, the young woman rises from the mossy shore and begins her walk back to her tribe. The normally short distance felt like circling the forest moon, having been through the prescient process. Her legs feel heavier than the trees around her, and her eyelids beg to close. Regardless, with a look of pride Talia reaches and enters the hall of the Terra Sixian Council.

"Contact the Centre Planet," Talia says with certainty. "It is my fate to be the advisor to our God, Earth Leader Ion."

"So it shall be done," Drake says, rising from his seat and nodding to Talia.

"And prepare a ship, Drake. Gods Ion and Crow will have some additional visitors when we arrive."

Chapter XXX

Earth 2130 – Exile Island, The Pure-Human Revolution

I have heard time and time again that war – regardless of the reasoning for it – is as close to hell as any living thing can experience. Veterans have told me of their horrific experiences, which effected their lives forever. With or without physical injuries, the mental toll it had taken on them is much too dreadful for me to ever try and describe. And what did they come home to? An unthankful government and - more often than not - apathetic citizens. Whilst they continued to suffer, the upper 1% laugh over cigars and bottles of expensive liquor from their Ivory Towers. No more, my friends. As long as I shall lead, I will do everything in my power to keep you from hell, and I will never permit my peoples' good will and warm hearts to be taken advantage of ever again.

-Leader Ion, after the 2116 Election

Moments ago where a field had been flooded with the sounds of war cries, a deafening silence looms. The immense form of a giant, non-microscopic bacteriophage looms over the now stunned earthlings. The icosahedron dome rests impossibly above a grandiose, drill-like tail. Six pillars drive themselves into the Earth to keep the rest of this entity's physical form standing.

The rigid head, separated by [9]20 triangular sides and 30 edges, is a rich green. The tail a soft pink, and the legs a sunny yellow. If one were unwise, they would take a moment to laugh at the obscure colour palette of this creature. Thus, of course, wasting their final moments mocking the very thing that would bring their demise. To be fair, it would not make a difference if any living thing tried to run away in terror. This unholy virus was known to wipe out entire species; leaving none but the lesser intelligent creatures to try and communicate the tale.

Very bad news for Earth indeed: once this bacteriophage-esque creature took a DNA sample of the dominant species, it would not leave until anything resembling that structure no longer existed on-planet. Tales of this evil had been spread throughout the Galactic Imperium, and it was believed that once these Phages came, they could not be stopped. Not a one had been destroyed in known history.

Thus, Ion knew what he must do. Even though he had been squabbling with these people, he had to get them to safety. His biggest concern would be the unconscious ones; they couldn't possibly do anything for themselves in their current state. The massive amount of conscious humans would have to fend for themselves for a moment, while Ion simultaneously finds a way to get them off-planet. With his minions out to get Life-Admiral Crow, Ion makes a mental note for he and his brother to extend the distance of their brainwave communications.

---

[9] https://www.britannica.com/science/bacteriophage

A tiny, barely noticeable disc ejects from Ion's back as he rushes toward the Phage. As he begins to put up a force field, the disc goes beneath the pile of unconscious Pure-Humans. It then expands flatly out, as if putting them on a plate. The plate then levitates upward, creating a border several feet high so its contents cannot come off. It then abruptly speeds off in the direction of the First Utopian Floating City.

As this is occurring, Leader Ion courageously plants himself mere meters away from the Phage. His metallic feet grip deeply into the dirt as he projects a massive density shield that stretches to the horizon. A translucent, pulsating red and tawny orange surface appears. The wall itself is held together in a series of smaller, triangular shapes. The still conscious Pure-Humans then look to Ion with both awe and confusion.

"Get to safety!" Ion's metallic voice bellows.

"What is that thing?!" inquires a Pure-Human rebel.

"Your demise if you don't head to your village now! I am sending a space craft to lift you just outside of the planet."

"How do we know that we can trust *you*?" demands another voice.

"Don't be a fool!" is the answer. The Phage's drill begins to burrow into the dirt. "It's not like you have much of a choice anyway. I know what this is, and you clearly do not. Just know that if you stay here you will die!" There is a silence for a moment, before Ion adds extremely authoritative tones to his synthetic voice. "Stop wasting time and MOVE!"

Evidently that had been enough for the numerous Pure-Humans to begin making a break for their village. Unfortunately, it was too little too late for a number of them. Ion can feel the Earth shaking beneath him as tendrils from the Phage worm their way through the ground. Moving under the density shield, the extensions of this entity move quickly and precisely toward its targets.

One tendril strikes Ion – not moving him but no doubt frustrating the creature. Many others appear behind Ion, surging to the would-be escaping Pure-humans. It would only be a matter of seconds before a dozen of them will be turned into samples for this monstrosity to base its cleansing on.

"NO!" Ion shouts incredulously. It appears as if a layer of his hands come off, maintaining the structure of the density shield as the Leader rushes to save as many Pure-Humans as he can. Despite the leader's incredible speed, it is the flimsy bodies of the Pure-Humans that forces him to move at a pace that would not break their necks. This reduced speed prevents him from grabbing more than seven Pure-Humans before the Phage takes a small handful of victims.

The gigantic Phage in the distance pulsates. Its 20 sided, triangular faces change colours as it receives the genetic information of its victims. The Pure-Humans themselves have their mouths agape, screaming in agony as their flesh is pierced. Within moments, the normally solid looking bodies of these poor individuals appear to liquefy from beneath the skin. An obscure ooze flows from their orifices as the Phage's extensions release the now limp, lifeless bodies.

Unlike most if not all known bacteriophage [10]viruses, it does not appear that this intruder inputs its own [11]DNA into its host. Therefore, the ooze which spills from the deceased apparently does not release more Phages. Ion makes a mental note to make sure he and Crow get a sample of this substance when this is all over.

However a more prevalent task is at hand. Ion flies as quickly as he can to the village, drops off the Pure-Humans (who don't even thank him, they unappreciatively just run to a nearby bunker), and heads back to hopefully save more of his exiled people. He zooms back to ground zero, taking down the evidently ineffective density shield as he does so. The pieces that had essentially been the palms of his hands float back into their place, and the Phage is fully visible once again.

What has happened, brother? Crow inquires over their mental link.

The Phages that we had been warned about are here for a purge, is the straightforward answer.

Well…that is less than ideal. Do you have a suggestion of what we should do?

Get the Pure-Humans just outside of the planet's orbit. In theory if their target is off-world, it should think that its task is done.

---

[10] **https://www.youtube.com/watch?v=Yl3tsmFsrOg&t=130s**

[11] **https://science.jrank.org/pages/715/Bacteriophage-Bacteriophage-structure.html**

Brilliant! Crow exclaims. *Kindly send me the coordinates of the Pure-Humans in this area, and distract the Phage. Once we are done here, we will have to check on the separatist countries.*

Indeed….I truly hope they have not gotten to them already, Ion states telepathically.

As instructed, the Earth Leader sends the Life-Admiral the specific coordinated of both the village, and the sad folk running from an unstoppable monster. Whilst doing so, Ion soars to where the Phage's tendrils are still maliciously attacking their defenseless victims. He does his best to grab the tendrils, rip them, super-heat them, anything that would prevent any further casualties. For some reason, to no avail. He leaves a scanner to follow a tendril in the hopes it may figure out what it is made of, while he himself soars over to the gigantic body of the Phage itself.

The Phage's large physiology makes even the nine foot height of Leader Ion seem a bit minuscule. It appears uncaring as it covers the sun before its current and soon to be victims. Ion stares at it for a moment, then flies up to its icosahedron dome of a head. The Earth Leader reels back, fires the arm rocket accelerators in his elbow, and delivers an incomprehensibly powerful blow.

The blue-white fire that accelerated Ion's punch seems dark in comparison to the light that blares as Ion's metal fist hit the Phage's head. A shockwave of energy tears at the ground beneath the Phage's feet, as well as anything within a one hundred mile radius from the point of Ion's aggressive impact. In a disc-like pattern, the force is visibly seen etching through the sky. Yet, the Phage seems unabated.

Ion tilts his head in minor confusion. Surely nothing organic could have withstood that much [12]pressure! The Earth leader then speeds all around the Phage, hitting it with great force over nearly its entire surface; the Earthling is looking for a weak point to this supposed organic, giant virus. As he carries on, however, Ion finds there to be no notable points of potential weakness…on its surface.

The Great Leader looks back to see that there had been too many Pure-Human casualties. He takes but a moment to mourn them, before launching himself toward the direction of the victims as those still running for safety. He flies across the battle field; which now has a series of craters from which the Phage's tendrils had risen, as well as oozy bodies. Ion soars right up to a Pure-Human who is seconds away from being consumed by a one of the Phage's tendrils, before grabbing the Phage's extension.

"Life-Admiral Crow will be taking you all off planet from your village, go while I deal with this," Ion says calmly. The Pure-Human looks as though they are about to thank their Tyrant, looking at him as he holds the squirming tendril in his metallic hand. However they simply turn and run for the village. Ion sighs, then shoves his arm within the tendril.

It feels as though the Phage's extension is trying to push Ion's arm out, but the Earth Leader notices that it is simply trying to send the chemical through and into a host. Ion shoves his other arm through, then his head. The previously abundant sound of screaming Pure-Humans becomes muffled as he pushes himself into the tube. With great force he pulls himself in, before his entire upper body is within the murderous creature's weapon.

[12] https://www.washingtoncitypaper.com/columns/straight-dope/article/13039270/straight-dope-the-physics-of-punching-someone-in-the-face

Ion then uses rocket boosters from his arms, surging into the tube a meter at a time. Eventually, his entire body is encased within the tendril. The heat from his rockets seems to have no effect on the host, as he uses them to propel through the tube and up into the Phage itself.

To his relief, Ion finds himself inside of the Phage. Currently, the cyborg is within a chemical producing sack within the monster's tail. Fortunately for the Earth Leader, breathing is no longer a requirement. He looks up from within this membrane, propping himself above the tendrils' source, as not to be sucked back through (it continues to try and push the chemical through, no doubt having already grabbed another victim).

From his right arm, Ion produces a plasma blade. He swipes through the membrane: this causes an alarm to sound from the Phage. The sack from which he had just been contained ruptures, leeching the chemical from within (what would be) the Phage's tail. In this cylindrical space, Ion can see some very non-organic materials.

It would appear these Phages are not, in fact, a virus that had gained sentience. No; this is a deliberate creation by some species long forgotten. Wires, an unfamiliar alien language, and beaming red lights flash and convulse as the Earth Leader realizes he does not have time to inspect this specimen.

He flies up the cylindrical tube and into the icosahedral head of this synthetic monstrosity. From within, it appears as though this dome collects the DNA of its victims both digitally and with genetic samples. The inside of the dome itself is also etched with lettering from an unrecognizable language. Ion wastes no more time trying to decipher the origin.

The Heroic and Powerful Leader Ion uses his plasma blade arm to sever the dome from the tail. As he does so, the alarm sound falls silent. The Phage itself begins to fall, with Ion still within its dome. With a massive BOOM, the Phage lands on the ground – useless.

Ion begins grabbing samples from the head, when he hears a beeping. He looks over and sees a light flashing sporadically, gradually quickening. "That can't be good," he thinks to himself. Ion exits the Phage's insides, picks up the two severed halves, and launches them into the sky.

The setting sun gleams off of the Phage's surface. Brilliant shades of yellow, pink and orange are seen dancing through the sky. That is until the remains of the Phage erupt into a ball of fire that surely would have turned Ion's (ecologically) reclaimed island into a smouldering heap. The additional Pure-Human casualties were less than ideal as well; Ion estimates that the entire island would have been destroyed by this explosion. Bits of hot metal fall to the ground from above Ion. What could have been a catastrophe has been averted.

However, Life-Admiral Crow's ships are still gathering the Pure-Humans. Ion knows the potential of there being other Phages on planet, and feels immense determination to take them down before they obliterate any of the non-Utopian countries. Surely by this point, there is still time to save the majority of them.

Later, on Exile Island

The Indisputable Earth Leader rests in the centre of the Exile Island battlefield. The carnage that just occurred on it is still very evident and visible. Piles of actually dead bodies (unlike the unconscious ones Ion had made) are strewn about, massive holes in the ground are steaming and spaced sporadically. The ooze from the Pure-Human bodies lay in lumpy puddles alongside their former flesh containers. The dirt circle itself is on fire here and there from the fallen Phage debris.

Ion had just returned from the separatist countries (one of which is now known as "Rukrasia"), and was able to take down the Phages there with little difficulty. Countless lives were saved that day, humbly by the Utopian Prime Minister. There had been a number of casualties, unfortunately; the other countries thought it wise to send in their military forces in defense – only to send them to their graves. Still, the casualties were minimized, and there remained a large and thankful amount of citizens from every country.

Since, Leader Ion had gone into the stratosphere, in order to communicate with Life-Admiral Crow. He requested that the Pure-Humans return back to Earth, and that the "leader" of this revolution finally take a moment to listen to Crow and Ion's offer. Vena - considering that Ion had went out of his way to save the exiles - agreed and is currently on her way back from being off-planet.

The authoritative Leader stands stoic in the blowing wind. Arms crossed, and prepared to finally put this very sad situation behind him. Humanity has fought for much too long and - despite his efforts - this will be one of the last three battles he will have to face from his own species. The cyborg sighs as a series of Utopian ships land around him. All of the Pure-Humans exit the borrowed crafts uneasily, with Mrs. Vena leading the way to Leader Ion. Crow rests in a ship slightly above them, observing what he hopes to by the final ultimatum between he and his brother's people, and the exiles.

"Why did you save us?" Vena asks as she approaches the cyborg. Her eyes are narrowed and she appears steadfast in her previous opinions on their situation.

"Regardless of whether or not the Phages had come," Ion begins, an air of calm within his synthetic voice. "There has been too much death and war on this planet. Though our perspectives may differ, I do not which death upon any of you."

"We think the world would be better if you were never a part of it," Vena responds coldly, leering up to the immense metal man.

"You are entitled to your own perspective," Ion answers, still calm and with a nod. "In the same breath, are you willing to hear our offer?"

Mrs. Vena, now covered in dirt and orange-ish yellow ooze from her fallen kin, tries to still appear strong. She had just lost a great deal of exemplary soldiers. People who had families, agreeable views on how the world should be, and had dreams of seeing Earth as it once was again. Regardless, she closes her eyes for a moment, then nods consent to hear Ion's offer.

"I think I have found a solution that we can both agree with," Ion states, bringing a hologram into sight from the palms of his hands. "These ships we used to take you off planet…they still have plenty of fuel to make it to at least one of these locations." The hologram displays four separate planets from within an astronomical chart. "These planets have similar features to Earth, do not house any sentient life, and all give you the opportunity to begin anew."

"We will provide these means of travel, as well as items that will help you establish a home there. Life-Admiral Crow and I are happy to speak with the Centre Planet, and have you recognized as an individual and new planet within the Galactic Imperium. All we ask in return is that you allow us to run this planet as we see fit, and we will pay you the same respect. And no…more…war."

Vena stares at the Earth Leader for a moment, then to the sky pensively. Her lips are brought to a thin line, and Ion can tell that this was not her ideal offer…but a viable one. He takes a moment, while the rebel leader is thinking, to begin a list of what must be done to restore this island to its former glory.

"You will not dictate how we live?" she demands.

"I didn't while you were on this island, either," Ion responds baldly.

"And you will give us the resources we need?"

"I did say that, yes."

"How are we supposed to trust you?" she asks sternly.

"You trusted me to save your lives," Ion responds, uncaring and looking away from her. "Use that mentality to allow me to restore this island, and finally end this petty squabble."

After a brief deliberation with other Pure-Humans, Vena and her band of rebels finally agree to the terms. Contracts are signed, and time is allotted for the Pure-Humans to bury their dead, and prepare for a new life elsewhere in the galaxy. Crow and Ion had offered to help bury their deceased, but were forcefully refused.

Time goes on, and the Pure-Humans are ready to embark for a new life. As agreed in the contract, Ion himself would be present to make sure all of the exiles are heading to (what will be called) Terra Two. Life-Admiral Crow is on a diplomatic interplanetary mission at this time, so Ion makes sure his full attention is fixed on the exiles.

He watches as they clamour in, dressed for space travel and going over their supplies. All that had been offered by Leader Ion and Life-Admiral Crow was placed on the ship several days previously by this point; however the Pure-Humans chose to waste their time counting everything anyway.

As the people pour in, Leader Ion is shocked to see a familiar face there. One of the last Pure-Humans to enter the final ship: a woman with Blonde hair and a dazed look in her eye. She is escorting three individuals who unquestionably are her kin. From Great Grandmother, to the Grandmother, to Mother, and finally a teenage granddaughter. All with blonde hair, all with the same look in their eyes.

Ion floats over to them and scowls. Evidently the Oracle wasn't against using Life-Admiral Crow's age preserving serums, but extremely against sharing the reason she chose to leave one of the most brilliant men in the known universe. The group does not seem to notice Ion's approach. He makes a throat-clearing sound with his synthetic voice.

The group of women turn to Ion and bow their heads, as if in worship. Ion glares at them with irritation forced both on his face and his synthetic voice. The dazed look does not exit their faces, regardless.

"Hello Nancy," Ion begins, staring the woman down. "Would you like to explain to me why you are on my island with the exiles?"

"Great Leader," Nancy whispers, her eyes down as if she cannot look at Ion despite her best efforts. "I have seen the future-"

"I'll bet."

"And I knew I must come here, for this exact reason."

"Mmmmhmm….why don't you come with me. You owe my brother a very big explanation."

"Great Leader-" pipes the youngest of them.

"Silence," Ion spits, quietly yet venomously. "You are of no concern to me. Nancy, follow me, *now*."

Ion takes Nancy back to the village, and sits with her in front of one of the abandoned huts. The Pure-Human sits upon a small wicker stool, whilst the Earth Leader floats before her in the lotus position. He glares at the woman who claims to be an "oracle" with disgust on his synthetic face. Nancy however, still looks dazed, as if she had experienced this moment in time already.

"Explain," the cyborg commands.

"Leader Ion…oh, Great One…I know you are very adamant in you disbelief of my gifts-"

"Because they do not exist. Time is unknown to all of us, fool. It is not pre-written, and it cannot be pre-viewed. It must be experienced."

"You are right…it is not pre-written. There is no fate, there is only infinite possibility. I am able to channel this infinity, and find the optimal paths for the world to take."

"If a genius like my brother, one of the most brilliant minds in the *known universe*, cannot channel infinity…well, my dear, there is *zero* chance that you could."

"It is more complicated than intelligence."

"Yes, so complicated that it is a fallacy." Ion moves from his floating lotus and into a standing position, still floating over her. He looms over the woman. "Look Nancy, I am not here to discuss your delusions. I am here to have you tell me why you just disappeared from my brothers' life. Without so much as a goodbye or a note."

"Because I would have held him back," she answers honestly, as if on cue.

"Well, at least we can agree on that."

"And because, Great Leader...our shared genetics will one day lead to the greatest Oracle of all time...the one who will make sure that you are not the last of us."

Ion went to speak, then froze. What did she mean "our shared genetics"? She couldn't possibly mean-?

"That...was my niece back there?" Ion asks, his robotic voice shaking inexplicably.

"Yes. The daughter of Earth's Life-Admiral. Soon, a distant grandmother to the One Who Will Save Us All."

Ion did not know how to process this. Unable to feel anger or fear...sadness was the closest thing for him. Crow had been a father – is a father – and has no idea. Were he able to, he may have wept over what Nancy had taken from him.

"You...you are a monster," Ion says, turning his back to Nancy, yet with a still and quiet voice. "How *dare* you take that from him...my brother is the greatest man I know..."

"Now that you know...I need to ask of you something, Great and Powerful Leader."

Ion turns to her in disbelief. "You present me with that information...vital information you had hidden from us for almost a century...and you want to ask me a favour?!"

"I think you will be happy with what I ask of you," Nancy answers calmly. "I want you to kill me."

"What-?"

"I cannot see past this point in my future...I can only see what will become of our heirs...I believe that it is my time to die."

Up to this point, the Great and Merciful Leader Ion has not killed since the United Earth Coalition Cleansing. He had sworn off it, that he may better serve both his species and this universe. Ion fears that if he were to do as Nancy has asked – no matter how much he feels it justified – he may return to the easier method of eradicating an enemy. Choosing murder over trying to come to a mutual understanding through reason. He looks down upon the still seated, still dazed-looking "oracle."

"You and the heir will be the key to this universe's salvation, Great Leader. In time, you will bring Earth's Empire to the galaxy...in time you will be G-"

Leader Ion had heard enough. From his eyes ejected a beam of light that nearly severs Nancy's head. She falls to the ground, writhing in pain and looking desperately for mercy from the cyborg. Ion turns and begins to walk away.

"Consider me doing you this favour a mercy," Ion says as he prepares to fly back to the capital. "Consider your slow death a redemption to my brother."

Ion could never tell his brother that he found Nancy. It would hurt him too much, and Ion could not bear to see the Life-Admiral in sorrow. In his sorrow, the time it took for the duo to reclaim this Earth and make it a true haven would take too long. They had already wasted enough time with these "Pure-Humans." No, Crow must never know that his beloved brother had been the one to leave the mother of his child to die. Alone in front of an abandoned hut, while their heirs went forth to bring the Universe's salvation into fruition.

Chapter XXXI

The Great Utopian Floating City – Professor Anderson's Laboratory

"We's still workin' on the longevi'y, boss," Professor Anderson says to Leader Ion. The two are going over holographic charts and observing *sessienna* samples in the Botany Lab. "The time lapse chambah we pu' i' in 'as covered up t' faur millennia (as per the reques' of the Loife-Adm'ral). 'Owever, we will need maur toime to calcula'e the exact 'alf life of I', if dhere is any a' all."

"So, thus far, the chemicals within have only become more potent over time?" Ion inquires, reading through the notes.

"Tha's roight, boss," Anderson answers with a smile. He shows a time-lapsed video of several chemical extracts being viewed under a microscope. "I' reacts maur effectiv'wy wif da chemical we is alrea'y usin' to preserve our brains…which a course is an 'uge plus for 'umanity! As far as we've seen up to this poin', there's no sense in considerin' eternal loife impossible."

"My word…it is greater than I'd hoped! Well done, Professor!"

"Le's no' get too e'cited yet there, boss," Anderson warns gently. "I' could be tha' over too long i' loses i's po'ency. Nuffin we know of in dis gawaxy lasts fo'eva."

"Humanity could…" Ion states, staring longingly at the samples before him. They rest within petri dishes on a metal slab within the botany lab. "Humanity very well could…"

"Tha's the 'ope!" Anderson bellows with a massive grin. "Now, we 'ave to use the brains of moice to tes' wheva' or no' the chemical 'as any ne'ative effe'ts. Admi'edly, boss…that will take the most toime."

"You cannot rush greatness, Professor," Ion says, laying a reassuring metal hand on the other cyborg's shoulder. "And you have proven to be one of the greatest."

"Thank you, boss!" Anderson says, glowing with pride. "Means a lo' that oive done yeh proud!"

Leader Ion's mind begins to swim with the possibilities. With humanity's concepts reborn, the legacy of his species could change from a long line of wars, to one of peace. The prospect of being viewed throughout the galaxy – and possibly the universe – as a caring and compassionate people is within their grasp. Time could become the slave of Ion, rather than he waiting for death to take him far too soon. There is still so much to be done.

Ion prepares to exit, congratulating Professor Anderson and his team. Suddenly, an alarm goes off. An alarm that – though implemented pre-emptively – Leader Ion and Life-Admiral Crow figured would never sound. The Great Leader pauses, puzzled, and looks to the botanists.

"I cannot be hearing that correctly, can I Professor Anderson?"

"Grea' Leadah…" Anderson swallows. "Why would anyone even consi'er-?"

"That's not particularly important, Professor," Ion answers casually, approaching a communications screen. "What matters is how many there are, and what I will have to do to keep you all safe."

Meanwhile, on Frosk

Life-Admiral Crow is preparing for his departure from Frosk. Within his extended memory bank is a series of files the Frosks have given him to look over, and a series of tasks that would help design a more efficient engine for space travel. He and Trius walk side by side, discussing the potential source of the brainwaves they had captured.

The bug-like journalist walks with his staff, ever ornate with its display of Frosk's suns. They trade ideas, laugh, and generally do a quick catch up from Crow's last visit. Nila dances around them playfully, evidently more excited for another adventure from within a ship than Crow is.

The Life-Admiral is a bit taken aback as he sees a very rushed looking Shickles dash into a nearby ship and take off without so much as a "farewell." He had looked as though just noticing he was late for something very important. The Representative had been holding something similar to a briefcase as he surged his way up the ship bay. Crow furrows his brow, and turns to Trius.

"Have you the faintest idea as to what has Shickles in such a rush?"

"My guess, interplanetary business," Trius answers with a shrug. "Such is the life of the interplanetary representative, I suppose. He consistently seems to be going off-planet like that. Perhaps he needs an assistant to help keep himself on time."

"Indeed. I-"

Code Eclipse brother. Code eclipse. It was Leader Ion communicating through their artificial telepathy. His voice sounds very serious, and thus a great concern to both he and his brother.

You don't mean-? Crow asks.

Unfortunately I do.

The Life-Admiral pauses for a moment. He looks tersely at the sentient bug standing before him, his brows furrow once again. This could only mean one thing, so Crow believes.

Are the Frosks there? Crow inquires.

They don't appear to be yet, is the concerned reply. *However many of them are…only the Centre Planet representatives and the Xerophs definitely are not.*

I am just about to depart…should I take my leave?

I wish I knew, brother… Ion answers somberly. *It is tough to say who we can trust right now.*

"Is everything alright, Life-Admiral?" Trius asks, a look of genuine concern on his face.

"I'm not sure, Trius," Crow answers, turning his truth-telling programs on. "You wouldn't happen to know about some kind of...invasion, would you?"

"I-"

Just as Trius is about to answer, the Head of Torture approaches the duo. Life-Admiral Crow now has his defense mechanisms prepared to go off at any moment. Nila floats defensively over to the cyborg herself.

"Life-Admiral Crow..." the Head of Torture begins nervously. "We had forgotten to...tell you something. I think it would be best if you followed me."

"Indeed," Crow says, glaring threateningly at the insect. "There seems to be some explaining to do, Head of torture."

Meanwhile, on the Centre Planet

Head Representative Pamphias leers over the readings. The proper forms had not been signed for this, no permission had been given…why are there so many ships from so many different planets heading to Earth? More importantly; what punitive measures must be implemented? And how would she enforce it on such a large scale?

"It may not be malicious, Head Representative!" Observer 138 tries to assure optimistically. "Perhaps they are bringing a thank you to Earth for saving them during the Centre Planet attack by the Perusaks!"

"*OR*…they are looking to overthrow us with Ion's leadership…" Pamphias ponders. "It could also be that my fears are shared throughout the Galaxy."

"Fears?" Observer 138 says quizzically, turning to the Head Representative.

"Sometimes, Observer," Pamphias begins, still staring at the holo-screen displaying all those ships outside of Earth. "There is a species that we encounter who believe they are superior. Even to us. Thus far, we have snuffed those pests out. However, I am not sure we could stop this one…"

Observer 138 looks worriedly back to the screen. So many ships – nearly one for every planet is there, waiting. A thought strikes the Observer then, one that had never even crossed the mind of any Centre Planet member: could their authoritative reign come to an end? What sort of future would the Galaxy face if there was no neutral ground for all to stand on? Not enough answers, and perhaps at this point, not enough time.

"I am not noting a Xeroph ship within this fleet, are you Observer?" Pamphias inquires.

"Running scan."

Sure enough, the scans come back negative. Whether or not Technicorum II had been invited to this potential treason or not, Pamphias sighs in relief seeing that they definitively have a powerful ally on their side. Regardless, a series of extreme measures must be taken.

"I must head to the Com Bay," Pamphias informs, striding at a great pace toward the exit. "The Xerophs shall be informed, and our defense fleet must get prepared."

"For what, Head Representative?"

"War!" she calls back from half way down the hall. Observer 138 gulps nervously.

Earth – the Great Plains of Alberta, Canada

Helios sits in the middle of a field just after dusk. They had spent the entire day tending to the wildlife, and is now feeling exhausted. Not physically exhausted no – mentally. The Great Gift of a robotic body from Leader Ion and Life-Admiral Crow did not come with the suffering of aching muscle. Regardless, Helios feels accomplished after a hard day's work, and they seek to relax beneath the stars before heading back to the Utopian Capital.

The cosmos – though evidently accessible for hundreds of years – is still a great mystery to this cyborg. They had never been off-planet within their memory, so it held a certain intrigue. However, Helios feels this intrigue is best explored at a distance. For the unknown may be foreboding, but undoubtedly hold much less beauty and perfection than that of Helios' home world.

Indeed, since Leader Ion's Earth restoration program, Helios feels certain that any beauty that could be found elsewhere within the Galactic Imperium would pale in comparison. Regardless, "perfection" is still held in a broad term to the Earth citizen. Helios is greatly familiar that the restoration program still has a great deal of steps to follow before true perfection is achieved. Hence, staring into the cosmos is gratification enough for this citizen.

Looking up to them from the luscious fields, Helios can feel the true magnitude of their role in this universe. We are all but a blinking and dying light within this vast universe. A fleeting memory held in the hearts of other dying stars. Though with the help of Ion and Life-Admiral Crow life spans have been prolonged, nothing lives through eternity. It is up to we as people, to make the most of our minute time here. Helios heaves a grateful sigh knowing that the Omnific Ion grants his citizens to make a true difference on this planet. Others within the Galactic Imperium – so Helios understands – are not all granted the same opportunity.

Just as Helios is preparing to rise and make their way to the Utopian Capital, they notice something unnerving. Barely visible in the non-light polluted sky, there appears to be a series of alien ships. Not from one species, no – seemingly countless, visibly different ships are making their way in the direction of the Utopian Capital. Abruptly, the Invasion Alarm goes off. All citizens are required to head to the Capital and await further instruction.

Helios begins to make their way to the Capital as is instructed. However, the cyborg does not intend to wait for action. The Earth citizen has decided in their synthetic heart that they must do whatever it takes to defend their planet, and keep their beloved Leaders safe. At a break-neck pace the cyborg citizen zooms through the air, determined to stand for and protect their beautiful Earth.

The Utopian Capital –Leader Ion's Inter-Galactic Landing Pad

Leader Ion stands alone in the middle of the landing pad. The breeze from the ocean below wafts about, while the iron jungle's sirens blare without relent. All citizens have been taken from the Dreamscape, and asked to enter evacuation pods. Ion would not lose a citizen today.

Despite his fears of this situation not being diplomatic (and how could it be, the way things look to he and Crow, this could be nothing other than an attempt at a hostile take-over), Ion has his holographic suit of diplomacy overlaid. The very same he had "worn" during Titus's previous visit to Earth. Mentally, however, Ion is prepared to take each and every invading ship out individually if he has to.

His synthetic face shows an expression of stoicism, and an unwillingness to move. Even as the large ships from countless galaxies become visible in the night sky, he merely looks at them intimidatingly. From his wrist, a holographic message sent by one of the ships is being beamed to him. He answers, leaving the expression on his face, and ensuring an authoritative and fearsome tone rests in his voice.

"Leader Ion!" the image of the Neophide exclaims. The [13]porp oise-looking entity floats dutifully from within its tank (which itself is projected within the hologram). The Neophides are known peace-keepers within the galaxy; held in similar regard to the Centre Planet. Were this an attack, Ion is confused as to why the others had chosen this particular species to represent them. A Schleurghlting, Xeroph, or Perusak would have been more likely candidates.

"I am interplanetary representative Phoca," the Neophide continues, their language being translated for Ion as they speak. "Representatives of each Galactic Sector – including myself – are seeking permission to be sent down to your location."

Outside of the risen questions, this seems an acceptable term. Rather than several billion representatives being sent to speak with Ion – as it is done within the Centre Planet Senate – only a couple thousand would stand before him. Regardless, Ion needs an answer as to why they are here to begin with.

"For what purpose, Representative Phoca?" Ion inquires, unmoved.

"You may consider it an...award for your gracious acts during the Centre Planet attack," is the response. Ion ponders, but only for a moment.

Meanwhile, in the office of the Froskian Head of Torture

"They WHAT?!" Crow shouts, revulsion, confusion and anger welling up inside him.

"It is...more of a formality than a definitive ideology," the Head of Torture states, trying to be reassuring.

---

[13] **https://www.wwf.org.uk/wildlife/yangtze-finless-porpoise**

"Formality? FORMALITY?! We are talking about a complete alteration of philosophical and governmental alteration!"

"Life-Admiral…do you truly know what this will do to the galaxy?"

Crow turns from the sentient bug and throws a tool of torture against a wall. Nila, having never seen her companion in such a fury, scuttles toward the door where Trius stands. Trius himself winces, and looks worriedly at the cephalopod as he clutches his staff.

"Could it possibly bring any good? I fail to see how as of yet," Crow exclaims, slamming his hand on a metal table that separates himself from the Froskian Head of Torture.

"I, as well as the people of Frosk, see it as a unifying option within the galaxy," is the Head of Tortures answer. He stands before the Life-Admiral, blank faced and with his upper tarsus behind his back. "What this will do is bring every entity within the galaxy in a way that has never been seen. Do you not see the benefit? Countless beings following a concept that has not only been proven to be successful and effective, but generated an era of peace on your planet for centuries."

The Earthling leans forward on the table, elbow planted down and his fist against his mouth. This was much too soon for anything like this. The plane he and Ion had developed over the centuries would have to be altered in a way that could not have been anticipated or planned for. Not to mention the fact that Crow knows much more about Ion's true self than anyone else within the Imperium.

"I hope you are righ, Head of Torture," Crow says, distain etched within his voice. "Because with the Colosseum coming, I doubt even an oracle could predict the best outcome."

Earth: Mid-communication with Ion and Phoca

"I agree," he states, softening slightly. "Please give me a moment to generate more space to fit you all before making your way."

The holographic communications are shut down, and Leader Ion uses his brainwave technology to alter the current landing pad. It rises from its position, and begins to expand its circumference outward as it does so. This would generate a more comfortable platform for the representatives (each of whom vary in size and shape) for when they arrived.

Ion is taken by surprise, however, as an Earth citizen springs up from behind him using their propulsion system (the citizens had very similar mechanics as the Leader's own synthetic body. In times like this, they are also given access to their defensive weapons – weapons approved by the Centre Planet, of course). The cyborg turns and looks quizzically at the citizen. He looms over the six foot tall cyborg and opens his arms in a welcoming gesture as this individual takes a defensive stance slightly behind their Leader.

"Hello friend!" Ion says to them, smiling. "You should be heading to an evacuation pod. I am afraid I do not know the intent of these ships."

"With all due respect, Great Leader," the citizen replies, remaining steadfast. "I would much rather be here with you. I fear we may have to defend this planet that we collectively have worked so hard to replenish."

"What is your name, citizen?" Ion inquires, his tone fatherly.

"Helios," they answer. Ion smiles internally at this. How far they have come since their memory had been altered.

"Helios, friend," Ion says, laying an assuring hand on their shoulder. The Earthling remains unmoved. "I assure you that whatever happens, I can handle."

"I want to be here!" Helios exclaims. "Regardless, you may want to tell the rest of them in case they change their minds."

"Rest of wh-?"

Before the Earth Leader can finish his inquiry, thousands of citizens fly up to the still rising, still expanding platform. They rise up the same way Helios had, and take the same stance as them. Words like "we are here for you, Great Leader," "We will be by your side, Leader Ion," and "Together friends! For the benefit of Earth!" are all declared as they take their places. Ion physically smiles as they all clamour up around him.

"Very well, friends," Ion says, turning to where the Interplanetary Representatives had begun to land. "Please make sure your defensive weapons are on 'stun' if you wish to be here."

"Yes, Great Leader," is the immediate reply by all.

The Representatives from each Galactic Sector begin to pour down via beams onto the platform. Entities from every species one could imagine (and even a few one couldn't) land gracefully before the Earth Leader and his dedicated citizens. Despite there evidently being an army behind him, the representatives smile at the Earthling, as if to reassure that there is no malintent from them.

"Thank you for having us, gracious Leader" Phoca says, having been beamed down at the forefront of all the Representatives. The Representative themself had been beamed down with their tank. No doubt their species - not unlike the non-sentient species here on Earth – could be classified as (at least something similar to) mammal. "We apologize for coming to you without notice, and in such a large group."

"I must admit," Ion states, returning to his authoritative stance. His arms are crossed and the holographic cloth he is wearing acts is if affected by the breeze. "You have left my imagination to wander only to the worst."

"And for that we apologize," Phoca continues, bowing from within their tank. "We feared you may come to that conclusion, however we assure you that we do intend to give you a form of reward."

"…What form of reward?" Ion asks after a moment. The citizens surrounding him remain in a defensive stance, their weapons all set to stun (Ion verified this as the Interplanetary Representatives beamed down).

"Well, it is not a very cut-and-dry situation, if we are all being honest," they continue, pulling a hologram onto their tank. Upon the hologram is an image of a sort of constitution, upon which billions of signatures have been written. "However, I will deliver it in the most concise way possible, whilst sharing the collective views of our planets:"

Leader Ion, we many Representatives have come before you today to seek your approval. For quite some time we collectively have admired your courage, generosity, and graciousness. You have proven to be a highly influential, respectable, and ideological Leader. With that said, many of us within the Galactic Imperium would like to ask you the question larger than all questions. After you had saved us all from the Perusak Attack on the Centre Planet, it seemed the optimal way for us to proceed. With your blessing, Great Leader, we would like to expand upon the Terra Sixian religion, and view you as a God in our eyes. What say you?

The humble cyborg is at a loss for words. The citizens behind him move from their defensive stances, and bow to their Leader. Ion, still trying to remain stoic, finds himself at a loss of comprehension.

"...Is this some sort of trick, Representative?" Ion inquires.

The entire cast of Representatives bellow, "No Lord!" in unison. They then themselves (to the best of their capability, based on the entities physical traits) bow before the immense cyborg. Ion can do nothing but watch as seemingly countless entities throw their wills at his feet.

"We do not wish to trick you, Lord," Phoca assures him once all (figuratively) bow before him. "We wish to worship you."

Bibliography

http://www.veronicasicoe.com/blog/2014/04/the-kardashev-scale-0-to-6/

This is a site that gives an in depth but digestible description of the Kardashev Scale. This scale is referenced throughout the novel, and demonstrated by use of the parameters outlined (in part) with insight from this site.

https://www.royalsignalsmuseum.co.uk/ww1-ww2-communications/

This site is a credible museum website that shows a variety of methods used in World War I and II for communication and espionage. These methods were used to share information with allies without it being seized and deciphered (hopefully) by whomever the enemy was at the time.

https://www.dailymail.co.uk/sciencetech/article-2124581/The-worlds-quietest-place-chamber-Orfield-Laboratories.html

This site provides a journalistic article on the anechoic chamber built in the Orfield Laboratories. This astounding space uses a variety of scientific methods to create the quietest space on Earth (at the time this book was written).

https://www.youtube.com/watch?v=sNhhvQGsMEc

This is an informative video created by the channel Kurzgesagt - In a Nutshell. It explores (and sources) the concepts of both the Kardashev Scale and the Fermi Paradox.

https://mayfieldclinic.com/pe-anatbrain.htm

This site provides a scientific and anatomical look at the human brain. The information here was used to ensure a variety of anatomical information (mostly with the Citizen) was accurate.

https://www.gia.edu/alexandrite

This site outlines specific details on the gemstone Alexandrite, and provides a plethora of information on a variety of other gems.

https://www.yogiapproved.com/om/3-sanskrit-mantras-boost-meditation-practice/

This is a blog post that gives a variety of information on yoga poses, mantras, breathing techniques and mantras.

https://www.britannica.com/science/bacteriophage

A highly prestigious site that gives an in depth analysis of the microscopic entity known as the bacteriophage.

https://www.youtube.com/watch?v=YI3tsmFsrOg&t=130s

Another visual reference from the youtube channel Kurzgesagt - In a Nutshell. It further explores information and facts on the bacteriophage.

https://science.jrank.org/pages/715/Bacteriophage-Bacteriophage-structure.html

Further analysis and information on the bacteriophage.

https://www.washingtoncitypaper.com/columns/straight-dope/article/13039270/straight-dope-the-physics-of-punching-someone-in-the-face

An interesting article on the physics of what happens when punching another person in the face

https://www.wwf.org.uk/wildlife/yangtze-finless-porpoise

A site I used to better understand a variety of important needs of a porpoise. Trying to maintain scientific integrity for this novel required the information provided on this site to make the appearance of the alien species realistic.

Manufactured by Amazon.ca
Bolton, ON

28455926R00179